Gangsta

Gangsta

K'wan

URBAN
BOOKS

www.urbanbooks.net

Urban Books, LLC
97 N18th Street
Wyandanch, NY 11798

ISBN 13: 978-1-60162-618-9
ISBN 10: 1-60162-618-5

First Mass Market Printing August 2014
First Trade Paperback Printing January 2013
Printed in the United States of America

10 9 8 7 6 5 4 3 2 1

Distributed by Kensington Corp.
Submit Wholesale Orders to:
Kensington Publishing Corp.
C/O Penguin Group (USA) Inc.
Attention: Order Processing
405 Murray Hill Parkway
East Rutherford, NJ 07073-2316
Phone: 1-800-526-0275
Fax: 1-800-227-9604

Gangsta

by

K'wan

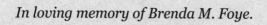

In loving memory of Brenda M. Foye.

Walk With Me
One More Time

Nearly eleven years ago I found myself at a crossroads in my young life. I was working a high-stress job, a higher-stress relationship, and studying for a Series Seven license that I seriously doubted that I'd be able to pass. I didn't want to be an investment broker, but it was where I found myself at that point. As a multiple-convicted felon, I didn't have very many options when it came to gainful employment, so I took my blessings where I could get them. I was just coasting and playing the hand I was dealt.

One day I was sitting in my office, cold calling, and trying to block out the yelling of the other brokers and constant ringing of phones. I felt myself coming unglued. I stood up, tore off my tie and tossed all my contact cards in the air, laughing like a madman the whole time. My boss thought I was having a nervous breakdown—and it felt like it—but it wasn't that. I was tired. That day I walked out of my office, which sat in the shadow of the World Trade Center, and told them to mail my check because I wasn't coming back. The next day, 9/11 happened. The first plane hit at the exact hour that I'd have been making the morning doughnut run for the office at Krispy Kreme, which was on the ground floor of the WTC. My breakdown saved my life and it was the first sign that God had a bigger plan for me.

I traded in my briefcase and tie for a gun and pound of weed and found myself pulled back into a life that I had abandoned. I was going to hustle and get by as best I could until something else came along. About this time I got two pieces of news: Both would change my life forever.

I was informed by the young woman I was dealing with that I was about to be a father, which scared me half to death. I could barely take care of myself, so how in the world would I care for a child? My mother, who I hadn't had the best relationship with over the years, asked that we come to her house to discuss the revelation. Little did I know she had a revelation of her own. As we sat there on the balcony, talking about my reluctance to become a father, she told me she was dying. She had cancer and it was too far along for the doctors to do anything but make her comfortable.

I was in a very, very dark place. As I said, my mother and I hadn't had the best relationship. My parents spent most of the eighties and nineties on and off drugs and I spent most of my life living with different relatives, waiting for them to get it together. It wasn't until I was an adult that I was able to better understand the evils of addiction and let go of old resentments so I could build a relationship with my mother. No sooner than we began to bond, she was going to be taken from me. It was, yet again, another cruel trick that God decided to play on me. Everything was happening faster than I could process and I don't think it became real to me until I had to sign off on the DNR (do not resuscitate) papers. My mother didn't want to live life in anything but the fabulous fashion she'd always lived it and when her time came, she didn't want to fight it; she just wanted to go.

During this time my mother and I got very close. We talked about life, love, and responsibility. She told me how she wanted to hold on long enough to see her first grandchild come into the world. I think she wanted it more than I did. Among other things we talked about were her dreams to become a published writer. I promised that I'd help her by doing the legwork to find out what she needed to do to make it happen. You have to understand: Being a published author was never my dream, it was my mother's. I had toyed with writing, but I was a painter. I didn't have the discipline to sit down and write a book. Or so I thought. She was eventually released from the hospital, but this was the calm before the storm. My mother was on borrowed time.

During the day I was strong for my mother, but at night I was a train wreck. I would drink, rage, and cry until I passed out, then repeat the process the following night. In the midst of my tailspin I began to scribble on a piece of a paper bag. I didn't know I was writing a story, but I knew that my scribbling was the only thing that eased my pain. I had so many things rattling around in my head that I felt like if I didn't get them out, I was going to go completely mad. It began to consume me. I didn't realize it at the time, but my mother was passing me her gift. The weaker she got, the stronger I got, and the more I wrote. My paper bag scribbling graduated to a notebook and eventually my thoughts were coming so rapidly that I needed a quicker way to get them out. I needed a computer, but couldn't afford one at the time.

My uncle Eric, who lived on the other side of town, offered to let me use his computer, but the catch was I had to get to his place before he left for work. So every morning at about six o'clock, rain, snow or shine, I would walk across town to my uncle's. When he came home in the evenings I would be in the exact same place he left me, hunched over the computer, typing with one finger and surrounded by empty 40-ounce bottles. He wasn't sure what I was working on and he never asked; he just knew that it was helping me through my tough time, so he let me be.

Somewhere along the lines I sobered up enough to read over what I was writing. I was utterly shocked. I had been in such a deep state of depression that I was writing without thought, purely off instinct, and my ramblings had developed into a novel. Granted, not a very long novel, but it was mine. It was a gritty, yet poetically tragic tale of the very war that was raging within my soul: the Good Son vs. the Bastard Child. When I read it all I could say was, "That shit is gangsta!" And so *Gangsta* is what it was titled.

Even with this great miracle, I was still not able to process the fact that I had the ability to sit down and write a book. All I was thinking about was making some quick cash off the words I'd written so I could feed the child I had on the way. One thing I vowed that I would never do was feed my child with dirty money. I've always felt like being fed with dirty money is what brought bad karma into my life, so I wanted to spare my child that.

I had done some legwork for my mother's stuff, so I had a starting point as to how to get published, but everything beyond that was like Chinese arithmetic to me. Publishing was very different back then. There were no e-books, short-run printers, hook-ups, etc. To get your work to the people you had to *grind* until the soles of your feet bled then *grind* some more. The fact that chick-lit was what was selling back then—and I was writing about killers—didn't help my cause much either. I was a square in a roomful of circles.

My mother had been admitted back into the hospital. The last time I saw her, she was in a coma and breathing through a ventilator. From her thrashing I knew she was in pain and it crushed me to see her like that. My cousins and I sat around the bedside and laughed and joked with her like she was awake. The doctors said she would come out of it because her vitals showed that she was still fighting, and to an extent he was right. My mother held on long enough for me to sit with her one last time. When I walked in the door from the hospital, my phone was ringing. I knew what the caller would say before I picked it up. My mother was gone. She passed away three months before my first novel was published and five months before her granddaughter was born.

Losing my mother had stoked an already building fire. I was now more determined to get that book out. When I couldn't get two minutes with a major publisher, I decided to try and self-publish, but had no idea what I was doing. I went to some of my closest friends and told them my plan to self-publish and asked them to invest a few hundred bucks apiece. They laughed and told me it was a bad investment because there was no way anyone would ever read anything I wrote. I was a criminal and I should stick to what I knew.

Frustrated, I decided I would make a way regardless and wouldn't stop until I did. I can remember pulling all of the books I had off my shelves, and contacting every author who had their information listed. It wasn't the soundest strategy, but I didn't know any better. Some of them ignored me, some offered me a few kind words, and some dismissed me as a beggar. The thing about this was I wasn't asking these authors for deals or to put me on. I was simply explaining my dilemma and asked for some direction, but they acted like I was asking to borrow money. Not all of them were like that: There was a young woman named Vickie Stringer who I struck up an ongoing dialogue with.

I had just read *B-More Careful* by Shannon Holmes and asked my local vendor for something similar. He suggested *Let That Be the Reason*. What drew me to Vickie and Shannon's books was the fact that they were published in a genre that I kept being told there was no market for. Vickie's e-mail address was on the back of her book, so I took a chance and reached out to her.

My first message was something to the affect of: I'm a thirsty muthafucka; can you point me at a glass of water? I was disheartened and turned off by the publishing industry, and her being a fairly new author herself, she understood.

Vickie and I chopped it up about my dilemma at length and she shared stories of some of her publishing pitfalls. I showed Vickie a sample of my work and she loved it. She gave me two options: I could let her shop me for a deal and give her a finder's fee or she could sign me to a new publishing house she was working to get off the ground. I would be their first author. The way I saw it, if I signed to a house with multiple authors, I wouldn't be the focal point, but if I signed to a house that had no authors, I'd get the bulk of the focus. So I signed with Vickie and officially became the first author signed to Triple Crown Publications.

With nothing but a black cover with the title scrolled in white letters across the top, and *no distribution,* we sent *Gangsta* out into the world and held our breath. Vickie and I believed, but we had to get the readers to believe too. I got my first copy of *Gangsta* on Christmas eve of 2002. By the second week in January every copy of *Gangsta* we'd printed was gone and my career was born. Everybody was talking about the new kid on the block with the funny name.

I'll spare you the story of the boy who sold the family cow for a hill of beans. It's relevant to the chain of events in my career between now and then, but the fact that my first two novels are back home with me make that part of the story unnecessary. Looking back, none of us really had a grasp of what we were doing or how the moves we were making would affect a whole genre of books. The road to becoming a published author was far less glamorous than I thought it'd be, but I'd be lying if I told you it wasn't exciting. And for all my ups and downs, I can honestly say that I wouldn't have done anything different. Everything is growth, and I'm proud to say that I've spent almost my entire adult life doing something that I love for those who appreciate what I do. And this is the thing that keeps me going.

Chapter 1

The Beginning

"Lou-Loc," a female voice boomed from the other side of the door. "Lou-Loc, don't even try to play like you don't hear me. St. Louis Alexander, are you awake?"

Lou-Loc slowly pulled his head from under the pillow and tried to get his bearings. It took almost a minute for him to get his equilibrium right to sit up. Running his hands across his face, he pushed back his long, wild hair and wiped the sleep from his eyes, as he heard his name being called again. The first word that popped into his mind was *drama*. Whenever Martina called him by his government name it meant drama, and he wasn't up for it. His head was still throbbing from the party the night before. He knew that he would be no match for Martina in an argument, especially in his drunken condition.

All the homeboys and girls from the hood got together and threw a welcome-home party for Pop Top, a respected older homie who rolled with a small crew called the Park Avenue Crips or P.A.C for short. They were a rowdy, but small, bunch, and their numbers swelled when they consolidated under Harlem Crip. As Pop Top had been locked up when Lou-Loc first arrived on the scene, they didn't know each other that well, but had met in passing when Pop Top visited Cali a few years prior. Each knew how the other got down so there was always a mutual respect between them. Lou-Loc had originally considered skipping the party, but thought better of it. He knew that attending the party would be looked upon favorably by Pop Top and having the wild gunslinger on his side would only help to solidify Lou-Loc's already strong hold on the hood. Lou-Loc was a master strategist and understood that a general was only as strong as his army.

A lot of people thought Pop Top got his name from the fifty-cent sodas he was always drinking, but it had really come from his ill temper. Pop Top was one of those cats that could be calm and reserved one minute and on a murderous rampage the next, and it was this mentality that kept him knee-deep in bullshit.

The day Pop Top managed to get himself sent to prison was one the hood talked about for a while. He had only been in court on a steering charge, which would've been thrown out because he was clean when they picked him up, but things were never that simple. The lawyer tried to explain to Pop Top that because of his criminal record, it would've been wise for him to plead out to a year of probation, but Pop Top wasn't trying to hear that. He wasn't the sharpest knife in the drawer, but he knew a bit about law and knew that the cops didn't have anything on him. The legal aid ignored Pop Top's decision and pled him out to it anyhow, which turned out to be a painful mistake.

In front of the judge and everyone else watching, Pop Top lost it. He hit the lawyer in the face so hard that everybody in the courtroom heard his jaw snap. It took three bailiffs, the DA, and Top's sister to pull him off the legal aid. The judge wanted to throw the book at Top, but because he had a history of mental illness, the next legal aid assigned to him was able to use that to soften the blow. Pop Top did a little over a year on Rikers Island, where he stabbed a Blood over a cookie, but the bulk of his bid was done in various mental institutions around New York State.

Lou-Loc rolled his sleepy eyes over the digital clock and tried to focus on the numbers. When he realized that it was only ten-thirty in the morning and she had broken his rest, he wanted to go up top on her, but that would only succeed in prolonging the argument and he'd never be able to get any rest. His best offense was good defense, so he would listen to what she had to say and not argue back.

Martina burst into the room like a raging tornado. Her long black hair was wrapped around her head and held in place with colorful pins. A deep scowl had her luscious pink lips twisted and there was no sparkle in her rich brown eyes. "Damn, fool, I've been screaming your name so fucking long that the neighbors probably know it. You got a phone call," she said, tossing him the phone, "and tell your stupid-ass friends to have some respect when they call my house, cuz." She slammed the door.

"Bitch," Lou-Loc mumbled under his breath. He loved Martina, but she was a pain in the ass. How he had ended up with her was a mystery, but why he stayed with her was an even bigger brainteaser.

Martina was a typical hood rat: No job, didn't finish school, and really didn't aspire to do anything except make it through to the next day, but as fucked up as she was, character-wise, she was one of the baddest chicks Lou-Loc had ever seen. Martina was a honey-colored Dominican girl who was born, educated, and turned out on 149th between Broadway and Amsterdam. She stood five feet five, well curved, and with an angelic quality about her that made you stare even when you didn't want to. Even at six months' pregnant her body was still tight enough to hold her own with any video model on their best day. Looking at Martina, you could hardly tell she was pregnant, let alone had two more kids at home. Yeah, Martina was an absolute pain in the ass, but she was his pain and that was how fate had written it.

Lou-Loc cradled the cordless phone and croaked, "What's cracking?"

"Brims, blunts, and bottles," replied the voice on the other end.

"My nigga Gutter, what it be like, cuz?" Lou-Loc immediately recognized his comrade's voice.

Lou-Loc and Gutter grew up and threw up together on the mean streets of Los Angeles. From slanging, ganging, and hanging they had done it together and over the years had become like brothers. When things got hectic on the west and Lou-Loc made his way east, his crime partner made the move with him. They rested their heads in a few spots along the way, but it was New York where they eventually settled. In New York Lou-Loc saw a place where he could shed his gang affiliation and pursue his true dream, which was to become a writer, but Gutter had other plans. All a new city meant to him was more territory to conquer. Compared to L.A., New York was wide open. The streets of New York weren't prepared for a man like Gutter and the brand of ignorance he brought with him. They would either crown Gutter king or sadist, but New York would definitely feel his passing.

When Lou-Loc and Gutter settled in New York, they realized they had been blessed and jinxed. New York was overrun with Bloods, but there was also a good number of Crips who seemed dedicated enough to the cause, but they really didn't know too much about being Crips. They had the basic rules and foundation, but there was no passion in their movement and it showed in the fact that all of the small sets were disorganized and without real direction. Lou-Loc and Gutter had gone out to the scattered Crip sets and passed on the word as it had been given to them in L.A., the true word. Within a few months the word spread to the ears of other Crips around the city and who all came to listen to what Lou-Loc and Gutter were kicking.

The two L.A. refugees had convinced nearly 80 percent of the Crips in New York City to come together under one banner . . . *Harlem Crip*.

Everything is blue, homeboy," Gutter replied.

"What you on today?" Gutter asked.

Lou-Loc paused to light his Newport, "Can't call it, fool, how 'bout you?"

"Glad you asked. I gotta go see the boy Roc out in Brooklyn and I was gonna holla at you to roll wit a nigga, cuz."

"I don't know, Gutter. I got a mean hangover, and I had just planned on kicking it on the local side of things." Gutter bust up laughing at Lou-Loc's reply. "What the hell is so funny?"

"Ain't nothing," Gutter said, trying to catch his breath. "I'll understand if Martina won't let you out. I'm your boy; you ain't got to lie to me."

"Man, fuck you crab," Lou-Loc shot back. "I'm a grown-ass man, fool. I do what I want when I want. Just because Sharell be kicking yo' punk ass don't try to get me twisted!"

The two friends enjoyed a laugh.

"Nah," Gutter said, a little more serious. "I need you to watch my back. You know how these New York niggaz is, especially in Brooklyn. Shit, they worst than them fools in Compton. I'd end up having to blast one of them fools for trying to jack me."

"Okay," Lou-Loc moaned, finally having enough of Gutter's snow job. "I'll roll with you, G. Pick me up in two hours, Gutter—not one hour, not one and a half. Two hours, Gutter, you hear me?"

"Yeah, cuz." Gutter repeated the instructions, and hung up the phone.

Lou-Loc slid out of the bed and onto his feet. As he stretched, various bones cracked and corrected themselves. *Rough night,* he thought to himself, as he put on his slippers and shuffled to the mirror. Lou-Loc looked at his handsome brown face and smiled at the youthful image staring back at him. He had lived quite a hard life to be only twenty-five, but for as hard and as fast as he lived, he still maintained his boyish features. He was dark, but not as dark as Gutter; more of a rich chocolate. With perfect white teeth and bowed full lips, Lou-Loc looked more like a pretty boy than a gangster, but those that knew him knew that a monster lurked behind that pretty smile.

Lou-Loc shuffled over to the closet to find something to wear. When people were lucky enough to get a glimpse inside of the huge walk-in closet he had built for Martina, they couldn't help but to be impressed. Each side of the closet held three rows of hanging bars, like the ones you might see in a dry cleaner. Each row was filled to the brim with designer clothes from all over the world. There was Rocawear, Sean John, Prada, Dolce, Gucci, and quite a few designers that people had yet to hear about.

On Martina's side, she had minks, and leather jackets in just about every cut and color. She had dresses that wouldn't be available to the public for a few years. And shoes? Forget about it. She had every designer shoe you could think of. Lou-Loc liked to spoil his boo. His homies used to joke and call him a trick, but it wasn't tricking if you had it to blow, and Lou-Loc was sitting on bread.

Lou-Loc's side of the closet was a little different. He had some fly pieces for when he felt like stepping out, such as shoes made from different kinds of animals, Dobbs fifty hats, and scores of button-up shirts, but it wasn't really his thing. He was a street nigga, so he mostly dressed accordingly, but even in that department he was holding. He always got the newest sneakers at least a year or so before they hit the street, countless football and basketball jerseys with the matching fitted caps, and leather jackets in every color of the rainbow. When it came to stunting most dudes couldn't see Lou-Loc, but he was humble about it, unless it was a special occasion. For those events he went to the big guns and one of his most prized possessions. It was a full-length electric-blue mink coat, with a matching mink baseball cap, with the cap being the real showstopper, engraved with the letter *C* on the front covered in real diamonds.

After a few minutes of debating, he selected an outfit for the day: a pair of black Dickey pants, a blue Dodgers jersey, and blue Dodgers fitted cap. Since it was a business trip he didn't see the need to go heavy on the jewels, so he kept it simple with a white gold crucifix and a blue-faced Timex watch. To complete his outfit he reached under his pillow and retrieved his nickel-plated 9. Chrome matched pretty much anything.

With the outfit straight, it was time to handle the grooming phase. As Lou-Loc made his way to the bathroom, he was stopped in the hallway by Martina's son, Carlo. The boy was the spitting image of his mother, except his features were more masculine. Even though Carlo wasn't Lou-Loc's biological son, he still showed the boy love.

Carlo put on his best mean mug and greeted Lou-Loc. "What up, O.G. Lou-Loc, what that Crip like? We rolling today or what?"

Lou-Loc smiled and slapped the boy five, "Nah, li'l player. I got some things to do. Ain't you got nowhere to be this morning?"

"A'ight, that's blue, homie. We'll kick it on the later side, Crip." Carlo flashed a gang sign just as Martina was coming around the corner.

"Carlo, what the hell did I tell you about that shit?" she snapped, grabbing him roughly by the arm. "When you're eighteen and out of my house you can engage in all the fool shit you want, but while your little ass is under my roof you will be a child and not a damn thug." She slapped him in the back of the head and shoved him down the hall. "And you," she turned to Lou-Loc, "how many times I gotta check you about bringing that shit around my kids?"

"Martina . . ."

"Martina, my ass," she cut him off. "Look, if you and Gutter want to run around making asses of yourselves, you're grown and entitled to do so, but when it comes to my kids I ain't trying to hear it. I don't want gangbanging around them or the li'l one I've got cooking in here," she said, rubbing her stomach.

Lou-Loc sighed in frustration. "Look, Martina, you know what I am and what I'm about, so don't get all anti-gang on me now, especially when it was this hood shit that opened your nose on me, remember?" He pulled up his T-shirt, exposing the tattoo on his stomach that read *Crip or Die*. "That's who I am, a muthafucking gangsta, born in the slums and baptized by fire. Where I come from we ain't got a lot of choice—it's either bang or get banged on, ya heard? They start recruiting at thirteen, you know that? They snatch the babies and turn them into killing tools. It ain't like New York, where niggaz started banging because rappers say it's cool to do it. This is our way of life in L.A., Martina. I'm a beast and that's my cross to bear, but I would never poison yours or anyone else's kid with this, but I can't deny who or what I am. I'm going to be a Crip until they put me in the ground. I can't change that, but the burden is mine to carry."

"That all sounds good, but I can't see it. You and that fucking asshole Kenyatta or Gutter or whatever you want to call him, are always into something. Every time I turn around it's Lou-Loc did this, or Gutter shot that one. What the fuck!"

Lou-Loc paused to gather himself before answering. "Martina, you must be crazy if you think I'm going to be hustling all my days. Yo' man got a plan, boo."

"And what plan might that be?" She twisted her lips.

"I'm going to be a writer," Lou-Loc said seriously. "My name is gonna be bigger than Donald Goines, K'wan, and all the rest of them niggaz they checking for in the bookstores, you watch and see."

Martina gave a throaty laugh. "Nigga please, who's gonna buy anything you criminal-ass writes? Established writers have agents and publishers behind them.

"Who you got behind you besides fool-ass niggaz from Harlem? What you need to do is keep your mind on the money that's feeding us and stop daydreaming about this writer shit. I got kids to feed and we can't eat no paper and ink, Lou-Loc," she capped and walked back into the kitchen.

Lou-Loc was so angry at Martina for shooting down his dream that he wanted to follow her into the kitchen and choke the shit out of her, but he had a more pressing issue, which was the sudden bubbling in his gut from last night's liquor. He darted into the bedroom to get a few things he needed and rushed to the bathroom.

When Lou-Loc got into the bathroom he stripped naked and plopped on the toilet, just in time to pass the first wave of waste that was kicking up in his stomach. He felt a little better, but the battle wasn't over yet. While he relieved himself he removed some rolling papers and a bag of weed from the box he'd gotten from the bedroom, and started twisting a joint. Once the joint was rolled, he lit an incense and proceeded to get blazed while going over the things in his head he had to do that day.

He'd initially planned on spending the day in the house with the family and taking care of a few things, but his homie needed him and he couldn't leave him hanging, especially hearing the urgency in Gutter's voice. For as long as he had known Gutter he had never seen him show fear or uncertainty about anything, but the Brooklyn cats made him nervous—with good reason. The black gangsters in Brooklyn were bad, but these Middle Eastern dudes took it to another level. From what Lou-Loc had heard of Roc and his people, they were a deadly lot who were suspicious of outsiders, especially Americans.

It was a good thing that he was riding with Gutter. That way he would be free to think instead of concentrating on the road. But the way Gutter drove, he would probably have to watch the road anyhow. That was one of the setbacks of not driving your own whip.

It's wasn't that Lou-Loc didn't own a car. In fact, he had two of them in New York. One was a silver 2000 Camry that sat on chrome twenty-fours, and the other was his pride and joy, a 1979 Cadillac Sedan Deville that he had imported from L.A. The body was a forest green, while the tires were pearl white, with gold 28-inch hundred-spoke rims. He had even had his boy Wiz fit it with bulletproof plating in the doors, roof, and windows. When he had first busted it out in New York it drew the attention of everyone who was out that day. They looked at Lou-Loc as if he was riding in a spaceship when he threw the car up on three wheels and dipped it down Seventh Avenue.

When Lou-Loc was halfway through his joint and his dump, he noticed a manila envelope sticking out of the bathroom wastebasket. Upon closer inspection he noticed that it had come from the Borough of Manhattan Community College and was addressed to him. Some time back Lou-Loc had decided to finish his education and try to receive his degree. He had taken some courses at LBCC, but because of everything that was going on in the streets he had never had the opportunity to finish, so he intended to pick up where he'd left off when he got to New York. It had always been his dream to become a writer, so he planned to pursue a degree in journalism. He had been waiting to hear back from the school for weeks and wondered why he hadn't heard back yet. At first he couldn't figure out how it found its way into the trash, but as he thought about it he knew just how it got there.

"Negative-ass tramp," he cursed, because he knew it had been Martina's handiwork. He was trying to do something with himself and she was trying to sabotage it. Martina couldn't accept the fact that he wanted to leave the game and do something constructive with his life, because her heart was so set on being with a baller who would take care of her and her kids. Trying to trash his paperwork was sneaky as hell, but her little trick didn't work. According to the letter he still had time to turn in his paperwork before the deadline, so he would deliver the papers in person while he was out with Gutter instead of mailing them in. He was determined not to let Martina or anyone else sidetrack him from his plan.

Chapter 2

Lou-Loc felt better after he'd emptied his guts and taken a shower, but he was still pissed that Martina had thrown his mail away. He wanted to bark on her but didn't trust what he would say out of his mouth. His best bet was to dress quickly and slip out of the house to avoid a confrontation with her. No sooner than the thought entered his head, Martina appeared in the doorway.

"Daddy," she cooed in her sweetest voice. As soon as he heard her tone, he knew she was about to crack on him for some paper. "You know my sister's wedding is next week, right?" She waited for a response, but didn't get one. "Well, are you still going with me or not?"

Lou-Loc continued tying his sneakers. "I can't call it," he said, still not looking at her.

"What you mean, you can't call it?"

"I mean what I said, I don't know."

"Lou-Loc," she whined, "how you going to do me like that? You're supposed to be my man, but you would actually consider letting me go to my sister's wedding alone? Do you know how that would look to my family?"

"Like I could give a fuck how I look to your family," he said seriously. "Let's be real about this shit, yo' family don't like me and I ain't too sure I like them either."

"Lou-Loc, you're just being paranoid. My mother was just saying the other day how lucky I was to have a man like you in my life."

"Miss me with that bullshit, Martina. Every time I go over there they get to talking about me on some slick shit."

"That's not true."

"The hell it isn't. They think that because they're talking about me in Spanish that I don't understand, which goes to show how ignorant they are. Spanish is a second language in California, so I picked up on it early. Yo' mama is suspect and yo' sister be straight tripping. I ain't for that shit."

"What you mean, my sister be tripping? I know you ain't trying to play the blame game, because I can go there too with the way your sister came up to New York trying to style like her shit didn't stink. From the way all of y'all kept throwing gifts at her you'd have thought she was the queen of the fucking Crips," Martina shot back.

Lou-Loc had finally had enough. "Muthafucka please, Malika is a teenager but your sister and them is grown as shit, acting like they still in high school. That slum bitch be acting all high off the hog, knowing damn well she from the projects. And please don't get me started on that chump-ass nigga she always trying to brag on. Yeah, he's a lawyer handling a li'lchange, so I'll give him that much, but with the way them two snort up powder I'm surprised he ain't broke yet."

"You're just jealous because he's about to marry my sister and we've been together longer than them and I'm not even engaged." Martina twisted her lips.

Lou-Loc looked at her crazy. "You must've fell and bumped your head if you think I'm jealous of a hype and a damn gold-digging whore. Lets me ask you this: If she so in love with this nigga, then why li'l Snoopy seen her all hugged up on one of them fag-ass Brims from a hundred and twelfth street?"

"Please, that's probably just some shit one of your boys made up to start trouble. My sister has more respect for herself than that, so try again," Martina dismissed the accusation.

"Respect my fucking ass! The only reason your sister probably hate on me so much is because I didn't take the pussy when she threw it at me. Fuck her." Lou-Loc walked to the mirror and began combing his wild-ass hair. He knew he had just dealt Martina a low blow, but he was angry and that's what he did when he got mad. He tried to stick to his guns, but when he looked at the hurt on her face through the reflection in the mirror he felt like shit. Her full, sexy lips were drawn and pouted as she stood looking at her feet with her hands on her belly. When she looked at him, her big brown eyes were rimmed with tears. Martina was a pure hell-raiser, but at times she appeared so innocent and fragile. Lou-Loc stopped combing his hair and walked to where she was standing. When their eyes met, a lone tear ran down her cheek and he was hooked like a fish on a line.

Martina sat on the edge of the bed and parted her legs. She wiped the tears from her eyes and motioned for him to sit between her legs so she could help him with his hair. Lou-Loc sat on the floor and rested his head on one of her thighs. The warmth was comforting to him. She massaged his scalp, immediately calming the raging beast inside him. As he allowed himself to be wrapped in the comfort of his lady, he remembered all the good times they had when he first came out to New York. Martina was a lot to deal with, but the heart wanted what the heart wanted, so he would thug it out.

"I know you don't like my family, but you don't always have to throw it up in my face like that. I have feelings too, Lou-Loc," she said sincerely. "Look, you don't like being around my family and I can respect that, but I didn't want to start a fight with you. I just thought that if I started softening you up early that maybe I could convince you to come with me to the wedding. If I had known it would lead to all this then I wouldn't have bothered."

Lou-Loc felt bad. He had thought she was softening him up to crack for some bread, when all she really wanted was a date to her sister's wedding. "My bad," he whispered. "When your mama ain't on my back about going to church I guess she can be pretty good, but that sister of yours . . ." he shook his head. "We're like oil and water."

For a long moment they just sat in silence, each lost in their own thoughts. Lou-Loc got up from the floor and walked over to the mirror. Martina had parted his hair and put a French braid on either side. It wasn't much, but it would do until he had a chance to hit the African braid shop on 125th. Outside of their five-story walk-up, somebody was beating the hell out of their car horn. Lou-Loc's ride had come, and it was time for him to hit the streets, but not before Martina put her bid in.

"Daddy," she said as he gathered his keys and wallet. "I was going to wear those Prada shoes you bought for me to the wedding, but being that my feet are swollen I can't get into them. You think you could hook a sister up?"

"Don't this just beat all?" Lou-Loc shook his head. Reluctantly, he pulled out his bankroll and handed her $250. He didn't want to part with the money, but if it could get her to shut up it was well worth it.

Martina looked down at the money. "That's it?"

Lou-Loc gave her a blank stare. "You said you wanted a pair of shoes, not a trip to the Dominican Republic. So if that, plus whatever you peeled outta my pocket when I staggered in here last night, ain't enough then you're just assed out. I'm gone." He left.

On the Lower East Side of Manhattan it was business as usual. The fiends were out looking to score, and the young soldiers of the Latin Connection were more than willing to serve them the poison. It wasn't personal, just business. The Latin Connection was a faction of the Bloods, whose members were composed entirely of Latinos. They were the newest Blood set to pop up in New York City, but they were quickly making a name for themselves as one of the most dangerous.

The soldiers were huddled up on the corner making sure all the fiends were taken care of when a long, red Eldorado pulled up to the curb and drew everyone's attention. The driver stepped out of the car and rolled his broad shoulders. He easily stood over six feet four and was almost as wide as the Cadillac's grill. He carried an air of menace about him that made people shy away from him when they came across him in the streets. The driver was a no-nonsense head buster and the personal bodyguard of a very important man.

The driver held open the back door of the Eldorado and his passenger stepped out. He was slender and tan, with a neatly tapered beard lining his jaw. He brushed off the sleeves of his white linen suit before checking his fedora in the reflection of the Cadillac's window. With the hulking bodyguard in tow, the man in the white suit made his way toward the little Spanish restaurant on the corner. Everyone he passed greeted him with smiles and well wishes or got

out of his way, but they all paid their respects.
The slender man didn't appear very powerful,
especially standing beside the driver, but in the
game nothing was ever as it seemed. Though
he had been gone for a while, everyone on the
Lower East Side recognized Michael Angelino,
aka El Diablo, the true leader of LC Bloods.

"*Como esta*," he greeted Marco, who was
standing in front of the restaurant. Marco was a
soldier and LC Blood and Cisco's lieutenant.

"Everything is *bueno*, Michael. *Muy bueno*
now that you're back with us." Marco smiled.
"Cisco is inside waiting for you."

El Diablo brushed past the grinning Marco
and stepped inside the restaurant. When the
people inside noticed him they gave El Diablo
a standing ovation. Among the Spanish community El Diablo was somewhat of a folk hero.
They called him the man who cleaned up the
streets, but what they really meant was the man
who forced all non-Hispanics from the neighborhood.

El Diablo smiled and bowed. "Please, please,"
he said, motioning for silence. "I am just a man.
Save your praise for someone who deserves
it." After another cheesy bow, he made his way
toward a table in the back where his captain,
Cisco, was waiting for him.

"The people love you." Cisco stood and greeted El Diablo with a warm hug. "You make the streets safe for poor businessmen such as myself, and we adore you for it. Welcome home, my brother."

After the pleasantries were done, the two men sat down to discuss business. El Diablo was the leader of LC, but it had been Cisco who they answered to while he was away. After being gone so long, El Diablo was anxious to be brought up to speed on the progress of their movement. "So, how've you been while I was away? I trust business is good, yes?"

"Si, si," Cisco replied. "We are indeed prospering. Our sales have increased by over thirty-two percent just over the last six months. Don't worry, Michael, you left your business in good hands."

El Diablo smiled at his captain. "Very good, Cisco, and our plans to expand, these are progressing too?"

Cisco shifted in his chair uncomfortably. "Well, yes and no."

"Cisco, forgive me for being a poor, dumb country boy, but I do not understand. This yes-no; is it some sort of new slang? Explain, please."

"If you'll permit me." Cisco reached into his inside pocket and pulled out a folded-up city map, which he spread out over the table. Certain areas on the map were circled in red marker and some in blue. "These are our main borders," he said, sliding his fingers from Thirty-second Street to the tip of Brooklyn. "With the exception of Chinatown, and Little Italy, we are the controlling factors in Manhattan and are gaining territory in the Bronx also." He traced a line from Third Avenue to Fordham Road.

El Diablo looked at the map closely. "And what of this area marked *fire zone*?" He tapped the area on the map that marked Harlem. The words *Fire Zone* were written across it. "What do we have there?"

Cisco made a face like he smelled something foul. "Harlem, that's no good, Michael. Those blacks up there"—he shook his head—"they are killing each other in the streets."

El Diablo scratched his chin. "Cisco, I thought Harlem was Blood hood? If this is the case, then why have we not spoken with our comrades up there about an arrangement?"

Cisco shrugged his shoulders. "Michael, I spoke with Scooby personally and he assured me that if we were trying to get something going in Harlem that we would have he and his crew's full support as long as they got to eat from it."

El Diablo shrugged. "If we have their support, then what's the problem?"

Cisco knew this question would come. He had gone over it again and again in his head. Now that the time had come, his mind drew a blank. There was something about the way that El Diablo looked at him that made him cringe.

"Things have changed uptown," he finally managed to get out. "Though our membership is still strong north of a hundred and tenth street, Harlem is temporarily under new management."

El Diablo leaned in and peered at Cisco. "Who is so bold as to tell me that I can't feed my soldiers?"

"Crips, Michael." Cisco said and braced himself for El Diablo's reaction. To his surprise, El Diablo burst into a fit of laughter.

"Are you serious?" El Diablo tried to stop laughing long enough to catch his breath. "You mean to say that you allowed a handful of disorganized gangbangers to stop us from invading one of the most profitable drug areas on the east coast?" He back-handed Cisco to the floor. Before Cisco could gather his wits, the giant scooped him up by his neck.

"Michael, these are not the same disorganized street punks you remember!" Cisco gasped as the breath was being choked from him. "These two kids from L.A. came out here a few years ago and everything changed. They unified the gangs!"

El Diablo was interested in what Cisco had to say and Cisco motioned for the giant to release him. "Don't play me, Cisco. The Crips are too busy killing each other to unify. What are you talking about?"

"All true," Cisco said, gasping for air. "They touched down in New York about two years ago, if my information on them is correct. At first they were just getting money on a few corners, then they started recruiting workers. They didn't appear to be making major moves so they flew under our radar, but over the last year or so things changed. They sought out the leaders of the smaller gangs and started getting in their ears and the next thing we knew the sets were unified and started claiming Harlem Crip with the two L.A. niggers as they leaders. By the time we realized what was going on they had Harlem in the smash."

El Diablo sat back in his chair. "Cisco, why hasn't this problem been dealt with already? If these two men have the power to unify the gangs of New York, then the threat must be neutralized."

Cisco straightened his suit jacket before continuing. "Believe me, we've tried, but our attempts have been less than successful. A while back some Bloods from up around the Gun Hill section of the Bronx decided they wanted to get money in Harlem, but to do it they'd have to get rid of the two Crips. They sent down three of their best killers, and I'm not talking locals with guns. These guys were professionals. So these guys roll on one of the ones they call Gutter one night outside of a bodega. They're out there waving their guns and popping mucho crap and the whole time this Gutter cat is just laughing like he wasn't about to get his face blown off. So while these muthafuckas are trying to figure out what the hell is so funny, Gutter's partner Lou-Loc jumped out on some ninja shit." Cisco crossed himself. "When he got done with them there wasn't enough left of their faces for their families to identify them."

El Diablo gave Cisco a very disapproving look so Cisco tried to save face by shifting the blame. "I wanted to keep going at them, but some of the other Blood leaders decided that instead of wasting our troops and making the streets hot, it may be best just to leave them to their little corners."

"Cisco," El Diablo began, "you and I came up together since we were little pissers, robbing dealers for their packages and I love you like a brother. It is because of this love that you still live, but do not test the limits of that love. I will not tolerate excuses from you or anyone else. The Jamaicans couldn't do it, the Italians wouldn't, but you let these crab muthafuckas disrupt our flow and disrespect our set?"

"Michael, on everything I love, these two will be dealt with in due time," Cisco assured him

El Diablo removed a cigar from his jacket pocket and lit it, watching Cisco squirm the whole time. "Cisco," he blew out a cloud of smoke, "for as long as we've known each other I had never realized that common sense isn't one of your strong points. If a girl gives you crabs, you don't wait and give them time to multiply and cause you more discomfort. You get rid of them, immediately!" He slammed his fists on the table for emphasis. El Diablo rose from his seat and flicked the ashes of his cigar into Cisco's drink. "I will have Harlem, and you will get it for me or I will find someone who can."

Chapter 3

Lou-Loc stepped out of his building and was almost blinded by the crisp May sun. He threw on his sunglasses and peered up at the clear sky and smiled because it was looking like a beautiful day. His moment was soured when Gutter started beating on the horn again. "Kick back with that shit, fool!" Lou-Loc shouted.

Gutter stepped out of the car to greet his friend. With the blue bandannas tied to his wrists and the dark glasses covering his face, Gutter looked like he had stepped straight off a television episode of *Gangland*. He was a coal-black cat with a shaggy beard that looked like it hadn't been combed in a few days. Whereas Lou-Loc was more conservative about flying his gang colors, Gutter was G'd up at all times. He was dressed in an oversized Duke Blue Devils sweatshirt; blue Levi's, and blue All Stars with the blue laces. He was one of the most dangerous men Lou-Loc had ever met, as well as his best friend.

Gutter had gotten into gangbanging about a year before Lou-Loc got put on the hood, but Gutter had solider in his blood long before his feet had ever touched Los Angeles soil. He was born in Algiers, but moved to the States a few years after when his father was killed. When he and what was left of his family settled in Los Angeles, he began to see the world with new eyes. His uncles, aunts, and all his cousins were Crips and filled their foreign cousin with everything they knew about being a Crip. For Gutter to join the Crips was only natural, but for Lou-Loc it was an altogether different story.

When Lou-Loc was about ten, he and his father were doing some Christmas shopping in the Crenshaw Mall, lost in the holiday spirit. As they were heading back to the car with all their packages, they were surrounded by a group of young hoodlums. Lou-Loc didn't know too much about gangbanging back then but he knew they were Bloods from the red scarves covering their faces. The Bloods brandished weapons and demanded their packages. Lou-Loc was terrified but his father seemed strong and confident. But, looking back at it, Lou-Loc realized that he was probably afraid too but wouldn't show it in front of his son. His father simply told them that they could have whatever little money he had left on him, but he couldn't part with his family's Christmas gifts. It seemed as if he would rather have died than see his family not have gifts for Christmas, so they killed him.

Lou-Loc sat on the cold concrete ground of the parking lot, sobbing and holding his dead father's hand until the police showed up almost thirty minutes later. Two detectives whisked him away to the precinct, where they questioned him about what he saw. All Lou-Loc would say is that they were Bloods. The police showed him a book that contained pictures and profiles of active Blood gang members in the area, hoping that he could identify someone. Of course, Lou-Loc hadn't seen their faces so it was impossible, but he let them continue flipping through the book while he burned the faces of the men he saw into his memory. By the time they released him into the custody of his grieving mother, Lou-Loc was numb. He tried to force himself to go to sleep that night but he couldn't. The only thing he could focus on was revenge. He couldn't identify the men who had killed his father so he would punish the Bloods as a whole. It was on sight with his new enemies, and so began his walk into the darkness.

It didn't take long for word of Lou-Loc's exploits to reach the older homies from his neighborhood, which was Hoover territory. Lou-Loc had given the Bloods enough grief for them to place a bounty on his head and have his name on the wire in every Blood hood. It was terminate on sight for Lou-Loc and with him not being connected to anyone it would only be a matter of time before someone collected on the bounty, so the Hoovers decided to intervene.

Lou-Loc had heard through the grapevine that his presence had been requested by some of the older homies to discuss the heat he was bringing down on the hood, but he paid it no mind. He had too much work to put in to be sent for by anyone, so he blew off the homies' requests. When it became obvious that Lou-Loc wasn't going to come to them they decided to go to him. He was coming out of Jack in the Box when they rolled on him. He recognized the hulk of a man leading the pack as Big Gunn, a respected leader from Hoover Crip, but he didn't know the other five ragtag gangsters he had with them. When Lou-Loc found himself in the parking lot surrounded by the angry Crips he was terrified, but kept his gangsta scowl to hide his fear.

"What's cracking, cuz? Where you from?" Gutter asked in a less-than-pleasant tone. At the time they didn't know one another, but had seen each other in passing in the halls at school on those rare occasions when Gutter decided to attend. His face had always stood out to Lou-Loc because Gutter was coal-black with pale green eyes. It was a trait many of the men in his family carried.

"You don't know me to be questioning me." Lou-Loc tried to brush past Gutter but Big Gunn cut him off. The O.G. stood a full foot taller than Lou-Loc and was covered in muscles.

"That ain't the right answer, li'l homie. You can either answer my nephew's question or I can fire on you right now," Big Gunn said, raising one of his mallet-like fists.

Lou-Loc looked around and weighed his options. He would've knuckled up with either of the youngsters but the thought of getting a mouth shot from Big Gunn wasn't something he wanted to experience. He looked Big Gunn directly in the eyes and answered him honestly: "I ain't from nowhere."

Gutter sized Lou-Loc up. "You gotta be from somewhere with the kinda shit you're out here pulling, cuz. Anybody decides to wage war on the Bloods by his lonesome has either got a screw loose or a motive. What angle you working, cuz?"

"Ain't no angle, homie. My beef with them is personal, so I'm gonna keep busting on them niggaz until I feel like we even, and from what they took from me we ain't never gonna be even," Lou-Loc said passionately.

Big Gunn studied Lou-Loc. From the look of hatred in his eyes when he spoke of the Bloods, Big Gunn knew that whatever crime they committed against the young man was a heinous one. He had seen the looks of the faces of many young soldiers who had been driven to gang life through tragedy, so he felt his pain. "What they call you, cuz?"

"Crazy Lou," Lou-Loc said, as that was the moniker he went by in those days. He got the name based on some of the extremes he went to when he first kicked off his personal war with the other side.

"I heard of this li'l nigga," another young Crip spoke up. "They say that fool tried to run up in the projects by himself hunting Bloods and almost got his fool ass killed when they mobbed on him," he said, laughing.

"Yeah, they was twenty deep chasing me up outta there, but I'm still here and two of theirs ain't, so who would you say came out on top in that one?" Lou-Loc shot back.

The Crip stood toe to toe with Lou-Loc. "You think you hard, huh?"

"Homie, if you keep icing me like that you gonna find out firsthand what I think and what I know," Lou-Loc told him.

"Fall back, cuz." Big Gunn separated them with a sweep of his massive arms. "You niggaz wanna knuckle up, then you'll do it the right way, when we put li'l cuz on the hood."

"Dig, I respect Hoover to the fullest, but I don't need to join no gang for protection. I been doing okay protecting myself," Lou-Loc told him.

Big Gunn turned his green eyes on Lou-Loc. "Li'l nigga, I ain't trying to protect you, I'm trying to school you. I see li'l dudes like you every day, angry li'l hoppers running around with nothing and nobody, trying to find where you fit in. I been there, homie, and I know it ain't easy, so I'm reaching out to try and ease some of that pain."

"What do you know about my pain?" Lou-Loc asked emotionally.

"Li'l nigga, I've been killing and watching my homies die for over twenty years. What the fuck do you think I know about pain? You see, my li'l homies," Big Gunn motioned toward the young men with him, "to the outside looking in all we are is a gang, but we're more than that, we're a family. Yeah, you out here getting your stripes because you're dedicated to busting on slobs, but we're dedicated to each other. Each man here would kill or die for the other because we love each other, cuz, and that's how family does. Are you ready to make that kind of commitment?"

Big Gunn's words touched Lou-Loc because they danced so close to the truth. His sister was still young and his mother was so busy trying to get over the loss of his father, so there was nobody who truly understood what he was going through, but Big Gunn did. In the ranks of the Crips, Gunn offered Lou-Loc something that he had been searching for since he'd lost his father: love.

"A'ight, I'm in. What do I have to do?" Lou-Loc asked.

"Survive," Big Gunn said with a smile and stepped back.

Before Lou-Loc could make heads or tails of what he meant, Gutter stole on him. The blow dazed Lou-Loc but didn't drop him. Lou-Loc came back with an awkward swing, which Gutter easily evaded, and hooked him in the gut. Lou-Loc doubled over and Gutter went for the knockout, just as he had expected. When Gutter swung, Lou-Loc weaved and landed a crushing right cross Gutter's chin, which sent him spilling to the concrete. Before Lou-Loc could savor his small victory, he was descended upon by the teenage Crips. They punched and kicked him in every exposed part of his body, but Lou-Loc gave just as well as he got. Someone caught him in the back of the head and dropped him to one knee. He knew that if he hit the ground they would surely kill him, so he kept swinging. After what seemed like forever he heard Big Gunn's voice.

"A'ight, that's enough." Big Gunn parted the crowd and helped Lou-Loc to stand. Everyone who had participated in the fight was bruised or bloodied, but Gutter looked like he had caught the worst of it. He took a step toward Lou-Loc like he wanted to keep fighting, but Big Gunn pushed him away. "I said enough, nephew. The l'il nigga held his own so let it be. L'il cuz," he addressed Lou-Loc, "you knew all you had to do was go to the ground and it would've been over, so why did you keep fighting, knowing that you couldn't win?"

"Better to go out fighting then to just lay down and die," Lou-Loc mumbled. He felt like his jaw was broken and his teeth felt loose.

"Sho ya right." Big Gunn patted him on the back. "And that is your first lesson about Crip'n, to stand up for what you believe in. Now you can go back to playing Rambo in these streets and possibly get yourself killed or bow down to something greater than yourself and become a legend." Big Gunn took the bandanna from his back pocket and held it out to Lou-Loc.

Lou-Loc was hesitant. He knew that if he stepped through the door that Big Gunn had just opened there would be no turning back, but what did he have to lose? "Fuck it," he took the bandanna. The moment he did he was greeted by a series of whistles and cheers from the homies as if he had just hit the winning shot in a playoff game. Even Gutter, who was still upset about his busted lip, embraced him. For the first time in a long time, Lou-Loc felt whole again.

As time passed he and Gutter would become thick as thieves. The two youngsters were recognized by the other members as loyal and efficient soldiers. They were the first to pop their guns and the last to roll out in every firefight, earning them reputations as young killers. And when Hoover allied itself with an up-and-coming hood called Harlem, Lou-Loc and Gutter's legend grew even bigger. It was made clear to all gangs across L.A. County that Hoover-Harlem wasn't to be fucked with. By this time Big Gunn's protégé had become a respected young lieutenant on the set, and had dropped the Crazy from his name and started going by Lou-Loc. But for as notorious as Lou-Loc and Gutter were becoming, it was a split-second decision that had made them legends and wanted men.

The O.G.'s from Hoover had called a meeting to discuss a narcotics detective who the homies in the hood had an arrangement with. They were already giving him 40 percent of their weekly drug take but he got greedy and tried to up it to 65. When they refused to pay, the detective decided to send them a message and killed one of the l'il homies from Harlem. When they found the kid he was hanging by his ankles from a streetlight on the corner of Hoover and 107th, in the center of their hood. Inside of his mouth was a note that read *Pay or join your friend in nigger heaven.* The police had no idea who had done it or what the note meant, but the homies did. The murder was not only a slight to Hoover and Harlem but to their allies, because they were all eating together. The leaders of several sets got together and decided that it was time to do something about Detective O'Leary.

A homeboy by the name of Fat Pat had a sister who did clerical work at the precinct O'Leary worked out of who provided them with the information they needed to pull off the caper. The plan was simple: Break into O'Leary's house, give him a good beating, and bust the place up. They didn't want him dead because it would bring the wrath of the entire LAPD down on the Crips, but they wanted to teach him a good lesson. Things in the hood, though, never worked out quite how you planned them.

The soldiers selected for the mission represented several Crip sets. This was Big Gunn's idea to promote the unity among their respective hoods. There was Stan from East Coast, Snake Eyes from Hoover, and Gutter, who would represent Harlem. Lou-Loc wasn't supposed to be there but because he and Gutter were crime partners he went along to back his homie up in case anything went wrong. The four desperadoes piled into the Buick they had stolen that morning for the mission, and headed for Carson.

The particular house they were looking for was right off Carson Avenue, near a housing complex that was still under construction. Carson was a relatively quiet town, but had a fairly large population of Crips. This was a bonus, because in the event that anything went wrong and they had to get low, they had several different pads to hide out in. The key to this mission would be Stan. He was one of those high-yellow dudes, with good hair and Anglo features. In the right light Stan could pass for white, which is what they were all counting on. Stan would ring the doorbell dressed in a FedEx uniform to get O'Leary's wife to open the door and the rest of the homies would rush the house and subdue the family and wait for O'Leary to come home and ambush him.

"A'ight nigga," Gutter said to Stan from his seat in the back, "once we get up in there, you go on up to the corner and look out for O'Leary's car. There's only one way to come down this street, so you can't miss the nigga. When you see his car, dial my cell. Let the phone ring once, and then hang up. That'll be the signal, you got me?"

Stan was so busy scooping pinky nails full of cocaine into his nose in the front seat that he was only half listening. "Cuz, why you keep acting like this shit is rocket science?" Stan asked in an irritated tone.

"Nigga, you need to put that powder down and pay attention. If we get caught up it won't be no county time for us, we going straight to the big league," Lou-Loc warned him.

Stan wiped his nose with the palm of his hand. "Stop bitching like a nigga scared to go to prison, I was born in that muthafucka so it'll be like going home for me. I don't see why we gotta do all this secret-agent shit instead of just peeling this nigga's wig back."

"Because killing a cop is a capital offense," Snake Eyes spoke up. "Which means if we get caught it's a free ride to the gas chamber." Like the rest of them, Snake Eyes was a gangbanger and down-ass Crip, but he was also a thinker. He had graduated at the top of his class from high school, and was in the middle of his third year of law school at UCLA. Much like Lou-Loc, Snake Eyes knew there was more to life than just gangbanging and intended to make something of himself, but he was fiercely loyal to Hoover Crip.

"Fuck all that yapping, I'm ready to put this work in." Gutter checked the .38 he was carrying. "You ready, cuz?" he said, looking at Lou-Loc.

For a long moment Lou-Loc said nothing. He sat there staring at the TEC-9 on his lap and wondered for the millionth time if he had made the right decision by going along on the mission. Since the day Big Gunn had put him on the hood he had come to love putting on work, but something about the caper they were on made him feel uneasy. At nineteen years old, Lou-Loc had committed God-knows-how-many crimes and shot at least a half-dozen people. So it wasn't fear that he felt; it was more like apprehension. Still, he kept his reservations to himself and went along with the mission.

"Cuz, if you don't want to you ain't gotta get dirty this rip. Me and Snake Eyes can handle this," Gutter whispered to Lou-Loc, noticing the worried expression on his face.

Lou-Loc looked at his friend and mustered his phoniest smile. "What I look like letting you take all the glory so you can go back to the hood and

brag on it. Let's handle this and get it over with."
Lou-Loc got out of the car, followed by Gutter
and the rest. They all covered their faces with
red bandannas instead of the traditional blue so
that when the deed was done the heat would fall
on the Bloods.

"Just so everybody is clear, we don't touch his
wife and kids. I could give a fuck what happens to
O'Leary, but we take it easy with his family and
when it's over we turn them loose, dig?" Lou-Loc
said seriously. Gutter and Snake Eyes looked
puzzled but both agreed to it. Stan just sucked his
teeth and continued toward the house, carrying
the fake FedEx box. Lou-Loc felt it in his bones
that Stan was going to be trouble.

Stan walked up the few steps and rang the
doorbell while his three henchmen concealed
themselves in the bushes. The living-room cur-
tain fluttered and a few seconds later the locks
came undone and the door opened. The young
lady who answered the door was very attractive;
with long blond hair she wore in a ponytail and
tanned skin. Her crisp blue eyes looked Stan up
and down playfully. The cool breeze coming off
the Pacific Ocean caused her nipples to stand at
full attention behind the thin baby-doll T-shirt.
She shifted her weight from one leg to the other
and gave Stan a pleasant smile.

After a long silence, and a bit of fantasizing, Stan finally found his voice. "Ah . . . package for the O'Learys."

The girl licked her lips and looked Stan dead in the eye. "Pretty big, huh?" she said seductively, "The package, that is."

"So where would you like me to put it?" Stan asked, matching her tone. Before she could answer, Gutter stepped from the shadows with his gun drawn.

"Don't move, bitch," Gutter snapped. She looked like she was going to scream until Gutter placed the gun to her head. "Let's do a little math, shall we." He backed her into the house. "You screaming plus this gun equals a dead white girl, ya dig?" The girl nodded. "Good."

Lou-Loc and Snake Eyes stepped into the house, followed by Stan, who was licking his lips hungrily. "Yeah, I need to taste a l'il of that pink flesh." He moved toward the terrified girl, but Lou-Loc pushed him back.

"Save them freakish-ass cravings you got for your own time, and let's stick to the business. You got somewhere to be, don't you?" Lou-Loc reminded him. He could tell from the way Stan was looking at him that he wanted to make something off it, but the East Coast Crip knew he couldn't see Lou-Loc, so he let it be and left the house. Lou-Loc turned his attention toward the girl. He motioned for her to sit on the couch and then knelt down beside her. "What's your name?" When she didn't answer he tried being a little softer with her. "Look, girl, ain't nobody gonna hurt you. Now, tell me your name?"

"T—Tina," she finally blurted out.

"Now we're making some progress. Next question: Who else is here with you?" he asked, but the girl remained silent.

"Look bitch—Snake Eyes began, but was cut off when Lou-Loc raised his hand for silence. Getting the girl all scared wouldn't help them any.

"Tina," Lou-Loc said very evenly, "I told you that no one was going to hurt you, but if you don't cooperate, all bets are off. Who else is in the house with you?"

Tina fidgeted but eventually answered. "My mother and little brother are upstairs in the bedroom, but please don't hurt them. They won't be any trouble."

"Let us be the judge of that," Lou-Loc told her. He turned to Snake Eyes and Gutter. "Round them up quietly if possible, forcibly if necessary."

Snake Eyes and Gutter darted off to the upper levels of the house. There were screams and the sounds of furniture moving upstairs, which worried Lou-Loc because he knew that Gutter could be quite unpredictable. A few minutes later Gutter made his way down the stairs with a middle-aged woman hog-tied and slung over his shoulder, with Snake Eyes bringing up the rear, leading a little boy by the hand. Gutter tossed Mrs. O'Leary on the couch next to her daughter. She didn't look to be harmed but she was less than happy about his manhandling of her.

"Blood, this ho started tripping so I had to tie her ass up." Gutter answered the question on Lou-Loc's face.

"Did these animals harm you?" Mrs. O'Leary inspected Tina.

"No, Mom, I'm fine. As long as we cooperate they're not going to hurt us," Tina told her mother.

Mrs. O'Leary looked at her daughter in disbelief. "Tina, are you insane? All these people know is violence," she said in a matter-of-fact tone.

"Miss, we didn't come to harm you or your daughter, so just chill out," Lou-Loc assured her.

"You expect me to believe that? I read about your kind in the news everyday and all you do is kill each other and try to blame decent white folks for your troubles," Mrs. O'Leary scoffed. "You bastards are parasites, and we have only ourselves to blame for brining you to this country."

Gutter, being of foreign descent, took offense to the remark and stalked over to Mrs. O'Leary. He snatched her up by the front of her bathrobe and rained spittle in her face when he snarled, "Who the fuck are you to judge? Bitch, your boy-loving ancestors plucked us from our native land and brought us here against our will and you've got the nerve to try and play the blame game. How dare you!" Lou-Loc tried to intervene but Gutter waved him away. "You hate black folks, but it's a black man who saved your life tonight because my father would turn over in his grave if he knew I wasted my time or my bullets on a trash whore like you," he said, tossing her roughly back on the couch.

Lou-Loc breathed a sigh of relief when Gutter walked away from the woman. Even if he told her, Mrs. O'Leary still wouldn't know how close she'd come to turning the break-in into a murder.

Outside, Stan stood on the corner kicking rocks, upset that he was away from the action. He would've loved to have had a chance to loot the O'Leary house, but what bothered him more was not being able to get a taste of Tina's sweet little ass. "Cock-blocking motherfucker," he spat, thinking how Lou-Loc had dismissed him like he was a boss. He might've run Harlem but he didn't run East Coast.

Stan perked up when he noticed a group of young Mexican girls walking in his direction. They were all wearing bikini tops and too-tight shorts, with beach towels slung over their shoulders. "*Hola, mamis, como esta*?" He kicked his weak game. One of the girls thought he was kind of cute so she stopped to talk to him. Stan was so wrapped up in the girls that he didn't notice O'Leary's blue Ford bend the corner and drive right past him.

Two hours had gone past since Lou-Loc and the others entered the house and there was still no sign of O'Leary. Gutter and Snake Eyes were both getting antsy, but Lou-Loc felt sick to the pit of his stomach. He felt that something was wrong, but they had come too far to turn back now. "Where this fool at?" He looked at his watch. "His shift ended hours ago and he still ain't here."

"Maybe he's out with his girlfriend?" Gutter said, taunting Mrs. O'Leary.

"My husband is a police officer, so whatever you're planning you're not going to get away with it," Mrs. O'Leary told them.

"We know who your punk-ass husband is— Why do you think we're here?" Gutter chuckled.

"If it's money you're after, there's three hundred dollars on my nightstand, and some jewelry in my box. You can have it all if you just leave," Mrs. O'Leary offered.

"Don't nobody want your money, lady," Lou-Loc said, dismissing her offer.

"Speak for yourself, cuz. I'm all over that scratch." Gutter tossed Lou-Loc the cell phone that Stan was supposed to be calling. "Be on point for the homie's call while I gots to see what these crackers is holding."

"Man, stick to the script," Lou-Loc warned, but Gutter was already gone.

Outside the house Detective O'Leary was just pulling into his driveway. He was a short, squat man with thinning gray hair. His brown suit looked like it had been slept in, and his wing-tipped shoes looked like they were ready to be retired. From the stains on his shirt, it was fair to say that the man was a slob. He got out of the beat-up blue Caprice followed by his partner, Bill Simms, who was a young, dark-haired man, wearing an expensive-looking blue suit. Together they made their way toward the house, continuing the conversation they'd started on the ride over.

"I don't know, John, it seems like for every spook we bust, two more pop up to take their place. Makes you wonder if it's even worth it," Bill was saying.

"All depends on how you look at it, Billy boy." O'Leary took a minute to light his cigarette. "Those poor bastards are doing us a favor by killing each other in the streets on the nightly basis. The comical part about it all is that they aren't even killing each other over money: They're waging war over colors and streets that they'll never own. I say we step aside and let 'em wipe each other out. It doesn't make me any difference as long as I collect my pension when it's all said and done."

The two men laughed together and headed for the front door. Neither one knew what waited for them on the other side.

Lou-Loc was pacing back and forth over the living room carpet, wondering why O'Leary hadn't made it home yet. This would be their best and only chance to get at him, so it needed to get done that night.

"Man, why don't you sit your ass still before you wear a hole in the damn carpet?" Snake Eyes joked.

Lou-Loc gave a halfhearted laugh. Just as he was about to go back to the window to check for

O'Leary the front door clicked open. Before Lou-Loc could shout a warning to Snake Eyes, O'Leary stepped into the house and looked around in horror. "What the fuck?" he barked. Stan had fucked up, big-time.

O'Leary was attempting to pull his gun, but his partner Billy was a little quicker on the draw and cleared his service revolver. He shoved O'Leary to the side and fired two shots at Snake Eyes. Snake Eyes managed to evade the first shot but the second struck him in the leg, folding him. The two detectives were so focused on Snake Eyes that they didn't even notice Lou-Loc, who was standing behind the door.

Lou-Loc reached around the door and grabbed O'Leary by his tie. Pulling with all that he had, he pulled the detective into the house, tripping him up and sending him spilling awkwardly to the ground. Billy tried to rush the house, but Lou-Loc slammed the door into his face, dazing him. With a killer's precision he lined the TEC-9 with Billy's head from the other side of the door and pulled the trigger. The hollow-point bullets shredded the door and most of Billy's skull along with it.

O'Leary made another grab for his gun, but a foot crushed his hand. He looked up, wincing in pain, and found himself staring into a pair of green eyes.

Chapter 4

"So good of you to join us." Gutter smiled down at O'Leary, whose face was twisted into a mask of rage. The detective's eyes kept darting from Gutter to the gun, which lay a few feet away. "By all means, keep reaching so I can have an excuse to blast yo' bitch ass." O'Leary wisely remained still. Gutter looked from Snake Eyes, who was bleeding like a stuck pig, to Lou-Loc. "Fuck happened down here?" Gutter snapped at Lou-Loc and Snake Eyes said with a smile, "Don't let me stop you. By all means, reach for it." O'Leary saw the murderous look in the masked man's eyes and changed his mind.

"Fuck happened in here?" Gutter asked, looking from Lou-Loc to Snake Eyes, who was on the ground bleeding.

"Ask your stupid-ass homeboy," Lou-Loc snapped as he rushed over to tend to Snake Eyes. "Homie slipped and let the fat bastard get the drop on us."

"Damn," Gutter spat, looking at the dead man in the doorway. "You hit bad, Blood?" he asked Snake Eyes.

"Nah, I think it just scratched me, no thanks to old boy," he said, grimacing and clutching his leg. "Where the fuck is that nigga at?"

No sooner than the words left Snake Eyes's mouth than Stan came running into the house. He took one look at the dead body on the floor and Snake Eyes stretched out and panicked. "What the fuck, Lou-Loc!"

Lou-Loc shot Stan a dagger warning him to shut up, but it was too late. O'Leary glared up at Lou-Loc and a light of recognition went off in his head. When all the pieces fell into place, all he could do was chuckle. "You think you're pretty smart, don't you, cuz?" he said to Lou-Loc, letting him know that he had seen through the ruse of the red rags. "If you're Lou-Loc, then that black bastard over there must be Gutter."

"Damn, he knows us, we're fucked," Stan said frantically.

"*Fucked* ain't the word," O'Leary said as he eased off the floor, with Lou-Loc's gun still on him, while Gutter kept his on the wife and child. They knew he wouldn't try anything stupid that would get his family killed. "Let me let you geniuses in on a secret: Killing a cop is a capital offense, so all you boys will get to keep each other company for what you did to old Billy." He motioned toward his partner's corpse in the doorway. "I'm gonna turn the gas on personally for this one."

Stan's eyes began to fill with tears as the panic started to set in. "You think this is a fucking game," he said, pulling a .22 from his pocket that none of them knew he was carrying and pointed it at Mrs. O'Leary.

"Homie, tuck that strap, before somebody gets hurt," Lou-Loc urged him. Stan was taking the situation from bad to worse at an alarming rate.

"Nah, cuz. I can't go to prison, that ain't gonna happen." He began crying and waving the gun nervously.

"Cuz, everything is blue. Just be cool." Gutter eased up on Stan. When he got close enough he lunged, and the gun went off. He slowly looked over his shoulder, afraid of what he would see and could only mutter, "Fuck!" Tina was screaming her head off, while her little brother sat there numb and in shock. Pieces of his mother's brains clung to his Spiderman pajamas, and the side of his face was splattered with blood. At hell had officially broken loose.

When Detective O'Leary saw what the gangbanger had done to his wife he came unhinged.

He caught Gutter with a stiff right hand that he had never saw coming. Before Gutter could gather his wits O'Leary hit him with a vicious three-punch combination and dropped him. Stan tried to turn his pistol on O'Leary, but was a half a second too late. O'Leary grabbed Stan's wrist and twisted until the bones popped, taking his gun.

"Shit!" Lou-Loc dove through the kitchen door before O'Leary could turn the gun on him, leaving Gutter, Snake Eyes, and Stan to deal with the grief-stricken detective.

"Muthafuckas." O'Leary kicked Snake Eyes in his already injured leg. "You come into my fucking house and hurt my family." He kicked Stan this time. He turned to Gutter and stomped him twice in the stomach before catching his breath. "Prison is too good for you niggers, so I'm gonna treat you to a little down-home justice." O'Leary sneered as he picked the cordless phone off from its base by the coffee table. He used one hand to dial and the other to keep the gun trained on the Crips. "This is Detective O'Leary, out of Central unit. I've got a code thirteen at my house, I need backup! They killed my partner, but I managed to kill three of them." Everyone from Gutter to Snake Eyes became nervous when they heard him say this. "Yeah, but there's still one loose on the property, hurry." He slammed the phone down. He turned his hate-filled eyes on the Crips. "Now let's have a little fun."

Lou-Loc peeped in the front window and saw O'Leary had his back to him while he was punching and kicking his homeboys. His gut had warned him to sit this mission out, but he just had to hold Gutter down and now they were all up shit creek. His mind turned over a million possible outcomes and solutions to the pinch they were in and none of them were good. He had made it out and could disappear if he so chose, but Lou-Loc would never abandon his comrades. From the way things were playing out, the only way Lou-Loc's friends would be leaving the O'Leary house was in bracelets or bags and neither option seemed very appealing. Stan had allowed them to be backed into a corner and the only way out was for O'Leary to die.

Lou-Loc crept to the door where Detective Simms was still laid out. The right side of his face was torn up so bad that Lou-Loc could see his chipped jawbone through what was left of his skin. He ignored the dead lawman and continued creeping into the house. Snake Eyes and Stan were handcuffed together to the coffee table, while O'Leary had Gutter in the middle of the living room, pistol-whipping him. Gutter's head lolled to one side and his eyes focused on Lou-Loc, who gave him a knowing nod. Gutter's bloodied lips parted into a grin as he knew it was about to be a wrap for O'Leary.

"So this is funny to you, huh?" O'Leary punched Gutter in the face.

Stan also saw Lou-Loc creeping and in true idiot fashion blew the element of surprise. "Help us, fool!"

O'Leary spun just as Lou-Loc squeezed off a burst from the TEC that punched holes in the wall and ceiling above Tina's head. O'Leary squeezed off two shots from the .22 but Lou-Loc was already on the move. As Lou-Loc fell to one side he pumped the trigger, swinging the machine gun across the living room, hitting O'Leary multiple times in the legs and torso. His body did a sick dance before finally hitting the floor, where it continued to twitch.

Lou-Loc walked over to O'Leary, who was lying on the ground and gasping like a fish out of water. He pointed the smoking TEC at O'Leary's face and told him, "This is for the l'il homie," before dumping several bullets into him. In the distance Lou-Loc could hear the familiar sirens of police cars approaching. He dug through the dead detective's pockets and retrieved the handcuff keys so he could free his comrades.

As soon as Gutter was free he walked over to O'Leary and kicked him twice. "Bitch-ass nigga," he cursed, rubbing his jaw, which felt like it was cracked.

"Leave that nigga alone and let's get the fuck outta here," Lou-Loc told him.

"Damn, it feels like my shit is on fire." Snake Eyes pulled himself painfully to his feet. He tried to stand and almost fell over, so Gutter helped him.

"It looks bad, cuz," Gutter said of his bloody leg.

"No worse than yo' face, nigga." Snake Eyes clowned him about his bruises. "Let's shake this place before I bleed to death."

"Y'all give me them slob rags." Lou-Loc collected the bandannas from his crew. Lou-Loc took the rags and began stuffing them into O'Leary's mouth, ignoring the blood that was soaking through onto his hands. He took the bandanna from around his face and used it to remove O'Leary's service weapon. "Let's go."

"Hold on," Stan hung back. "These kids can identify us. We can't leave them here like this. It's more killing to be done, cuz."

"The homie is right," Lou-Loc agreed. He tested the weight of O'Leary's gun before turning it on Stan. Stan opened his mouth to protest and Lou-Loc put a bullet through the back of his throat. "Stupid muthafucka." Lou-Loc wiped the gun clean and put it back in O'Leary's hand. For the first time that whole night nobody had to hear Stan's mouth. "We out," Lou-Loc led them out the front door.

When they stepped outside the house they could see flashing lights coming from the direction where they had parked the Buick "Shit," Gutter cursed, knowing they were now trapped.

"This way, my niggaz." Lou-Loc helped Gutter half carry Snake Eyes between the O'Learys and their neighbor's house through the backyard. They came out on the next street over, where lights were being cut on and people were coming out of their houses to see what all the commotion was about. Gutter and Snake Eyes hid in some nearby bushes while Lou-Loc broke into a minivan that was parked on the street and got the engine started. Once he and Gutter had gotten Snake Eyes secured in the back they pulled out of the neighborhood, careful to use their turn signals and not go over the speed limit. As they zipped east down the street, a contingent of police cars were heading west. None of them breathed until they were on the highway and safely out of Carson.

The next morning Lou-Loc went out and got the paper to see if their exploits had made the news, which they did. When he read the headline on the front page it made him smile: HOME INVASION TURNS DEADLY. The article went on to tell the story of how a group of Bloods botched a home invasion of a police detective, which left several dead. For the most part Lou-Loc knew all the details because he'd been there, but the article revealed information about Stan that he hadn't known. In addition to the slain detectives, the body of Stanley Jones, 22, of Inglewood, was found at the scene. Jones was a longtime police informant who had been providing information on both Crip and Blood activity over the last eight months.

He was totally stunned to find out Stan had been playing both sides, but he couldn't say that it surprised him. He'd always felt like there was something off about Stan, but the homies had branded him paranoid for it. "Switch-hitting muthafucka." Lou-Loc shook his head and crumpled the newspaper.

When the news of Stan's murder had reached the O.G.'s from East Coast Crips, they wanted to have Lou-Loc killed for taking out one of theirs, but Big Gunn wasn't having it. He made it clear that if anything happened to Lou-Loc both Hoover and Harlem would retaliate and nobody wanted those kinds of problems over a snitch. In the weeks that followed, the police were stomping on Blood asses from L.A. County to San Diego. Every top dog on every Blood set was leaned on to give up the killers and when the LAPD leaned on you it hurt like hell.

The Crips also felt the punch of the O'Leary murder. Not only were the police putting in overtime in the hood and stopping all cash flow, the Bloods had also gotten wind of their little charade and weren't pleased about it. The already intense rivalry between the two gangs intensified and bodies were dropping left and right. It got especially bad for Lou-Loc, who couldn't seem to go anywhere without getting shot at. That summer Lou-Loc was ambushed by a group of Bounty-Hunter Bloods while coming out of the movie theater and took a bullet in the leg. Sensing that he was living on borrowed time the longer he stayed in Cali, Lou-Loc decided to head east and get a fresh start. That was two years ago.

Chapter 5

Lou-Loc reclined in the passenger seat of Gutter's whip, trying to enjoy the blunt he was smoking, but it was hard considering Gutter had them feeling like they were on a roller coaster with the way he was driving. The speedometer read 80 when the posted speed limit was forty.

"You gonna make us crash, Andretti," Lou-Loc said sarcastically. Gutter glanced at his friend and returned his eyes to the road. In spite of Lou-Loc's comment, he pushed it to eighty-five.

Gutter cut his eyes at Lou-Loc. "Player, you just ain't hip? This here is New York City, cuz. Everybody out here already drive crazy as hell so we fit right in. Now quit crying and pass the weed, cuz."

Lou-Loc passed him the blunt. "Just slow down some before we get stopped with these guns in the car and end up on Rikers Island, and I have to let them slobs get at yo' bitch ass."

"Fool, you crazy. You could put me in a cage with fifty Brims and I can't C-faded. I'm the hardest nigga alive. Calm down and stop telling me how to drive. Don't worry; I'll get you back to Martina in one piece."

"Fuck her," Lou-Loc said and busied himself looking out the window.

"What's the matter, trouble at home?" Gutter asked, but Lou-Loc didn't answer. "Cuz, don't play me like we ain't come up on free lunch together. If something is bothering you, holla at ya boy."

Lou-Loc hesitated. "Cuz, you ever feel like you might be outgrowing Sharell?"

"Hell nah," Gutter said, speeding past a truck. "Let me put you up on something, cuz. When we moved out here, bitches was trying to see us left and right. They were all good to fuck, but that was as far as it went until I met Sharell. She was the only chick in this whole funky-ass city that I actually felt like I could vibe with," he confessed, while switching lanes without signaling and cutting off a truck. "That girl is a gem. She got a good job with the state and goes to school at night. If anything, I wouldn't be surprised if it's her that's outgrowing me."

Lou-Loc smiled at his friend. "You right, player. I don't know, sometimes I just feel like maybe

Martina ain't the one. I'm trying to get out of this shit, and she trying to pull me deeper in it and it's getting to me. If it wasn't for the fact that she's having my baby then I probably would've left her already." When Lou-Loc mentioned Martina being pregnant, Gutter shot him a look but didn't say anything. "What?"

"Nothing, cuz." Gutter tossed the weed clip out the window and lit a Newport.

"Nigga, if you've got something to say then spill it," Lou-Loc demanded.

Gutter exhaled the smoke and searched for the words to express himself without offending his friend. "Cuz, I've been your truest, bluest homeboy since that day we jumped your skinny ass on to the set. I would never put you in a cross or question your judgment, but I gotta get this off of my chest." Gutter paused to make sure he had Lou-Loc's attention. "You sure that kid she carrying is yours?"

Lou-Loc looked at Gutter as if he'd lost his mind. "How you gonna ask me something like that? What the fuck you done heard, Gutter?" No answer. "*Gutter!*"

"A'ight, Lou-Loc. I heard it through the grapevine that Martina been creeping with some offbrand nigga behind yo' back." he blurted out."

Lou-Loc was shocked. "Gutter, don't come at me with no rumors on this one. You putting shit on my lady so you better be sure."

"That's on Hoover and Harlem, cuz," Gutter said honestly.

"I don't believe this shit." Lou-Loc slammed his fist into the dashboard. "All the work I been putting in trying to keep her ass fly and she got the nerve to be tipping. On Crip I should push that ho!"

"Chill, Loc, blasting her ain't gonna change nothing." Gutter tried to reason with him.

"It'd make me feel better. G. Where you get this info from?"

"From Sharell." Gutter jumped across three lanes to get off the highway on Christopher Street.

"And how does she know?"

"Lou-Loc, you know hoes talk and other hoes listen. Few days ago, she was in the nail shop on a hundred and twenty-sixth street and that skinny bitch Nina, from Martina's hood, was in there with two of her girls talking shit about how much fun she and Martina had at this jazz club in Long Island last weekend."

Lou-Loc's wheels began to spin. He remembered that was the weekend Martina said she was going to spend the night with her sister to go over some last-minute arrangements. When Lou-Loc offered to drop her off she insisted on taking a cab. He didn't think too much of it at the time, but now the chickens were coming home to roost.

"Anyway," Gutter continued, "her homegirl asked her who they went with and she said some Blood nigga named Mac and his cousin who suppose to be ballers from Newark. Sharell was tight but she wasn't gonna follow up with that stupid shit, until she looked up and saw them hoes beaming at her. They were making sure to talk loud enough for her to hear them so she could run back and tell it. I didn't even wanna tell you, but I couldn't hold it and watch my brother get played like a sucker over some New York broad. I'm sorry, Lou-Loc."

"Ain't no need for you to apologize, my nigga. It's that bitch that's foul. When I get back to the crib I'm gonna sock that bitch, then I'm packing my shit and rolling."

"My nigga, don't wild out just yet. We gonna get all our facts straight and do it the gangsta way. Just hold yo' head for a minute," Gutter told him.

With everything going on downtown they knew they wouldn't be able to find parking on the street, so they pulled into an open-air parking lot, where they would leave the car and walk the rest of the way to BMCC. During their walk the two old friends talked shit and tried to keep their attention diverted off Lou-Loc's problem. Being around his partner lifted Lou-Loc's spirits, but what he heard about Martina still bothered him. He wasn't sure if the information was 100 percent, so he couldn't wild out just yet. One thing was for sure, he was going to find out sooner than later.

The northbound traffic was fairly light for a Thursday afternoon. Cisco wove his red M3 in and out traffic with a vengeance. He was mad as hell, and he wanted the world to know it. "Fuck Diablo," he said to no one in particular. Diablo had disrespected him one time too many and he was getting tired of it.

For several years he ran LC Blood while Diablo ran from a murder charge and the gang flourished under him. Now Diablo wanted to crawl from under his rock and start giving orders. If it hadn't been for Cisco's plan, the great El Diablo would still be hiding in Cuba with his head in the sand.

There was a poor soul who owed a debt to LC—a large one at that. The bag had already been dropped and his life was forfeit if he couldn't come up with the money. Cisco knew that a dead man couldn't pay a debt so he figured a way to use it to his advantage. In exchange for his life, the man would confess to the murder that El Diablo was being charged with. The DA knew the man hadn't committed the murder, but he didn't care as long as he got his conviction and it was someone of color that he could splash on the front page of the newspaper. The judge handed that simple bastard twenty years without batting an eye and Diablo was no longer a wanted man. Cisco's plan had saved El Diablo's life but the sour old bastard had never said so much as *thank you*.

"Diablo," Cisco said out loud. *Devil* was a fitting name for that black-hearted son of a bitch.

Cisco pulled a tiny cellular phone from his pocket and flipped it open. He quickly scrolled through the phone book until he found the number he was looking for. With a manicured nail, he hit *send* and waited.

"Hello," came a voice from the other end.

"What's going on, Tito?"

"Cisco, to what do I owe this pleasure?"

"I think I'll be needing your services, Primo. Are you dressed?"

"*Si*, Don Cisco," Tito told him.

"Good, then come downstairs. I'm getting off the FDR and on my way to your block to get you. I got some moves to make, and I want you with me."

"Drama?" Tito asked, now sounding more alert.

"If it were that serious, you'd be the first to know. We'll talk further when I see you." Without waiting for a response, Cisco ended the call.

He pulled the M3 to a stop on 129th Street as he waited for a red light to turn green. As he looked out his passenger window, he noticed a group of boys crossing the street. At first he paid them no mind, but at the sight of the blue bandannas hanging from their belts he felt himself become very angry. At the sight of his enemies, Cisco reached for the chrome-plated 9 mm on his lap. One of the boys made eye contact and Cisco put on his mean mug. The boy slowed his pace and returned Cisco's stare. Cisco spat out the passenger window and raised his gun so it rested on the steering wheel for the boy to see. At the sight of the cannon, the boy turned away and quickly caught up with his friends.

"Puto!" Cisco yelled out the window and sped through the green light.

By the time Cisco made it to 126th and Park, Tito was already standing outside. Tito was one of those people whose appearance didn't match their character. He was a very average-looking young man, neither short nor tall. He was slim, but at the same time very muscular. This was no doubt from the years of chopping cane in Puerto Rico. Tito had spend most of his life as a farm boy, and moved to New York as a teenager.

Tito's skin was an even tan complexion, making him look almost African American instead of Puerto Rican. Although he looked harmless enough, he was anything but that. It was his passion for violence that earned him the nickname L'il Major Blood. He was a dedicated soldier in the ranks of LC Blood and one of Cisco's most feared enforcers.

Tito came into the fold shortly after El Diablo went into hiding. He was young and eager to prove himself worthy of the ranks of LC, which Cisco learned firsthand when Tito cut the throat of a man who had made the mistake of stepping on Cisco's shoe at a club. Cisco hired him as muscle at first, and eventually promoted him to enforcer. When Cisco assumed control of LC he offered Tito a position as second in command, but Tito declined. He was more comfortable in the streets with the rest of the soldiers and didn't want the responsibilities that came with the position Cisco was offering.

Cisco sat in his car and watched the predator as he approached. He was decked out in a red Champion hoodie with red and white Air Force 1s. Being that the weather was nice and Tito was still wearing a thick pullover, Cisco knew the man was strapped. And he preferred it that way. To spite living in a Crip-controlled neighborhood, Tito always flew his colors and dared someone to say something about it.

"What's good, Cisco?" Tito asked as he hopped into the passenger seat.

"Tito, I don't see how you can stand to live among these people." Cisco was speaking of the Crips.

Tito shrugged. "Fuck 'em. There are advantages to living among the Crabs. In the event that we go to war or something to that effect, they would never think to look for me in their own backyard. Besides, I have an understanding with these young ones around here. They don't fuck with me, and I don't slaughter their families," Tito said with a snicker. "So what has brought you to the slums, Cisco?"

Cisco smiled like the cat who has just swallowed the canary. "Tito, my friend, there are about to be some drastic changes in our fair city, and I want to ensure that we reap the benefits. Listen carefully to what I am about to run down to you."

Chapter 6

Walking through the halls of BMCC, Lou-Loc looked like a lost puppy. He was having a hard time finding the admissions office and becoming very frustrated. Just as he was about to give up and say "fuck college," a feminine voice called to him from behind. "Are you lost?"

Lou-Loc turned around, ready to tell whoever was speaking to him to fuck off. When he saw the source of the voice, he was speechless. He was standing face-to-face with the most beautiful woman God had ever saw fit to plant on this earth. Everything around him seemed to fade away and there was only her. She was a smooth copper-skinned girl with long black hair and playful eyes. Dressed in an expensive-looking Donna Karan pantsuit with the matching shoes, she looked every bit the modern businesswoman.

"I asked if you were lost," she repeated, snapping Lou-Loc out of his trance.

Lou-Loc mumbled something that sounded like: "I have crossed an entire ocean, and at last I've found you"

"What?" she asked, confused.

"Oh—yeah," he said, trying to recover himself. "I mean—yes. I am a little lost. I didn't realize it was so obvious."

"Not really. I just noticed you looking around, but not really moving in any direction, so I figured you were either lost or waiting for someone."

"Well, actually, a little of both," Lou-Loc said. "I was looking for the admissions office, but I think I've found who I've been waiting for." The girl smiled bashfully. "And what a beautiful smile."

"Thank you, but didn't your mother ever tell you it's impolite to stare?" she asked playfully.

"Forgive me," he said, bowing slightly, "but you are quite beautiful."

"Thank you for the kind words, but I think it's only fair to warn you that if you're trying to pick me up, it isn't going to happen. I'm not that kind of girl," she said seriously.

"Wait a minute, sweetheart," he said, holding up his palms. "it ain't even that kinda party. I got nothing but your best interest at heart. My name is Lou-Loc." He extended his hand.

She looked at his hand as if it was dirty. "Your mother named you Lou-Loc?"

He was a little surprised by her response, so he hesitated before answering. "Nah, my full name is St. Louis. St. Louis Alexander, but if you repeat it, I'll just deny it," he joked.

"St. Louis." She let the name roll off her tongue. "It's unusual, but I like it. What made her name you after a city?"

"That's where she met my daddy. So, do you have a name?" He changed the subject.

"Of course I do."

"So, are you going to tell me?"

She turned her back and began to walk away. "You can find the admissions office down the hall on the left," she said over her shoulder. Her sudden departure left him standing there stuck on stupid, but he wasn't going to let her slip away like that.

He jogged after her and finally caught up to her at the front door. Lou-Loc gently touched her arm to get her attention. "You still haven't told me your name?"

She turned to face him and licked her lips seductively. "St. Louis, I am not presently, nor have I ever been, easy. So don't get it twisted. You seem like a smart young man. If you really want to get with me, I'm sure you can find a way to reach me." She winked at him and strolled out the double doors.

As he watched her walk across the courtyard, so did the rest of the men gathered in front of the school. Even some of the girls took notice of the copper goddess in the Donna Karen suit. Lou-Loc watched her as she climbed into her green Cherokee Jeep. To his surprise, she turned around and looked directly at him standing out in front, blew a kiss in his direction, and merged into traffic. Before she got too far, he made a mental note of her license plate number. With visions of the mystery goddess still in his head, Lou-Loc went back inside to the admissions office.

During the registration process all he could think about was her. He was so thrown off that he didn't even realize until he looked at his paperwork that one of the classes he'd signed up for was Introduction to Latino History. The line was too long for him to wait on it again to change the class, so he put it off for another day. He still had business to attend to and didn't want to spend all day line hopping at BMCC.

When he got outside Gutter was leaning against a car, sipping a pint of Hennessy. He noticed the goofy expression on Lou-Loc's face. "Fuck is you all cheeky about?"

"Cuz, I think I just met my future wife," Lou-Loc said with a smile.

"Future wife? What about your current wife?"

"I ain't wedding Martina, cuz. You had to see this broad. She was all that."

"So you mean to say a bitch you ain't even bone yet got you open like that? Cuz, we should've kept calling you Crazy Lou because you are outta ya fucking mind." Gutter shook his head sadly.

"You don't understand. It's like a feeling you get when you know you've found someone who's right for you, like God patting you on the shoulder telling you it's all right to love this one. You feel me, nigga?"

"Hell nah. You sound like you been reading one of them romance novels or some shit," Gutter laughed.

"I'm trying to have a moment wit a nigga and you acting all stupid and shit," Lou-Loc snapped.

"My bad, Loc. A'ight, so run it down to me, what's her name?"

"I don't know."

"Where's she from?"

"I don't know."

"She got any kids?"

"I don't know."

"Hold on, hold on," Gutter said, putting the top back on his bottle. "You talk'n that true-love shit, and you don't know jack about this girl? Youse a weird ma' fucka, Lou."

"Whatever, G. I need you to do me a favor."

"What?" Gutter asked suspiciously.

"Call Yvette and have her run a plate number for me?"

"Lou-Loc, you my bluest homeboy, but don't get me caught up in this I-spy shit wit you."

"Nigga, the one time I ask you to do me one and you bitch'n 'bout it?"

"A'ight, stop crying, damn." Gutter pulled out his phone and dialed a number.

"Hello?" spoke a female voice on the other end.

"Yvette girl, what's up?" Gutter said jovially.

"Who is this—Gutter? Don't *what's up* me, nigga! You had me waiting for yo' funky ass all that time, and you ain't never show. What's up wit that?"

"Girl, I got locked up. I was fucking with Hollywood and Rob and them in Yonkers and the police stopped us and found a gun in the car. Nigga ain't even let me know he was riding dirty," Gutter lied. "I spent the whole weekend locked up in Yonkers on some bullshit. I know you salty, but I promise to make it up to you."

"You better!" she snapped.

"Say, peep game, baby. I need a favor."

Yvette sucked her teeth. "You niggaz is all the same, wanting something for nothing."

"It ain't for me, it's for Lou-Loc. He needs you to run this plate number for him."

"Is that right?" she asked in a slick tone. "Well, if he wants me to do something for him, I need him to do something for me. My girl Sharon has been checking for that nigga for a hot minute, but he act like he don't know. I'll run the plate for him on my lunch break, but he gotta go on a double date with me, you, and her."

Gutter was hesitant. Sharon had the body of a porn star, but a face that only a mother could love. Lou-Loc knew she wanted to put it on him, which is why he had been ducking her for the last few weeks. Lou-Loc wouldn't like the terms of the deal, but it was his favor, so Gutter agreed. "A'ight, he'll do it. Handle that shit for me right quick and hit me back." He hung up without saying good-bye.

"What'd she say?" Lou-Loc asked, excited.

"Oh, you straight. She gonna hook you up in a few and get back."

"Cool, homie. Good looking on that, G."

"You my peoples, Lou."

"Oh, one more thing, G?"

"What's that, homie?"

"What exactly did you tell Yvette I was gonna do?"

***

After Yvette got back to Gutter, he began to relay the information to his crime partner. "The vehicle is registered to Ms. Satin Angelino. She's twenty-one, never been married, and ain't got no kids. Her last known address is down in the Village and her bra size is . . ."

"I get the point, nigga," Lou-Loc cut him off. "Cuz, I need to get on this ASAP. I need that chick like a junkie needs a fix and I'm gonna pull out all the stops to get her."

"I believe you, but this brings me back to the million-dollar question: What's Martina gonna say about all this? What are you going to do, go home and tell ya wife, 'Baby, I know we been together for almost two years, and you a few months pregnant, but I've fallen in love wit a broad I hardly know'? Martina's crazy ass ain't hardly having that."

"Apparently you still ain't understanding me." Lou-Loc took the bottle of liquor from Gutter and took a shot. "To you, shorty just another face in the crowd. To me, she's the only face. Don't get me wrong; Martina's about to be my baby's mama and all, so you know I got nuff love for her, but I ain't in love with her. To be truthful with you, cuz, our lives are going in two different directions. I wanna do something with this writing shit besides writing obituaries for my fallen comrades." Lou-Loc took a sip of the bottle.

"Here we go again." Gutter snatched the bottle while Lou-Loc was in mid-gulp, causing liquor to trickle down his chin. "Cuz I ain't off that preaching shit today."

"Fuck you, Gutter." Loc-Loc wiped his chin. "Ain't nobody trying to preach. Dig, I ain't saying it like I'm an angel or nothing, because we all did dirt. I'm just trying to do something positive with my life to offset some of that negative, feel me?"

"Yeah, I feel you what you're saying, but what you keep forgetting is that the streets are all that some of us know. This shit we do put food on a lot of niggaz tables."

"That's true, but on the flipside, for every table that we put food on out here we take if off three more. You know as well as I do, most fiends will sell their own children for a blast of that shit we serving."

"I understand what you saying, Lou, but a motherfucker gotta eat. A lot of soldiers from our side as well as the other side come from fucked-up homes with no daddy, and little to no income. How can we expect them not to take to the streets when they people starving? You of all people should know that, cuz."

Lou-Loc looked at him sideways. "I know you ain't even trying to run that shit on me, Gutter. Yeah, I did what I had to do when my daddy got killed and my mama died, but you had a family, so what the fuck is your excuse? Shit, your grandfather was a college professor."

"Yeah," Gutter said, lighting a cigarette, "Gramps was a professor, but he was also a revolutionary. When the Soviet Union tried to bully their way on to Islamic soil, Gramps was right there fighting alongside the Muslims. Being an American citizen, he didn't even have to get in the fight but he did, because Islam teaches us that our brother's fight is our fight."

"That was Gramps for you. He was a real gangsta."

"On Crip he was and they respected him for that. I remember the reception we got when my aunt Rashia took me to Islamabad to visit his crypt. The way those folks treated us and carried on about him, he must've been an O.G. or some shit. I couldn't speak their language very well back then, but from what I was able to pick up, Kenyatta Hamid Soladine, Sr. was an important man. He gave it up like a G."

"But your grandfather wasn't just fighting for the hell of it. He had a purpose when he picked up his gun and took it to the streets. What's our purpose? Don't get it twisted, I'm 'bout this Crip business wholeheartedly and I always will be, but sometimes I feel like what the fuck is the point?"

Gutter laughed as if it wasn't even a question. "Power, cuz. One day Crips is gonna rule all this shit."

For the next block or so, neither man spoke, each lost in his own thoughts. Lou-Loc glanced across the street and noticed a circle of young boys wearing red bandannas. Trapped in the center of the circle was a young white girl. Something about the girl reminded Lou-Loc of Tina. She had the same attractive features, except her hair was brown. Watching them harass her built a fire in Lou-Loc's stomach. He didn't know the girl from a hole in the wall, but seeing the young black boys gang up on her infuriated him. Before Gutter had even realized it, his partner was gone; Lou-Loc was halfway across the street.

One of the boys noticed him coming in their direction, and stuck his chest out in defiance. "Keep walking, nigga," the boy snarled.

Lou-Loc held his hands up, palms out. "I don't want no trouble, l'il homie. I just came to ask y'all to let the young lady alone."

Two more of the boys flanked the first one on either side. At the sight of his friends and Lou-Loc's submissiveness, the first boy's confidence was boosted. From his rear pocket the boy produced a razor blade and pointed it at Lou-Loc. "Breeze, before I eat your food, muthafucka."

Without a second thought, Lou-Loc went into action. With blinding speed he grabbed the boy's exposed wrist and twisted until he heard the bone snap and the boy dropped the blade. Lou-Loc kicked the boy in the back of his kneecap and sent him down to one knee. The boy's friends abandoned the girl and moved to help their comrade, but thought better of it when Gutter drew his twin Glocks.

"I twist slobs, young and old, so make a move and I'ma make you news," Gutter warned. The boys wisely backed off.

Lou-Loc lifted the boy so that they were nose to nose. "Li'l young-ass nigga, I should take that shank and fuck you wit it. You know who the fuck I am?" The boy shook his head from side to side. "Then let me introduce you. I'm Lou-Loc, Harlem-Hoover gangsta, any slob killer," he spat.

"Oh shit!" the boy blurted out. He had heard stories about the executioner from Harlem Crip but never thought in a million years that he would ever come face-to-face with him. Piss began to trickle down his leg because he knew that he was as good as dead.

"Take them fucking rags off, all of you!" Lou-Loc barked at the boy's friends. The boys quickly did as they were told. "How old are you, boy?" Lou-Loc asked the boy who he still held in his grip.

"F—fifteen," the boy managed to stutter out.

Lou-Loc slapped fire out of the boy. "Nigga, you ain't even old enough to pee straight, let alone be out here in grown folks's business. Y'all need to have ya assess in school somewhere instead of out here trying to rob folks. Now get the fuck outta here." Lou-Loc shoved him away. "And if I ever see one of y'all pussies out here calling y'all selves gangbanging I'm gonna make you eat a fucking bullet."

As the boys made to leave, Gutter stopped them. "Hold up." He walked into the center of their gang, tucking his guns, and addressed them. "Make sure that you tell ya peoples that the borough of Manhattan is under new management. Any and all Brims will be executed on sight." To make sure that they got his point Gutter stole the tallest of the boys in his mouth and put him on his back.

The boys collected their wounded friends and slithered away in disgrace. Gutter threw his head back and had a good laugh at their expense. Lou-Loc, on the other hand, said nothing. He just stood there, fuming with his fist balled.

The girl who the boys had been accosting approached Lou-Loc and offered her thanks. "Thank you so much. I thought those animals were going to kill me."

Lou-Loc spun around suddenly and grabbed her by the throat, slowly applying pressure. "You think I really give a fuck what would've happened to you? What I did was for those kids. You don't know how tired I am of seeing kids throw their lives away over mark-ass muthafuckas like you. There are enough of my li'l brothers behind the wall as it is over some dumb shit and they would've been four more, so save your thanks."

"Well . . . I—" she started, but was cut off.

"Well, you what?" Lou-Loc snapped. "You didn't mean anything by it? Man, you crackers kill me. And y'all say *we* got a lot of excuses. Bitch, raise yo' ass up outta here, and go back to West End Avenue."

The girl looked back and forth from Lou-Loc to Gutter. When she looked like she was about to respond, Gutter stepped in between them. "Take a hike, shorty," he said very coolly. She sucked her teeth, but held her comment and walked off.

"Boy, I was beginning to wonder about you," Gutter said, slapping Lou-Loc on the ass. "Thought them stories about you losing your nerve might've been true. The way you wigged out on them slobs removed any doubt from my mind about your O.G. status."

Lou-Loc rolled his eyes at Gutter and walked off.

"Fuck is wrong wit you, cuz!" Gutter shouted after him. "A nigga try'n to give you ya props and you get all funny style. Fuck is the deal?"

Lou-Loc turned and looked at his friend with sadness in his eyes. "Animals," he said softly. "She called them animals."

"So, what's ya point?" Gutter asked, confused.

"What's my point? Gutter, we used to be just like them. Is that how people see us, as animals?"

"Lou-Loc, we wasn't nothing like them li'l niggaz. We respected the G-code as well as our elders. These li'l bastards don't respect shit."

"Fuck the code, Gutter. What about respect for people and life, what happened to that?"

"I feel where you're coming from, but those rules only apply to civilians. We ain't civilians no more and we ain't been for a long time. Don't get all wishy-washy on me now, you knew what was up when you got down wit the set. I understand you, Loc, really I do, but I need you to understand me. We're in hostile times, my friend, and ain't no emotions in war. It's either us or them, cuz. This is banging, full throttle all day, every day. Ain't no vacations or days off, straight like that. Cuz, I need your head to be right if we gonna win this game. Niggaz that don't think right, they go out like Stan and there ain't no way I'm gonna let that happen to either of us."

"You right, Gutter," Lou-Loc admitted, "but you can't say I don't have a valid point."

"Look, just forget it," Gutter said, finally tired of arguing. Once Lou-Loc got started, he could go on for hours. Gutter knew that he had shit to take care of. "Let's just go check Roc, and get faded. After that we can check on ya li'l girlfriend," Gutter capped. Seeing Lou-Loc's eyes get a little brighter, he smiled. "I knew that would pick your spirits up, lover boy."

"Fuck you, Kenyatta!" Lou-Loc said playfully.

"Fuck you right back, St. Louis." The two friends shared a hug and a laugh. "You still down for me, Loc?"

"'Til the day I leave here, cuz."

"Gangsta?"

"Gangsta."

Chapter 7

The Cherokee Jeep moved casually through the traffic on the Avenue of the Americas. Satin gripped the steering wheel with a manicured hand, and made the 4x4 do as she wished, very much the same way she did with people. Satin may have appeared innocent and unassuming, but she was a very ambitious girl who knew exactly what she wanted out of life and how to go about getting it. It was something she adapted very early in life.

When Satin was very young, she lost her mother to cancer and shortly after her father committed suicide, leaving her and her two brothers in the care of her aunt Selina. Between her aunt and her older brother, Michael, Satin never wanted for anything. Michael was always showering Satin with gifts that most kids her age could only dream of. It wasn't until she was older that she realized her brother made his money illegally. This made her more hesitant to accept his gifts, but she still let him do for her when necessary.

When Satin was a junior in high school, she revealed to her family her dream of owning her own business—a publishing house, to be exact. Writing had always been one of her favorite pastimes, so she decided to turn her hobby into a business venture. Satin was a girl who took her writing as seriously as she took her income and for her that was *very* serious.

When she revealed her plan to her family, they all laughed at her for dreaming so big. Their philosophy was that a woman had no place in the business world, especially publishing. Michael felt that there was no money in books, so he refused to give her the seed money to get the venture off the ground. But that didn't deter Satin one bit. In fact, it only made her more motivated. After she graduated high school she put college on hold and got an internship with a local magazine while working in Macy's in the evenings and on weekends. It was while working at the magazine that she deviated slightly from her original dream. While book publishing still interested her, she decided to go another route and start her own magazine—but not just any magazine, one that catered to the interests of Latino women.

The editor, who was a Hispanic female, was so impressed with Satin's work ethic and ideas that she hired her as a personal assistant. She even arranged Satin's schedule so that she could enroll in community college, where she would take communications classes and pursue a degree in journalism. Satin became very fond of the editor, because she was the only person to ever encourage her to chase her dreams, which she did vigorously. Satin's mind was on her money twenty-four-seven, but not that day. She was thinking about the young man she had met at BMCC.

"St. Louis." she said out loud, letting the name roll around in her mouth and reflecting on the charming young black man. She had been checking for him since the first time she'd seen him, which actually was a few months prior on 125th Street. She and her friends were coming out of the bookstore when she spotted Lou-Loc going into the Magic Johnson Theater. He was rocking a powder-blue sweat suit with a pair of white-on-white Nikes. His hair was braided in zigzag parts with blue rubber bands holding them in place. She remembered the butterflies that were driving her stomach crazy and the feeling of disappointment when a Dominican girl walked up and grabbed him by the arm. She was cute, but didn't have anything on Satin.

"Bitch," she spat. She knew that had to be his girl, but then again it was hard to say. Satin had seen the girl in a few spots, keeping company with several different guys. The thought of the girl already having him and being stupid enough to cheat on his fine ass only made Satin want him more.

She didn't reveal any of this when they finally met in the halls of BMCC, because she wanted to play hard-to-get, especially knowing that he was involved with someone. She still didn't know why she had initiated contact with the gangster. Maybe it was to see how far he was willing to go or how far she was willing to go, it was still unclear. The one thing that she was certain of was that she was feeling Lou-Loc and intended to see him again. She might've been wrong for trying to get involved with someone who already had someone, but life was too short to let opportunities pass you by when they presented themselves. Wrong or not, Satin was a girl of ambition and when she wanted something it was in her nature to go after it.

Satin parked her car in front of her apartment building on East Seventh Street and killed the engine. As she was stepping out of her jeep, a long red Cadillac pulled up to her passenger side. The windows were tinted, so she couldn't see who was in it. She closed the jeep door with one hand and let the other slip into the purse, where she kept her .22. Growing up in the projects she learned to shoot first and ask questions later. If it was going to pop off, she would be ready.

The driver's-side window slid halfway down and revealed a hulking head, wearing dark sunglasses. He smiled at Satin, revealing a mouthful of stained yellow teeth. "Long time, Satin," the giant, aka Rico Runez, greeted her.

"What are you doing here, Rico? I thought I made it clear to Cisco that his advances were in vain."

"Easy, mami, it ain't like that. I brought someone here to see you."

"I doubt that there's anyone you know that I'd want to see."

"Oh, but I beg to differ," he said, grinning, "I think you'll be quite pleased to see who has come to call on you."

As if on cue, El Diablo stepped out of the back of the Cadillac. "Hello, Satin."

Satin stood there with a shocked expression on her face. It had been years since she had last seen her brother and wasn't sure how she felt about him popping up on her unexpectedly.

"Hello, Michael, or do you prefer El Diablo?" she asked venomously.

El Diablo dismissed her comment with a wave of his hand. "That is merely a name given to me by some of my associates, nothing more. So how have you been, little sister?"

"Fine, not that you care. How many years has it been since you left us high and dry?"

"Aye," he threw up his hands in mock surrender, "why so cold, Satin? You know I didn't have a choice. Besides, were you not taken care of in my absence?"

"Taken care of? If you call sending your yes-man Cisco here with money, and trying to get in my pants *taken care of*, yes, I was fine."

"My apologies, Satin. Cisco can be a bit vulgar, but I will see that he is reprimanded for his actions. But financially, you and the family were good?"

"Yeah," she said flatly. "But Auntie Selina hasn't been in the best of shape. She's at Saint Vincent's. You been to see her?"

"No." he said sadly. "I feared that I would not be welcomed. Your warm reception has confirmed that. I won't take up your time, Satin. I just wanted to see you, and to let you know I'm home. If you should need something you have but to call on me and if you don't want to see me, I can send Cisco."

"That's a fucking joke, right? Cisco is a piece of shit who cares about no one but himself. You told him to treat me like a sister; instead he tried to treat me like a whore, showering me with gifts to gain my affection. No amount of money would ever get me into his bed."

"As I said earlier, Cisco will be dealt with, but let's move on to another topic. How is our brother, Jesus? What's he been up to?"

"In and out of trouble." she said. "I don't blame him, considering his role model is a kingpin."

"Satin, I never meant for things to turn out this way. I only wanted to make things better for our family. Is that so wrong?"

Satin massaged the back of her neck as she looked into his sorrow-filled eyes. She knew that he meant well, but his methods were all wrong. "Michael," she said, taking his hand in hers, "I'm a big girl now. I appreciate all that you've done for me and our family, but I don't need a keeper anymore. You, on the other hand, could use a little guidance. Why don't you find yourself a nice girl to settle down with and stop playing in these streets?"

"I have many women, but it is the streets that have my heart." He smiled.

Satin shook her head. "You know what I meant. Look, if you want to make me happy, why don't you come with us to church, Sunday? It'd be nice to have the family attend service together like the old days."

"I'm afraid I cannot, little one," El Diablo said sadly. "I fear I am no longer welcomed in the house of worship." El Diablo pulled a piece of paper from his pocket and wrote an address down. "This is where I'll be staying," he said, handing Satin the paper. "if you need anything, you can reach me there. It was good to see you, little one." He turned to walk away with his head hung low.

Seeing the sadness in her brother, Satin's conscience began to eat away at her. Michael was a gangster and though she didn't approve of how he lived, they were still family. "Michael," she called after him. When he turned around, Satin threw herself into his arms and gave him a warm hug. "You're an asshole, but you're still my big brother. Welcome home."

Chapter 8

Lou-Loc and Gutter strolled in silence down Church Avenue in Brooklyn on their way to meet Roc and his boss Anwar, head of the Al Mukalla crime family. Lou-Loc had met Roc once or twice in the past, but he didn't really know much about him. No one did. All Lou-Loc really knew is that Roc was the underboss of the Al Mukalla, and Anwar ran the operation. The Al Mukalla was a gang of Middle Easterners who operated out of Brooklyn and had their hands in everything from gambling to gun trafficking. They turned a profit from all sorts of vices, but their main source of income was heroin. Anwar and his men ruled their little corner of the city with an iron fist. Although they were few in number, they more than made up for it in viciousness. Each member of the organization was ready to die for what they believed in.

Gutter had gotten connected to Roc during a visit to At Taif, where their two families had prop-

erties in the same province. Their grandparents
had been a part of the same regiment so they
had that in common, as well as their fascination
with the streets. Gutter returned to the States
while Roc remained in At Taif, but they'd kept
in contact and when Roc came to America they
promised to hook up and do some business. After
a few months of going back and forth about it,
Roc finally agreed to introduce Gutter to Anwar.
The Al Mukalla was very suspicious of outsiders,
especially Americans. The only reason Anwar
even agreed to meet with Gutter was because he
was a Muslim.

Gutter tapped Lou-Loc's arm, snapping him
out of his daze. "There it is, cuz," he said, pointing to a shabby-looking corner market.

Lou-Loc looked at the place skeptically. "Ain't
much to look at."

"Looks can be deceiving," Gutter told him and
led the way inside. They spotted Roc behind the
counter, handing a little girl a pack of Skittles
and her change. Roc noticed Gutter and greeted
him with a nod and a smile.

Roc was a jovial-looking man, standing around
five feet eight and sporting a buzz cut. With his
stained smock and potbelly he looked more like
the shopkeeper he was masquerading as than the
killer he really was. His hands were his favorite

killing devices and the reason for his nickname. It was said that he could crush the bones in a man's neck to powder with the lethal devices.

At the end of the line were three young men waiting to pay for their 40-ounces. All three of the young men were wearing red scarves and staring daggers at Gutter, who was sporting blue bandannas on each wrist. "Punk-ass crabs," one of the boys mumbled.

"What you say, nigga?" Gutter stepped forward. Sensing that violence was about to erupt, the customers abandoned their purchases and made for the door.

"You heard him, motherfucker," another boy added. "You in the wrong neighborhood to be rocking all that blue."

Lou-Loc snorted. "I don't give a fuck what hood we in. My advice to you is, Pay for ya muthafucking beer, and beat street. We ain't starting this shit, but we sure as hell can finish it. What's up, cuz?" Lou-Loc put a southern twang on the last word just to irk the East Coast hoodlums.

The first boy, whom Lou-Loc assumed to be the leader of the group, hesitated. When Lou-Loc noticed his hesitance he knew that he had the boy's heart, which meant the fight was halfway over before it started, but his partner had balls. From under his sweatshirt, the boy produced a small .22. He was quick, but Lou-Loc was quicker. By the time the boy raised his gun, Lou-Loc had closed the distance between them, and had the barrel of his 9 mm to the boy's chest.

Lou-Loc smiled and leaned in so he and the boy were nose to nose. "You wasn't trying to draw on me, was you, boy?" Lou-Loc whispered. The boy saw the savage look in Lou-Loc's eyes and suddenly didn't feel so tough. Before anyone else could react, there was a loud *click*, and the room went still. Everyone turned to see what the noise was, and were completely thrown off by what they saw.

Standing between aisles two and three stood a little boy. He was skinny, but not too much so. He was somewhere between frail and recently malnourished. He wore camouflage fatigue pants and a plain tank top. In his hands he held a large machine gun.

"Please," said Roc, stepping from behind the counter, "neither violence nor weapons are permitted here. I would urge you to take heed to the laws of the Al Mukalla." He said something in Arabic to the boy with the gun. In response to whatever the command was, the boy pulled a burlap sack from one of the shelves and stepped forward. "Place your guns in the sack, gentlemen," Roc ordered. The boys knew Roc and knew he wouldn't ask twice, so reluctantly they complied.

"This is some bullshit," one of the boys spat, dropping his gun in the sack.

"Hey, hey, don't tell me what's bullshit!" Roc barked. "Everyone in the neighborhood knows Anwar's rules about guns in his place, so be glad I'm just disarming you instead of dismantling you. Now, if you think you can keep yourselves from causing any more trouble, I'll return the guns to you later on."

"Come on, Roc, you know us," one of the boys whined.

"Yes, which is why I'm having Hassan take your guns instead of your lives. Now do as I say and go." The boys lowered their heads and slunk out of the store.

"What was that shit about, Roc?" Gutter asked.

"Nothing for you to worry about, Kenyatta. We have an understanding with the locals about keeping the peace and anything less is unacceptable, no matter what personal conflicts exist between your two factions. Let me show you something." Roc led them to the store window and pointed across the street to a playground. "That is Al Mukalla Park, founded and built by us. Even though we built it, the park is open to all children. It is a safe haven where parents don't have to fear for their children. We patrol it constantly and it's covered from all angles by video cameras. In that park, no one is allowed to sell or use drugs. The penalty for violating the rule is death. The children are the future of us all, so we must ensure that they grow to fruition."

"That's deep," Lou-Loc commented.

"That's Mukalla," Roc responded. "We are about the betterment of our people as well as those in our community. Allah has been good to us, and it is only fair that we spread the love to those around us."

"I can respect your gangster, Roc," Lou-Loc said.

"And I yours," Roc responded.

"So what's good, Roc?" Gutter interrupted. "I been looking forward to this gathering for some time now. I'm ready to do the damn thing."

"Easy, Gutter," Roc said, patting his shoulder. "Anwar is waiting for us in his war room. Before we go to join him, I would ask you also to remove your weapons."

"What's all this shit about?" Lou-Loc asked, looking at Gutter. "After what just went down, I'm keeping my strap right the fuck here."

Roc and Lou-Loc stared each other down for a moment. Neither man wanted to give ground, but this meeting was in both their best interests. Roc finally broke the silence.

"No disrespect to you," he said, looking Lou-Loc square in the eye, "but it is the policy of our war room. It keeps negotiations from becoming unpleasant."

"Come on, Loc. We straight in here so let's go along with the program," Gutter dropped his guns in the sack. Lou-Loc didn't like it, but he did as his friend asked.

"Thank you," Roc said with a smile. "Now if you will please follow me. Anwar is waiting." Roc instructed Hassan to put the confiscated weapons into the safe and run the register while he escorted the two guests to the war room.

Lou-Loc and Gutter followed Roc through the aisles and into the storeroom in the back. The small area was cluttered with boxes of supplies and file cabinets. There was a large meat freezer that stretched along the entire back wall. Roc turned the knob and the massive door slid open with a loud *hiss*. "This way, gentlemen."

Lou-Loc looked at Gutter, puzzled, and then turned his attention to Roc. "You want us to go into a freezer?"

"You Americans are so distrustful," Roc said with a chuckle. "This is the way to the war room. Once you step inside, you'll understand."

Gutter and Lou-Loc stepped into the freezer cautiously, with Roc bringing up the rear. Lou-Loc had an odd feeling about the whole situation. Once all three were inside, the massive door slammed, and the freezer went dark. "Shit," Lou-Loc cursed and pressed his back to the wall, fearing they were being set up. Several infrared beams of light passed over them and then disappeared as suddenly as they had appeared. The freezer rumbled and began descending.

"Hope that didn't unnerve you too much. The lights were sweeping you for concealed weapons," Rock explained.

"You boys sure are paranoid," Lou-Loc retorted with a hint of sarcasm in his voice.

"Afraid we must be," Roc said, while unlocking another door that Lou-Loc was sure wasn't there when they entered the freezer. "People these days aren't always honorable. Paranoia will help me to live a very long life."

The three men left the freezer-elevator and found themselves in an underground passage. It was a long corridor that appeared to not have been used in some time. The walls were crusted with mold and filth. The tiny holes in them showed signs that a gunfight had transpired at some point.

"Must've been quite a gunfight down here," Lou-Loc whispered to Gutter as he examined the holes. Upon closer inspection he noticed that some of the holes were glassed over like camera lenses. When he turned to rejoin the group, he noticed Roc watching him. Lou-Loc was tempted to ask about the holes, but he didn't. And Roc didn't volunteer the information.

At the end of the corridor there stood an iron door. Along the edge of the door was something written in Arabic. Lou-Loc couldn't translate the words, but they seemed to mean something to Gutter.

"This is Anwar's war room," Roc said, motioning toward the door. "While you gentlemen remove your shoes, I will notify him that you're here." Without waiting for a response, he disappeared behind the door, leaving Lou-Loc and Gutter in the hall alone.

Once Lou-Loc was sure Roc was out of earshot, he decided to ask Gutter about the writing. "Say, Gutter," he said, tapping his friend's arm, "what's that writing all about? What that shit mean, cuz?"

Gutter looked at his friend and smiled. "Well, the first part says: *Justice for the sons and daughters of Allah.* The second part says: *Death to the Almighty Devil.*"

Lou-Loc looked at Gutter, confused. "Who or what is the Almighty Devil?"

"America," Gutter said flatly.

A moment later, Roc came into the hallway and summoned them inside. As the two men entered the room, they were quite surprised by what they saw. Unlike the filthy corridor, the room was quite plush. The floors were carpeted from wall to wall, with a high-arched ceiling. The interior of the room was soundproofed and completely without windows. The only light, other than the few scattered candles, was given off by a vast network of monitors on the back wall.

There wasn't much in the way of furniture, either. There was a white-leather sofa that took up most of the wall to the left of the monitors. In another section of the room, there was a conference table surrounded by seven chairs. In the center of the room sat an oak desk directly in front of the monitors. Even though it was draped in shadows, Lou-Loc could tell that someone was sitting behind the desk, watching them.

"Please step in," said a voice in clipped English. "Step in and be seated. You are amongst friends here."

Lou-Loc and Gutter moved cautiously across the carpeted floor and took up seats on the couch. As Lou-Loc sniffed the air, he could smell a familiar aroma through the scented candles. It was the smell of death, old death. Lou-Loc tried to recall where he had smelled it before and when it hit him he gasped. He narrowed his eyes and scanned the shadows, but saw nothing.

A figure stepped from behind the desk, snapping Lou-Loc from his thoughts. As the figure came into the light, his features became clear to them. He had long black hair that was braided into a ponytail and tied off with a golden ribbon. His olive-toned face was smooth and bare, much like Lou-Loc's. The garments he wore were simple: green army fatigues and a black turtleneck.

Roc stepped in the center of the room and bowed from the waist. "Gutter, Lou-Loc, I present to you Prince Anwar Bien Mustaf."

When Anwar stepped forward and shook their hands, Lou-Loc noticed that his were warm, which put him slightly more at ease, but he would still stay on his toes. If the smell he had picked up when they came in was what he thought it was, then there was more to the Al Mukalla than even Gutter would believe.

Anwar was not at all what they had expected. He appeared to be no more than a teenager, but it was his eyes that told a different story. They were the eyes of a warrior.

"Thank you for coming," Anwar said politely. "We have many things to discuss, but first, may I offer you some refreshments. We have soda, juice, liquor or something a bit more exotic if you wish it." He gave Lou-Loc a knowing glance when he said this. There was definitely more to Anwar then what met the eye.

"You got any yak?" Gutter asked greedily.

"Of course I do. And for you, my friend?" Anwar looked at Lou-Loc.

"Yak is fine," Lou-Loc said. He didn't like the game Anwar was playing with him.

Anwar turned to Roc. "Would you mind, brother?"

"Your will is mine," Roc said with a bow. "I'll return shortly." With that, he was gone.

Anwar motioned for the two men to join him at the conference table so they could begin the negotiation. "Kenyatta," he said, bowing to Gutter, "when Roc told me of your long-standing friendship, I asked him why he hadn't brought you to my attention sooner. How could I deny a member of the Soladine family?"

"You are familiar with my family?" Gutter asked, surprised.

"Indeed I am. Believe it or not, I owe your grandfather a great debt. When I was a young boy, visiting my family in Afghanistan, the Russians invaded my uncle's village and it was your grandfather and his men that helped my family get out. Your grandfather was a great man. Even though he was not of our lands, he fought for our people. We were all saddened by his passing, as well as your father's."

"Thank you," Gutter said with a nod. All was silent for a moment. It was as if the men were paying their respects to the fallen soldiers. Roc came in with the drinks, and took up the seat next to Anwar.

"Now, to the business at hand," Anwar said, breaking the silence. "What can the Al Mukalla do for you, gentlemen?"

"Well, it's like this," Gutter started, "it ain't really what you can do for us, but what we can do for each other. You feel me? Me and my partner," he said, motioning toward Lou-Loc, "we doing big things in Harlem. We got paper coming in, and we holding shit down. Now things are cool uptown, but the shit is twisted everywhere else, so we're trying to expand to downtown and the lower, but with all the rival sets it's easier said than done. We're trying to make this happen without spilling a bucket of blood and bringing the police down on everyone's head in the process."

"And this means what to me?" Anwar asked.

"Hold on, Anwar, I'm getting to that. We heard about your little problem out here with the Bloods jacking your customers and fucking up business."

"Very true," Anwar answered honestly. "People are becoming more and more afraid to come out here. We hold sway within the heart of our turf, but we are stretched very thin along our borders. I see you've done your homework, Kenyatta."

"Thank you, Anwar."

"So, how do you and your bunch propose to help us with our problem?"

"Glad you asked," Gutter said with a grin. "We propose an alliance of sorts. Let us set up shop on the Al Mukalla borders. We'll cut you in for fifteen percent of our gross profits in Brooklyn for the first six months, and ten percent thereafter. In return, you hit us wit the dope at a discount. This way, your customers are guaranteed safe passage, your borders are covered, and we get to expand. Everybody gets paid. How you love that?"

Anwar paused for a moment to consider what was being laid out before him. "It sounds good, Kenyatta, but I do see a flaw in your plan."

"And what would that be?"

"Allowing your people to operate in our area will be looked upon as a slight to the Bloods in the area; some might even see it as us taking sides in your little war. We, Al Mukalla, are what you might call separatists. It is not our way to involve ourselves in outsider feuds. It isn't that we don't want to help you; it is quite the opposite, actually. It's just that this color war is not ours. To involve ourselves in this thing of yours, could cause serious problems. If anything negative were to come of this, it would not go over well with my people."

For a long while no one spoke. The Al Mukalla refusal to aid Harlem in the feud was something Gutter hadn't counted on. Gutter knew that if he couldn't sway Anwar, he would be back to square one.

"I have a suggestion," Lou-Loc said, surprising everyone in the room.

"I'm listening," Anwar said, leaning forward on his elbows.

"Tell me something," Lou-Loc started, "if hostile parties were to initiate violence on Al Mukalla turf, and you handled it, would you be in the wrong?"

Anwar looked at Lou-Loc, puzzled. "Technically, no. it is common knowledge amongst all the gang leaders in the area that we will brook no violations of our set, as you call it."

"Well, there's your solution," Lou-Loc said, sitting back in his chair.

"I'm afraid I don't follow you, Lou-Loc," Anwar said flatly.

"Well, let me break it down to you, Anwar. We'll keep dealing with the problems in Harlem; that isn't a problem for us. Now in Brooklyn, we'll do it like this: We'll handle the new spots, and the threats to the borders. The Al Mukalla will lend additional muscle, when called for. The best part of it is it'll all be done anonymous, if you'd prefer it that way. Other than me and Gutter, none of the homeboys know about this little meeting. If someone were to discover your involvement, it would be as if you were just protecting your turf. No harm, no foul, and we all win."

Anwar sat for a moment, rubbing his bare chin. A smile crossed his face as he turned his attention to Lou-Loc. "Lou-Loc, you are a snake and a brilliant strategist. You should be with Al Mukalla, my friend. You could've easily been a general in our army back home."

"Thank you, Anwar, but the Crips are my army."

"So, what it is, Anwar?" Gutter interrupted. "Do we do business or what?"

"So eager," Anwar said, smirking. "First things first. We need a binding agreement between us to make this work."

"Like a contract?" Gutter asked.

"Not quite. In olden times pacts were sealed in blood."

"So, you want us to prick our fingers or something. I ain't too fond of nothing red, but I ain't no punk. Let's do this," Gutter said eagerly.

"I had something different in mind, something to ensure our loyalty to each other in this relationship."

Lou-Loc had a bad feeling as to where the conversation was going. "What you talking 'bout, Anwar?"

Anwar leaned forward and looked Lou-Loc dead in the eye. "A life for a life. You kill someone for us, and we for you."

Gutter breathed a little easier. "Shit, is that all? I was more nervous when I thought you wanted me to cut myself. Nigga, I'm always down for that one-eight-seven. Who you want dead?"

"A local," Anwar started. "He runs this little group of five-percenters out of Bed-Stuy. He and his like are becoming a pain in my ass. Because of certain mutual spiritual beliefs and acquaintances, I can't strike him down directly so I am forced to call on outside help."

"Ain't nothing," Gutter said confidently, "I'll dust his ass myself."

"Afraid not," Anwar interjected. "You are also Muslim, and therefore, it would not be wise for you to embark on such a task. And because of our anonymous relationship, the task cannot be trusted to one of your underlings. I do have a candidate in mind, though," Anwar said, looking at Lou-Loc.

There it was. Lou-Loc had killed quite a few people in his life, but that was before. He had no desire to damn himself anymore than he already was. There was some bullshit about to go down, and he knew it.

"So," Anwar said, with a devilish smile, "will you do this thing for us?"

Lou-Loc wanted to tell Anwar to go fuck himself, but he knew how much the alliance meant to Gutter and the Crip organization. Still, he knew there was more to it than Anwar was letting on. "Why me?"

"You are my brother's brother. If Kenyatta trusts you, then I trust you. Besides, you are one of the most qualified killers I know of." This statement caught Lou-Loc off guard. "Don't look so surprised, St. Louis. I am very familiar with your work. To date, you have sixteen bodies to your credit, two of which were police officers. I know you, Lou-Loc."

"What the fuck, are you writing a book on my life?" Lou-Loc asked defensively.

"Not at all. I just make it a point to know all potential threats in every city we operate in. I know quite a bit about you, gang lord." Anwar smirked.

This made Lou-Loc's blood run cold. There was only one person who called him that, which made his mind go back to the smell. "Anwar . . ." Lou-Loc began, but Anwar cut him off.

"No need worry, your secret is safe," Anwar assured him. "As a matter of fact, I owe you somewhat of a debt. A few years ago, you killed a Blood called Two Shot. This particular Blood murdered a cousin of mine in a convenience-store holdup. You saved me the trouble of having him executed.

"Now back to the business at hand. If you help us on this I will make it worth your while. There's thirty thousand cash in it for you, and I will owe you a great debt. I have friends in the publishing industry, who owe me favors, and I would gladly convince them to take a look at your work."

Anwar knew a lot about Lou-Loc, more than he was comfortable with. When their business was concluded, he and Anwar were going to have a one-on-one conversation. "A'ight, I'll twist this pussy for you."

A broad smile crossed Gutter's and Anwar's faces. "My friends," Anwar said, raising his glass, "let us toast to success."

Lou-Loc toasted with them but he wasn't happy about the situation he had allowed himself to be roped into. He was trying to avoid shit and Anwar had just taken a dump in his lap.

Chapter 9

The sun was setting and evening was approaching as Lou-Loc made his way through the streets of the West Village with the day's events weighing heavily on him. Lou-Loc wanted to distance himself from the set, but something was always pulling him back. It was his sincere loyalty to the set that was slitting his own throat. Against his better judgment, he'd accepted the contract from the Al Mukalla, and in return, they would eliminate a certain rival gangster. Lou-Loc would fulfill his end of the bargain and then he was going to step to Anwar. That kid was playing some serious mind games, and Lou-Loc didn't like it. He valued his privacy, and people invading that rubbed him the wrong way. Connected or not, he and Anwar were going to have a chitchat. If need be, he could get it too.

Lou-Loc pushed those thoughts from his mind and concentrated on the business at hand, which was finding out what kind of games Martina was playing. After all that he had gone through with her, she must've been out of her mind to tip out on him. She thought that she was slicker than a pig in shit, but when it was all said and done Lou-Loc would show her how slick he could be.

Lou-Loc ducked into a small pub off West Fourth Street. It was an out-of-the-way spot that was inhabited by mostly goths and miscreants, so he stuck out like a sore thumb when he entered. Trying to be as inconspicuous as possible, he sidestepped through the crowd and took a seat at a corner booth. When Lou-Loc was finally able to flag down one of the leather-garbed waitresses, he ordered a rum and Coke. After a few moments, the waitress returned with his drink and sat it on the chalky table in front of him. Lou-Loc gave her his winning smile, and instructed her to keep them coming. The waitress smiled and made her way back to the bar area. Lou-Loc sipped his drink and waited.

About an hour and three drinks later, he spotted who he was waiting for. The man who entered the bar was surprisingly young looking. In fact, he really didn't look old enough to be in the bar. Strangely enough, no one bothered to stop him or ask to see his ID. It was as if they didn't even notice him. The young man must've felt Lou-Loc watching him, because he turned and stared directly at him from across the room. The stranger held Lou-Loc's gaze for a moment, then continued on to the bar, where he exchanged hushed words with the old bartender. The waitress cut off Lou-Loc's line of vision when she placed another drink on the table and when she moved the young man was standing there, glaring at him.

His skin was dark and smooth against his high cheekbones. With his emerald-green eyes, angular chin, and black trench coat, he looked right at home among the goth crowd. Although he appeared to be no more than a high school student, he carried himself like someone of an earlier time. All of his movements were fluid and easy. Lou-Loc didn't seem the least bit disturbed by the young man's presence. Without waiting for an invitation, the stranger sat down with his drink and faced Lou-Loc.

"What brings you to this part of town, gang lord?" the man asked in a deep voice that didn't quite match his appearance.

Lou-Loc swallowed the last of his watered-down drink and sized the stranger up. "I'm looking for a friend," he responded, "and I'm no gang lord, goth boy."

"Boy?" The young man laughed. "I'm way older than you, fuck you very much."

"Nah, fuck you," Lou-Loc shot back. When the two men noticed some of the people turning in their direction, they both burst out laughing. As the threat of violence passed, the patrons went back to their drinks.

"Lou-Loc, you are so fucking dramatic," the young man said with a smile, showing off the whitest teeth Lou-Loc had ever seen.

"No more than you are, Cross, dressed like something out of *The Matrix*. When are you gonna retire that ratty old duster?"

"When you hang up your soldier rag, which will probably be never. You might wanna watch how you talk to me before I kick your ass," he joked.

"Cross, I could take you on my worst day."

"I doubt it, but that cannon you're hiding under your shirt might help a little."

"Very little." Lou-Loc shrugged.

"So," Cross began. "This isn't your kind of place, so I gotta ask: What brings you down here to hobnob with the stiffs? You thinking about coming over to our side?"

Lou-Loc laughed. "Nah, I enjoy the little things, like getting drunk and long walks in the sun, so I ain't ready to give that up just yet. Thanks for offering, though. But straight-up, though, I need a favor. I hate to even come down here and ask you after all you've done for me already."

Cross waved him off. "Go 'head with that, Lou-Loc. If anything, I owe you!"

"You don't owe me nothing, Cross. That time them cats shot me, you came through for the kid."

"Man, that was just a scratch. That night you found me, I was in a bad way. You could've left me out to fry, but you didn't and even after that you never gave away my secret, not even to Gutter."

"You asked me not to say anything, so I didn't. I don't get down like that. Besides, who would've believed me?"

"True. But anyway, how can a child of the Gehenna service the general of Harlem Crip?"

"I need you to do a little detective work, and if it comes down to it, maybe hit something."

Cross picked up his beer and pretended to sip from the bottle. "That serious, huh?"

"It might be," Lou-Loc said, leaning forward, as if someone might overhear their conversation. "It's Martina."

"You want me to kill your girl?" Cross asked, sounding a little more excited than Lou-Loc was comfortable with. It was no secret that Cross had never cared for her.

"Slow down, Cross. I want you to follow her. I think she might be cheating."

"I'm sorry to hear that," Cross said honestly. "So, what's the plan? I mean, if she is cheating, how do you want to handle it?"

"Follow her; see where she goes and who she sees. If she's seeing someone else, kill him. Her, I'll deal with. You'll be paid for your services, and you can do what you want with his body. As an added bonus," Lou-Loc slid a manila envelope across the table, "those two are suited to your refined taste. You'll get the locations when the job is done."

Cross removed the contents of the envelope and his mouth began to water when he saw the picture inside. "So tender," he mumbled. "Done deal, Lou-Loc. I'll get on it tonight."

"Thank you," Lou-Loc said, standing to leave. "Oh—and Cross, no harm is to come to Martina. Are we clear on that?"

"Don't worry, I wont hurt the lady, but I can't say the same for her little friend. A slight upon you, is a slight upon me. And that, my friend, is unforgivable."

With that last comment, Lou-Loc left the bar. He was quite sure that Cross would carry out his wishes to the very letter. Cross was big on repaying debts, especially those in blood.

Long after Lou-Loc had gone, Cross continued sitting at the table, staring at the pictures that had been in the envelope. There was no doubt in his mind that Martina was up to no good because he had seen her creeping with other men on more than one occasion, but it would've broken his friend's heart if he'd told him, so he kept quiet. There had been plenty of nights that he wanted to step from the shadows and bleed Martina, but he knew how much Lou-Loc loved her and wouldn't hurt him like that, no matter how much he hated her.

It went without saying that Cross was going to make whoever Martina was foolish enough to creep with suffer unimaginably before he killed him, and while he was at it he was going to teach Martina's trifling ass a lesson once and for all. He had promised Lou-Loc that he wouldn't kill Martina, but never said anything about leaving her totally unharmed. Before it was done she would know the error of her ways.

Chapter 10

Cisco sat in the waiting area of the Roosevelt Hospital emergency room, waiting for Miguel to bring the car around. He touched the fresh stitches on the side of his face, and thought back to the meeting he had with El Diablo a few hours prior. That bitch Satin had told El Diablo of his advances, and he was rewarded with twelve stitches in his face. That just made Cisco despise his former mentor even more. El Diablo would have his day, and LC Blood would belong to Cisco again.

Miguel pulled up in front of the glass doors and beeped the horn. Cautiously, Cisco stepped from the emergency room into the night air. As he slid into the car, he kept looking around as if El Diablo were going to pop out of thin air and cut him again.

"Damn, Cisco," Miguel said, looking at the scar. "Diablo fucked you pretty good." Cisco looked at Miguel coldly and Miguel knew enough to shut his mouth.

"Don't test me," Cisco snapped. "Did you provide Tito with the information I gave you?"

"Yep, and I took care of it as soon as I dropped you off. He said he'd be good alone, but I told him to send Franco and Scales ahead just to test their defenses. If they can't get it done, he'll step to it personally."

"Very good, Miguel. Contrary to popular opinion, you aren't a complete idiot." Miguel looked at Cisco from the corner of his eye, but held his comment. "The winds of change are blowing, *mi amigo*," Cisco said while lighting a cigar. "The ways of the old-timers are fading. It is time we step into the twenty-first century. New times call for new leadership. Wouldn't you say, Miguel?"

Miguel wasn't sure where Cisco was going with the conversation, so he figured it best to just play along. "*Si*, we need to step it up like the Italians and the Chinese."

Cisco grinned, seeing that he and Miguel were reading from the same page. "El Diablo has played a large part in the strengthening of our chapter, but he's getting old. He thinks we're still living in the eighties, where people still respected and feared a name. These are the dog years, Miguel. The only thing people respect anymore is money and power. If you want something, you must take it. These old farts are losing their edge. We need fresh blood."

"So, what are you saying, Cisco?" Miguel asked keeping one eye on the road, and the other on Cisco.

"What I'm saying is that during my time as boss of LC, we prospered and made money. When El Diablo is removed from power, we will again be the head of the food chain. LC will be mine again. There are others among us who feel the same way. They too would like to go back to living large, instead of squabbling and dying over bullshit. By force or by choice, El Diablo will step down."

Miguel knew that Cisco was talking about a mutiny. If anything were to go wrong, those involved would surely become outlaws or be put to death. But on the other hand, if all went well Miguel would be able to get in on the ground floor. He didn't know whether he was going to side with Cisco or El Diablo, so Miguel decided to play both ends from the middle. Whichever way it went, there was something in it for him. He figured he might as well play it out.

"I assume you have a plan, Cisco?"

A broad smile crossed Cisco's face. "Indeed I do. Now listen carefully."

Satin was coming out of Barnes & Noble, going over the day's events. As she rounded the

corner of West Eighth Street, she noticed someone sitting on her jeep holding what looked like
a stick. It was dark on the block, so she couldn't
see who it was. Satin quickly retrieved her pistol
and moved cautiously toward the jeep. As she
got closer to the stranger, his features became
more familiar to her.

"*Hola, senorita*. Good to see you again, Satin,"
Lou-Loc greeted her.

Satin was surprised when she realized it was
Lou-Loc. "St. Louis? How did you find me?"

"As you said, I'm resourceful. Oh, and you can
ice the gat, I'm harmless." He nodded to the gun
in her hand.

Satin blushed, a little embarrassed that she
was still holding the gun. After an uncomfort-
able pause, she put the gun back in her purse.
Lou-Loc stepped forward and extended his arm.
What Satin had assumed to be a stick was actually one long-stemmed white rose.

"For you, gorgeous."

Satin inhaled the sweet fragrance and blushed
like a schoolgirl. "Why thank you, St. Louis. It's
beautiful."

"No thanks needed. But do me a favor and
cool out on my government. My friends call me
Lou-Loc."

"So we're friends, huh?"

"For now. Maybe further down the road it'll get a little deeper."

"Let's not get ahead of ourselves, Lou-Loc. One step at a time, okay?"

"Fair enough. Listen, why don't we go some where and rap a little. You know, get to know each other?"

Satin's face took on a look of disappointment. "I wish I could, but I have plans. They're having a black writers' convention at the Garden, and I want to see if I can get some of these signed." she said, holding up her B&N bag.

"Damn, ain't fate a bitch? I come all this way to see you and you hurt my feelings. Guess another time then?" Lou-Loc looked at her with puppy-dog eyes and Satin damn near wet herself. Satin wanted this man in the worst kind of way, but she had to be cool about it. As Lou-Loc turned to leave, she stopped him.

"Hey wait," she said, grabbing his arm, "I got an idea. You could come with me. I mean, only if you want to?"

Lou-Loc had already decided that if need be, he would follow this girl to the ends of the earth, but he couldn't hip her to it. He had to play hard to get so he wouldn't seem thirsty. Lou-Loc scratched his chin and shook his head. "I don't know, Satin. I'm not even dressed properly. I don't wanna cramp your style."

"Don't be that way," she said, rubbing his hand. "You might even enjoy it. You said you wanted to get to know me, right? So here's your chance."

"Okay, Ms. Angelino, you've convinced me. Give me a sec to make a phone call, and we're in the wind." Lou-Loc called Martina, but she wasn't home. After leaving a message, saying that he wouldn't be home until late, he turned his attention to Satin. "Okay, Satin, everything kosher. If you like, we can take my car?"

"I told you, I'm not that kinda girl," she said, faking an attitude. "We'll go in my car, and if you try something I will put one in you." She patted her purse.

Lou-Loc gave her his winning smile and said, "Shorty, I ain't no pervert that's hard-up for a nut. You're safe with me. Shall we, Ms. Angelino," he said and extended his arm.

"Indeed we shall," Satin answered as she took his arm. The two lovers strolled arm and arm to Satin's jeep. They were smiling like they had both hit the lotto, looking forward to what the future might hold.

***

Martina sat listening to Lou-Loc's message, putting lotion on her legs. She was tight at the fact that Lou-Loc wouldn't be there tonight, but she didn't sweat it too much. She had plans of her own.

After she finished dressing she called a taxi and went downstairs to wait for it. All she could think about was her secret rendezvous and how much she was looking forward to it. She was so wrapped up in her own shady thoughts that she had no idea she was being watched. When the taxi pulled up Martina hopped in and gave him the address where she was going.

The whole time Cross had been hanging from a ledge on the second floor, watching and listening. He was so angry that he wanted to pounce on her right then and there, but he didn't. Lou-Loc was a good man and Cross refused to do him dirty, no matter how much it would've pleased his own desires. Hopefully, when Lou-Loc realized how much of bitch she was, he'd ask Cross to take her. Until then, he was just going to watch.

When the taxi pulled off, Cross released his grip from the ledge and dropped soundlessly to the ground. He made hurried steps to the curb where he had left his motorcycle. It was a custom-built Harley-Davidson with what looked like an infant's skull mounted above the headlight. With a swipe of his boot, the hog roared to life. When Martina's taxi had gotten about a block or so, he pulled out behind them. He wasn't worried about losing them because he had Martina's scent, and once the Cross had been set on your trail there was no escape. As thoughts of his payment came to mind, he licked his cold lips and smiled. Although he couldn't touch Martina, the same didn't apply for her would-be lover. Whoever had been foolish enough to cross Lou-Loc by shacking up with the whore, had stepped into the demon's maw.

Chapter 11

Gutter strolled casually from the corner bodega, smoking a Black & Mild and scratching a scratch-off with a quarter. He was proud of how well things went with the Al Mukalla, and even more pleased that Lou-Loc had accepted the contract. Soon the dough would be rolling in and their crew would be in good shape. Lou-Loc was a true-blue homeboy. Gutter knew that he didn't want to accept the contract, but he did it off the strength of the set. He was a real nigga.

Gutter felt a little sour about the whole situation. He knew Lou-Loc wanted out of the game and all the bullshit that came with it, but he put his dreams on hold for the good of their gang. The only reason Lou-Loc was still putting in work was because of his love for Gutter. All the years they had spent putting in work would soon have to come to an end. Gutter had already decided that once this thing had been done for Anwar, he was going to set Lou-Loc free from his oath. The time they spent getting down with and for each other had been sweet, but Gutter knew Lou-Loc had bigger plans and he respected that.

Gutter pulled out his wallet and removed a bank deposit slip. After the two grand he had deposited the day before, it had brought the total to thirty thousand. It was money that Gutter had been secretly saving up for his friend. Once their business was conducted, he planned on giving it to Lou-Loc to help him out with whatever he wanted to do with his life. It was a good deal of bread, but you couldn't put a price on a friend like Lou-Loc.

Gutter was brought out of his thoughts by a flicker of movement in the corner of his eye. With reflexes born from years of street training, he dove to his left and pulled his gat in one motion. Just as Gutter hit the ground rolling, a hail of bullets ripped through the car he had been standing next to a second prior. As Gutter got to his feet, he saw two young men wearing red scarves over their faces charging at him. Gutter's brain screamed out a warning: *Enemies!*

The first Blood raised his Mac 10 to let off another burst, but Gutter beat him to the punch. Gutter let off two quick shots and both hit their mark. The Blood dropped his gun and howled in pain as the first shot slammed into the meat of his thigh, and the second shattered his cheekbone. Gutter took a second to admire his handiwork and that second cost him dearly. As he tried to move out of the second attacker's line of fire, he got hit. The bullet slammed into his stomach and sent him flying backward through the window of a dry cleaner's.

As Gutter tried to get to his feet, he was greeted by two more bullets. One struck him in the arm and the other hit him in the chest, sending his pistol flying. It seemed like the party was over for old Gutter, as the Blood called Scales moved in to finish him off. Gutter was fighting to stay conscious, but it was a losing battle. Scales raised his .45 and smiled at the fallen gang leader. Just as Scales began to tighten his grip on the trigger, a cry shattered the darkness.

"Harlem muthafucka!"

Before Scales even had a chance to turn around, he found himself being ripped to shreds by a hail of bullets. The unknown attacker pressed down on the trigger of his .380 and didn't release his grip until the clip was spent. As Scales lay on his back bleeding and twitching, the stranger stepped over him and bashed his skull in with the end of the oak cane he'd been carrying.

Gutter could hear the chaos erupting around him, but couldn't find the strength to move. The

stranger was tugging at Gutter and calling his
name, but he was having trouble focusing. Between the pain and the loss of blood, he was losing
his will to fight. For the briefest of moments, Gutter forced his eyes to focus on the stranger, and
the face was familiar. It was Snake Eyes. Gutter
managed to force a smile onto his lips, and then
the darkness claimed him.

Lou-Loc and Satin sat sipping coffee at a small
shop not far from Madison Square Garden. They
had just come from the convention and decided
not to call it a night just yet. At first Lou-Loc had
been a bit skeptical about going to the event. In
fact, the only reason he even bothered was to
spend some time with Satin. Once they reached
the convention, Lou-Loc was quite astounded by
the whole affair. There were people and books of
all shapes, sizes, and colors. Most of the books on
display were books that he'd read already. There
were a few he hadn't checked out, so he bought
them and got them signed by the authors. Some of
Lou-Loc's favorite writers were at the convention.
He wanted to run around grinning and shaking
hands, but he couldn't come across as a groupie
in front of Satin on their first date.

Satin was very impressed by the fact that Lou-Loc was so well-read. He knew a little something about all of the books there. He had either read them or heard of them. He even bought Satin a book about a girl who wanted to have the best of both worlds. It was written by that guy with the dreads who kind of resembled Jerry Rice ten years ago. He was a brilliant writer and his books were always juicy.

As Satin sat stirring her French vanilla coffee, she decided to pick Lou-Loc's brain. "So, Lou-Loc," she said, licking her stirrer seductively, "how come you know so much about books?"

"What, you surprised I can read or something?" he asked playfully.

"No, I don't mean it like that. It's just that when you talk about books and writing, there's so much passion in your words."

"Writing is something I'm very passionate about. It's my escape from the hustle and bustle of everyday bullshit."

"So you write, then?" she asked, leaning in a little closer.

"Sure do," he responded. "I've written two books and a bunch of short stories."

"I'm impressed, Lou-Loc. You don't strike me as the type."

"Why, because I rock my pants a little looser than most folks or 'cause my hair is all braided up? Tsk, tsk, Satin, how stereotypical of you."

"Cut it out, Lou-Loc. You know what I mean."

"I know. I'm just messing wit ya. I get that a lot, though. People tend to judge you for face value instead of who you really are. It's a'ight though; I kinda like it that way. People tend to give you a wider berth when they think you're some kind of sick cat. And what about you, Satin, what's your story?"

"Don't really have one, to tell you the truth. I'm just a young girl trying to work her way through school, and make a better life for her family. Since my aunt's been sick, I've kinda had to bear the burden. You know, taking care of my little brother and all."

As Satin spoke, Lou-Loc felt closer to her. She was such a deep person; he wanted to hear all she had to tell. Lou-Loc moved closer to her and placed his hand on hers. His pager went off, but he ignored it and listened to her.

"So, it's just the three of you?" he asked.

"No," she said turning her eyes away, "I have another sibling, an older brother. He doesn't come around much. My aunt calls him a street person. She doesn't agree with his lifestyle."

"And you, Satin, how do you feel about his lifestyle?"

"I don't condemn it, nor do I condone it. It's just how he is. I wish he would give those damn streets up."

"I see how you feel, doll, but for some of us, the streets are the only way out."

"Oh, you mean like you? Will the streets be your escape, as you call it?"

"Hey, hold on now, Satin. I ain't never say I was an angel. I make no excuses for what I do and as far as your question, no. Believe it or not, I've grown quite tired of the game."

"So, why do you still play it?"

Lou-Loc was caught off guard by that question. He didn't really have an answer, so he just spoke from the heart. "I don't know why I play it. I guess because I don't know how to stop playing it."

Satin looked up at Lou-Loc with tears in her eyes and shook her head. "Hey, come on," he said, moving around the table to her side. "I didn't mean to upset you."

She waved him off, but didn't push him away. "It's not you," she said, wiping her eyes, "it's this fucked-up world we live in. So many talented brothers like you get pulled down by these streets. I'm just sick of it."

"Satin," he said, taking her in his arms, "people can change. Your brother can change; there's still time."

"And you, Lou-Loc, can you change?"

"Who knows—maybe if I had the right person in my life to help me? Will you help me change, Satin?"

Satin looked into Lou-Loc's eyes and saw sincerity. This only made her cry more. Here was this man who she hardly knew, and she was falling for him face-first. She wanted him, and she knew he wanted her, but what about his girl?

"Lou-Loc," she said, pulling away, "this can't be. I have to be honest: I want you. I've wanted you from the first moment I saw you going into the Magic Theater. We want each other, but you got a girl, and I can't rock like that."

Lou-Loc stepped back, completely taken by surprise. How the hell did she know about Martina? He could've lied about it, or denied the fact that he was still with her, but he didn't. There was something about Satin that made him want to be totally honest with her, no matter what the consequences.

"Satin, you're right about me having a lady—I won't lie to you—but it's not what you think. That chick is way bogus. I used to be so in love with her that I was blind to the bullshit she was pulling on me. As we speak, I got somebody following her because she's been tipping out on me, but I haven't been able to prove it. I gave her everything, including my heart, but I guess it wasn't good enough."

Satin looked at the tears welling up in Lou-Loc's eyes and her heart went out to him. She saw so much pain inside him that she had to turn away. Satin knew Lou-Loc was the man she wanted to be with, but she was afraid of getting hurt. "So, now what?" she asked.

"Well, we can wonder what might have been, or we can take a chance on the future, one step at a time."

"One step at a time?"

"One step at a time."

The two of them walked from the shop, hand in hand, talking and trying to make sense out of life. Neither one of them noticed the young man in the red sweat suit watching their exit.

It was about 3:00 a.m. when Martina finally finished her little date. It was just as Lou-Loc had expected: She was tipping. Every time Cross would see them hug or touch each other, he got a thrill. He was going to make this little task as painful as possible.

From the lowdown Cross had gotten from his associate, Jasper, the man with Martina called himself Mac. He ran a Blood chapter out of Newark. He and Martina had been seeing each other off and on for about three years—sometimes as a couple; other times they were just fuck buddies. Cross really didn't know what Martina saw in the guy. He could tell the boy was getting money from the expensive jewelry he was wearing and the nice car he drove, but he had no style whatsoever. Even from a few yards away Cross could smell the cheap-ass cologne he had bathed in. He wasn't particularly attractive, either. He was short with lumpy brown skin and chemical waves. He wore gold caps to hide the few teeth in his mouth that were rotten. What caught Cross's attention was the monstrous ruby that he sported on his left pinky. He could probably fetch quite a few dollars for it on the open market.

Cross waited quietly in the shadows of a doorway while Mac kissed Martina and put her in a taxi. *No sense in tipping the little bitch to the fact that she's busted*, he thought to himself. Soon the taxi was well away, and Mac was taking a slow stroll back to his car. A stroll he would never get to finish.

Just as Mac reached for his car keys, Cross leapt out of the darkness with a snarl. He could've taken Mac without making a sound, but it was more dramatic this way. Cross was a sucker for drama. Mac spun to face what he thought was a stray dog from the sound. He was totally surprised to see a man moving toward him. He reached for his gun, but was stopped short by Cross's viselike grip on his wrist. Cross leaned in and twisted his face into a mask of death.

At the sight of this slobbering thing that was standing not even two feet away from him, Mac pissed his pants. Cross let out a demonic laugh as he tightened his grip and crushed Mac's wrist. He began to whimper, which only excited Cross more. Popping open his switchblade, Cross slashed Mac's face. The heady aroma of fresh blood sent Cross into a frenzy as he tore savagely at Mac's already shredded face with his teeth. Mac begged and pleaded for his life, but it was too late. The beast had been let loose, and his life was forfeit.

Chapter 12

When Lou-Loc got home, the house was empty. No Martina, no kids. Didn't really surprise him, though—she had been slipping out quite often lately. It seemed like every time he was out for an extended period, she would slip away and come home with a lame excuse.

Fuck her, he thought to himself. If she was doing dirt, Cross would find out. Every time Lou-Loc thought of Cross a chill ran down his back. They were good friends but Cross was really out there. Lou-Loc had known some scary cats in his lifetime, but Cross made them all seem like choirboys. He was a walking reminder that there really were things that went bump in the night.

Lou-Loc stripped down to his boxers and stood in front of the mirror. He touched the spot where the bullet wound would've been if Cross hadn't intervened. Lou-Loc had saved Cross, and Cross had returned the favor down the line. The score was even, but the two chose to remain friends.

Lou-Loc flopped down on the bed and sighed. The answering-machine light read twenty messages. "Lazy bitch couldn't even clear the machine." Lou-Loc didn't care who called, he had some thinking to do, and most of it was about Satin.

From the moment he first saw her, she had been on his mind. At first he thought she might've been just a stuck-up little chick, but after he had spent time talking to her and getting to know her, he realized he was wrong. She was deeper than he thought possible, and that just made him want her more. Satin was the kinda lady that had ambition. She knew what her goals were and busted her ass to reach them. She had a deep appreciation for life and a hell of a lot of class. Satin carried herself like a lady at all times. She hardly swore, and articulated herself very well when she spoke. Satin was one of those women that when she spoke to someone, her voice commanded their undivided attention. She was definitely someone he could learn from.

It was all like a fairy tale to Lou-Loc. They say when you find your soul mate you know it from your first encounter. Lou-Loc was really beginning to think there was some truth to that. Then his thoughts shifted back to Martina. What if he had been wrong about her tipping? He loved Martina—at least he did at one point—but his feelings for her had begun to die until she announced that she was pregnant. Knowing that he was about to become a father was what kept him around, but he really didn't want to be there. He could've easily broken up with Martina and still did what he had to do for his kid, but the thought of his li'l one growing up without a father in the house—like he did—wasn't something he was comfortable with.

Lou-Loc heard the front door click and knew Martina was home. He quickly closed his eyes and pretended to be asleep.

Martina removed her shoes in the hall and slipped silently in the house. She was still a little tipsy from the bottle of champagne she and Mac had been sipping on. It wasn't the smartest thing in the world for her to do, being pregnant and all, but she figured, *It's only champagne, what could it hurt?*

When she went into the bedroom, she saw Lou-Loc stretched across the bed, knocked out. Sometimes she felt bad for creeping on him, but fuck it. Her logic was: If he was more sensitive to her needs, she wouldn't have to tip on him. She cared for Lou-Loc, that was true enough, but the main reason she stayed with him was because the boy was worth paper. Lou-Loc was indeed a hustler's hustler.

When she had first met him, she already knew who he was because her friends had given her the rundown on the boss player from L.A. Lou-Loc had money, style, and on top of all that he was pretty as hell. The word was out that he was the dude to get with, so Martina wasted no time in snatching him up, which wasn't too hard to do. Lou-Loc was a gangster, but beneath the bandanna he was a sweetheart who had a soft spot for Spanish pussy. Once she put it on him it was a done deal.

Martina walked to the bed and looked down at Lou-Loc's sleeping form. She felt kinda bad about her secret rendezvous. Lou-Loc was a lot of things, but to her knowledge he hadn't been unfaithful. Sometimes she didn't understand why she even fucked with Mac. Lou-Loc was better looking and his paper was just as long, if not longer. The thing with her and Mac was just something that always was. She'd been fucking with him since before Lou-Loc came east. Maybe she would cut Mac off and be true to Lou-Loc. That was a big maybe, considering the fact that she wasn't sure if the baby she was carrying belonged to Mac or Lou-Loc. "If it ain't broke, don't fix it," she told herself.

Martina stripped down to her birthday suit and slid into the bed next to her man. She moved her body against his to steal some of his warmth. She loved him so much, yet she just had such a hard time being true with him always being away. Maybe in time. Maybe.

Satin got home that evening with mixed feelings about the way the day had gone. First Michael popped back up on the scene, then Lou-Loc showed up and took her on one of the best dates she'd ever gone on. If anything, the day had been eventful.

Satin removed her clothes and put on her white-laced nightgown. She flopped on her bed and looked at the purple-and-yellow book Lou-Loc had bought for her. Every time she thought of him, her underwear got moist. He was so damn fine and he wanted her as much as she wanted him. Satin was far from stupid; she knew niggaz was good for playing games, but not Lou-Loc. She could tell from the first time he opened his mouth that he was a man of honor. He was truly into her. It wasn't unusual for a guy to fall head over heels for her, but that was usually lust. With Lou-Loc, it was something much deeper.

Satin had never encountered a man like Lou-Loc. He was so passionate about everything. That was odd for a young man, especially a gangbanger. The thought of his gang affiliation presented Satin with another problem. Even though she didn't get down with the whole gang thing, she was guilty by association. What would Lou-Loc think if he found out who her brother was?

To her, the whole concept was stupid. Young Blacks and Latinos killing each other over bullshit, colors and property that neither side owned. First it was Michael, and then her youngest brother Jesus. Both had fallen victim to this thing they called *street life.* Now she had to sit idly by and watch someone else she cared for fall victim. Then there was the fact that he had a girl. Though Lou-Loc claimed he wasn't feeling her like that, she could tell he still had love for her. That dizzy bitch had a winner on her hands, but still felt it necessary to cock her legs for anybody with a kind word for her. Satin knew how Martina was getting down, but she felt it wasn't her place to put her mouth in that. The good thing was Lou-Loc was finally starting to get wise to her shit.

Satin felt kinda stupid feeling the way she did about Lou-Loc. Even though he seemed sincere, she knew that nine outta ten niggaz was full of shit. Again, she pushed those feelings out of her mind. She kept telling herself that Lou-Loc was the real thing. Every girl dreams about that knight in shining armor, but she had finally found him. As long as Lou-Loc didn't play himself, they'd be all good.

Satin popped some chamomile tea in the microwave and lit some scented candles. After her tea was done, she got into bed and tried to relax. Every time she tried to close her eyes she saw Lou-Loc. When she inhaled, she smelled his cologne. When she touched her hand, she still felt his print. Satin had a problem, and she knew it. She was in love.

Chapter 13

Lou-Loc was awakened at the crack of dawn by the phone ringing. He was dead tired from the night before, so he decided to let Martina's lazy ass get it. It was probably for her anyhow. He heard her mumble a groggy "hello" into the receiver. She sucked her teeth and began to shake him. Fuck could it be calling him this early?

"Who is it?" he asked, annoyed.

"Somebody named Tariq," she replied with attitude.

For a moment, Lou-Loc's still half-asleep brain couldn't place the name. It was a familiar one, but he wasn't sure where he knew it from. As the fog began to clear, he recognized who the name belonged to. Tariq was the government of his partner Snake Eyes. "What it is, my nigga?" he asked, sitting upright. "Shit, it's like three something in the morning back home. What gives, homie?"

"Ay, what's up, cuz?" Snake Eyes replied. "I ain't home, I'm in New York."

"New York?" Lou-Loc asked, surprised. "Fuck you doing here, and why you ain't call me to pick you up from the airport? Shit, I would've—"

"Man, this ain't no social call," Snake Eyes interrupted. "We got a situation. These mutha-fuckers hit Gutter."

Lou-Loc could feel all of the blood drain from his face. He was just with him that afternoon so it had to be some kind of mistake. Gutter couldn't be dead. Fighting back the tears that were trying to make their way to the surface, Lou-Loc spoke calmly into the phone. "My nigga dead?"

"Nah," Snake Eyes said, exhaling, "he still with us, but it ain't looking good. He was woke for awhile, but they got him all doped up. He was asking for you, though. How soon can you get here?"

"I'm leaving as we speak. What hospital y'all in?"

"Where else, nigga, Harlem."

Lou-Loc let out a slight chuckle and hung up the phone. Martina was sitting up and looking at Lou-Loc inquisitively. He knew she was wondering what was going on, but he ignored her. Lou-Loc jumped into his clothes in record time and was breaking for the door.

"Baby," she called, "what's wrong? is Gutter okay?"

"Nah," he said, snatching his car keys from the dresser, "the nigga got shot."

"Oh my God, is he okay?"

"I don't know yet. I'm going to the hospital now."

"You want me to go with you?" she asked, getting out of bed.

"Nah," he said, waving her back down, "I'm going solo. I'll call you when I know something, boo. Go back to sleep and don't worry yourself." Without waiting for her to protest, as she surely would, he was out the door.

Martina sat up in the bed, not knowing what to make of the situation. She was worried about Gutter. Even though she and Gutter didn't always see eye to eye, that was her man's best friend, so she too had love for him and wouldn't wish harm on the brother. It could've just as easily been Lou-Loc laid up in the hospital, or even worse: the morgue.

With these thoughts in her mind, she began to reflect on the decisions she had forced Lou-Loc to make to support their lifestyle. She began to wonder if having the finer things in life was worth her man's life or her sanity. Suddenly the thought of Lou-Loc getting out of the game and living a normal life with her and the kids didn't sound like such a bad idea.

The hospital wasn't far from where Lou-Loc lived, so he got there within minutes. He double-parked on Lenox and rushed into the emergency room. After some quick questioning, he found out that Gutter was up in ICU, so that's where he needed to be.

Five minutes and an elevator ride later, Lou-Loc stepped out of the tiny car into the waiting area. He detested hospitals. Ever since he watched his mother wither and die from cancer, they made him uneasy. To Lou-Loc, hospitals stunk of death, a smell he was quite familiar with. Lou-Loc looked around the tiny green room and looked amongs the different faces, people from all walks of life all gathered together for common causes: sickness and tragedy. He hated coming to hospitals because they always reminded him of his routine visits to see his mother when she fell ill. It was hard for him to watch the cancer eat away at her while he watched helplessly. She suffered so much that in the end he was happy that she passed away, because it meant that she wouldn't have to suffer anymore. After dealing with that, he steered clear of hospitals. Even when his homies were laid up he wouldn't go visit them. Everyone who knew what he had gone through understood and didn't hold it against him.

Lou-Loc shook off his fears and strutted through the waiting area. After some searching, he spotted his partner Snake Eyes, sitting in a corner chair reading a magazine. Snake Eyes had put on some weight since the last time he saw him and even sprouted facial hair, but for the most part his homie looked the same. When Snake Eyes saw Lou-Loc coming his way, he braced himself on his cane and stood up to greet him.

"What it is, cuz." Lou-Loc embraced him. "I'm glad to see you; I just wish the circumstances were different."

"Me too, man. Me too," Snake Eyes said sadly.

"Snake, why didn't you call and tell me you were coming? I could've at least picked up from the airport."

"It's all good. I didn't fly anyhow, I took the train up. You know they don't let you on no airplanes with these," he said, showing him the .380 he had tucked in his pocket.

Lou-Loc smiled and took the seat next to him. "You still rolling wit that raggedy-ass gun?"

"Nigga, this li'l bitch done got me out of plenty of scrapes," Snake Eyes told him.

"Snake, you still putting in work? I thought you was a square peg?"

"Shit, I am, but you know how it is in the hood. Honestly, this is the first time I've used a gun in a long time. With this bum leg of mine I ain't really fit to put in no real work, so I had been focusing on school and this damn LSAT."

"How's that working out for you?" Lou-Loc asked.

"It's going great, I just passed the bar. I was actually coming up here for an interview with this firm. I'm gonna be practicing law on the East Coast."

"Sho ya right, cuz," he said, patting Snake Eyes on the back. "I'm going to need a good lawyer at the rate I'm going."

"Man, don't talk like that," Snake Eyes snapped. "You got a lot going for you, cuz, you just gotta stop jamming ya self with this street shit. It's like my dad used to tell you, you're a smart nigga, but you ain't got no common sense."

"Yeah, I remember. How's the old man?"

"He a'ight. He semiretired last year and moved to the Valley. Him and his girl got a nice li'l crib and he opened up a consulting firm. They're doing big things!" Before they could roll into more detail about it, Sharell came out of the back.

Gutter's lady was a pretty little brown-skinned thing with a bright smile and a kind spirit. She was on the thick side, but she wasn't fat because all her weight was in the right places. As far as personality went, she and Gutter were polar opposites. He was a gangster who smoked, drank, and operated outside the law, whereas she was a working girl who didn't do any of that and went to church twice a week. They said that opposites attract and they were proof of that.

"Hey Lou-Loc." Sharell greeted him, trying to hide the shakiness in her voice. Lou-Loc could tell from the way her eyes were red and puffed out that she'd been crying.

"What up, girl?" Lou-Loc hugged her. "You a'ight?"

"I'm trying to be strong," she said, wiping her eyes.

"I know that's right, how's my boy?"

Sharell had to fight off another wave of tears. "They tore my baby up something awful, but he's still alive, thank the Lord. He's awake, but in a lot of pain, so the doctors have him doped up. He asked me to send you in when you got here."

"A'ight, guess I'd better go check him, then. You and Snake go on and relax, I'll be back."

Lou-Loc got up from his chair and made his way toward Gutter's room. The corridor to Gutter's room was a pale blue, lined with plain wooden doors. All of the doors were the same wood brown with cheap tin lining. The only distinctive features were the cold gray numbers etched on the outside. Lou-Loc strolled through the hall, peering into the various rooms, inspecting the occupants. All of the patients' faces held the death mask Lou-Loc had become so accustomed to. Some would make it and others wouldn't. That was just the way shit worked in the hood. Actually, life in general was kinda like that, he reasoned. People were born just to die. Sometimes Lou-Loc wondered what the point of it all was.

He stood outside of Gutter's room, opening and closing his hands. He constantly wiped his hands on his sweats, but the moisture never fled. For some reason he couldn't shake the visions that were bombarding him. They were visions of the time he spent in the hospital with his mother. Some of the patients harbored that same skeletal glare as she did toward the end. It was painful for Lou-Loc to watch his mother waste away like that. After his father was murdered, she was the only person he and his sister had left. She did as best she could with her government checks, but they just weren't enough. That was one of the main reasons that Lou-Loc started hustling. He had to man up and hold his family down.

Lou-Loc stood in front of the door and tried to put on his game face. It was hard, but he knew he had to be strong for his brother and the set. When he opened the door, he almost broke down at what he saw.

Gutter was laid up in one of those cast-iron-type beds. There were bandages wrapped around his entire torso as well as one of his arms. He was hooked up to all kinds of tubes and devices to monitor his vitals. To see this once-proud warrior so helpless brought a lone tear to Lou-Loc's eye. Just as he was about to lose his nerve and back out, Gutter turned around to face him.

"You just gonna stand there or come holla at ya nigga?" Gutter said groggily, trying to muster a smile.

Lou-Loc took up a seat at Gutter's bedside. From this close he got a better assessment of the damage. The would-be hit men really did a number on Gutter. His face and arms were covered with bruises and scrapes from falling through the window. The bandages that covered his wounds were soaked through and caked with dried blood. The fucking nurses probably hadn't changed the dressing in a while. That's how they did you when you don't have any insurance.

Gutter noticed Lou-Loc giving him the once-over and spoke up. "Fucking Brims tried to do me in, cuz."

"Muthafuckas can't fade you, G. You're invincible." Lou-Loc patted Gutter's hand. Gutter tried to laugh, but broke out into a fit of coughing. "Easy, soldier," Lou-Loc said softly, "we need you healthy. We got big plans, you and me. You gonna fuck everything up by dying, punk."

Gutter regained his wind and began speaking again. "I think it was them LC niggaz, cuz. I recognized that kid, Scales. These busters done started some shit," Gutter managed to get out before he started coughing again.

"Don't even worry about it, cuz. We gonna hit these faggots and we gonna hit 'em hard."

"The contract—" Gutter coughed.

"Nah." Lou-Loc shook his head, "I gots to be here wit my nigga. Fuck Anwar."

Gutter gripped Lou-Loc's arm so hard that he flinched. "Business first."

Lou-Loc started to protest, but when he saw the look in his friend's eyes he didn't. This was important to Gutter. Lou-Loc wanted to believe that his friend would pull through, but in reality, it wasn't likely. The boy was in bad shape. If this was to be Gutter's last request, he would not be denied.

Lou-Loc's thoughts were interrupted when Gutter coughed out a word: "Freedom." He said it so low that Lou-Loc almost didn't catch it.

"Freedom," Gutter said again. "When this bullshit is done . . ." Gutter's words were cut off as he was rocked by another fit of coughing. It seemed like he was having a hard time catching his breath but after a few minutes he was good. "You gotta get outta this, Loc."

"Cuz, you know that ain't an option. I'm gonna Crip until they lower me into the ground," Lou-Loc boasted. He was trying to get Gutter to smile but his face was very serious.

"Look at me." Gutter flung the covers off him as best he could so that Lou-Loc could see the extent of his injuries and it didn't look good. "These niggaz tried to finish me, but I ain't mad because this is the road I chose to walk. I might die in this hospital, and if that's what Allah has willed, then so be it."

"Cuz, stop talking crazy," Lou-Loc told him. He couldn't bear the thought of being without his best friend and crime partner.

"I'm serious as a heart attack. I wouldn't say this in front of Sharell, but I'm fucked-up, homie," Gutter confessed. "I'm in a bad way and I don't want this for you. I'd break my heart for the homies to have to escort ya li'l sister to your funeral. I don't want this for you, Lou-Loc. Do something with your life."

"And what about you, Gutter?" Lou-Loc asked, with tears forming in his eyes. "What are you gonna do when you get out of here?"

"You mean, *if* I get outta here," Gutter corrected him. "Loc, you of all people know how I get down, so you know if I make it through this I'm going right back to the trap and gonna bust on the first slob I catch. I'm gonna gangbang until Allah calls me home." Gutter tried to sound like he wasn't worried but Lou-Loc knew better. He saw something in his friend's eyes that night that he had never seen before: fear. "I gotta tell you something. I was gonna surprise you, but I don't know if I'll get a chance to tell you later. I'm going to give you the number to a bank account where I got some paper stashed and I want you to—" Gutter started coughing again. This time blood spilled over his lips and he was clearly in a lot of pain. All sorts of alarms started going off and the machines monitoring his vitals started beeping frantically. Not knowing what else to do, Lou-Loc called for the nurse.

The doctors and nurses rushed in like linebackers, knocking Lou-Loc out of the way so they could attend to Gutter. Lou-Loc wasn't sure what was going on, but it was scaring the hell out of him. Gutter went from seizing violently to not moving at all and Lou-Loc knew something was dreadfully wrong. He tried to peer over the doctors' shoulders to see what was going on, but the nurses rushed him from the room so they could work. The nurses slammed the door in Lou-Loc's face and left him in the hallways feeling like he was trapped in a bad dream. This couldn't be happening.

Sharell came streaking down the hallway, with Snake Eyes hobbling behind her. The look on Lou-Loc's face filled her heart with terror. "Lou-Loc, what's going on? Is Kenyatta okay?"

Lou-Loc just looked back and forth from her to Snake Eyes. He tried to form words, but his lips wouldn't cooperate.

"Damn it, tell me something," she said, grabbing him by the front of his shirt.

Finally he found his voice. "Try to stay calm, Sharell. The doctors are working on him. He had some kind of seizure."

"Father God, please no!" Sharell dropped to her knees and started bawling. Most of what she was saying was gibberish. She was just rocking back and forth, rubbing the iced-out cross Gutter had brought her for her birthday. With Snake Eyes's help, Lou-Loc was able to get her to her feet and into one of the chairs in the waiting area. The trio sat in the waiting area, hoping the doctors would bring them some positive news.

Martina was blowing up Lou-Loc's pager, but he ignored it. He sat with his friend, trying to be strong for Sharell.

Finally, the thin, balding doctor wearing blue scrubs came out of Gutter's room looking exhausted. "Who's here for Kenyatta Soladine?" he asked.

Seeing that Sharell was in no condition to handle whatever news the doctor had, Lou-Loc stepped to the plate.

"That would be me," he said walking across the waiting area. Seeing the doctor's uneasiness at his gangsta appearance, he extended his hand and introduced himself. "I'm his brother, St. Louis Alexander."

The doctor relaxed a little and spoke in a hushed tone that only Lou-Loc could hear. "Your brother's not doing too good," he said, wringing his hands together, "We've managed to stabilize him for the moment, but his vitals are very weak. You and your family are welcomed to stay, but there isn't much you can do for him at this point. My advice would be for you to all go home and get some rest. We'll call you should his condition change."

Lou-Loc thanked the doctor and made his way back over to Sharell and Snake Eyes. After speaking to the doctor, he felt a little better, but he knew Gutter wasn't out of the woods yet. Snake Eyes and Sharell looked at him with expectant eyes. He didn't want to alarm Sharell any further, so he figured he'd just tell her a half truth.

"He's stable," Lou-Loc said with a huff. "He's still real weak, so we can't see him anymore for a while. They got your number already, Sharell, and I gave them mine. They'll call us if anything changes."

"Oh, praise God," Sharell said, wiping her eyes. "I don't know what's wrong with y'all, Lou-Loc. When are you gonna get out of this life? It's all genocide."

Lou-Loc was in no mood to be lectured, but he understood that she was going through something, so he tried not to be short with her when he spoke. "Listen, Sharell. I know you don't dig how we get down, but sometimes the end justifies the means. We ain't trying to live like this forever, especially me. Everybody comes around in their own time."

"I didn't mean to sound like I was screaming on you," she said, composing herself. "I'm just scared. I mean, that's my heart laid up in there. I couldn't go on without Ken and Lou-Loc, you know I love you like a brother, so if anything were to happen to either of you I'd lose it."

"Don't even think like that," he cut her off. "Me or that nigga in there ain't checking out no time soon. What kinda nigga would I be if I wasn't there to be best man at y'all wedding?" He pulled Sharell close and hugged her. "Quit that crying," he whispered in her ear, "everything gonna be blue. I'm gonna have Snake Eyes take you home while I go handle a few things."

"Lou-Loc, I know you. Just let it go. Getting at them boys who shot my Ken ain't gonna do nothing but make it worse. Let it go," she pleaded.

"Sharell, don't you worry your pretty little head about me doing nothing stupid." Lou-Loc smiled at her. "I just got some stuff that needs to be attended to so I can free up some time to be here for Gutter. Now you go on and get the car while I rap a taste with Snake Eyes. He'll be along in a minute."

Sharell was still suspicious, but she did like Lou-Loc asked and went to fetch the car. As soon as she got on the elevator the smiles faded and the two Crips immediately went into war mode.

"What you scheming on, cuz?" he asked.

"The lives of these faggots who touched my brother," Lou-Loc said with ice in his voice. "These muthafuckas got themselves an asshole full of trouble for what they done, and that's on Harlem."

"Just tell me what you want me to do, cuz," Snake Eyes told him. It had been a while since he'd been active in combat, but for his brother he would gladly pick up his gun and do what he had to.

"I need you to go up to Hunts Point and see my man Wiz at the auto shop. Tell him to get my toy ready ASAP. When you get done with that, hit my pager. I need to have a meeting with the homies to let them know what's up then I got some shit that I gotta handle."

"You know I'm wit you, cuz. Let's put the work in on these niggaz."

"Nah, brother. You ain't a combat soldier no more. I need you to be there for Sharell because she's gonna need a shoulder to lean on and my hands are gonna be full."

"Cuz, don't do me like that. Gutter is my family too and I got a right to be a part of this," Snake Eyes demanded.

Lou-Loc didn't want Snake Eyes in the middle of what was about to go down, but he had just as much right to ride out as anyone. "Have it your way, then. I'll call you with the details. Right now I gotta breeze." Lou-Loc slapped his homeboy a five and headed for the stairs.

"What you gonna do, cuz?" Snake Eyes yelled after him.

Lou-Loc turned around and smiled. "What I do best, my nigga." With that, he was down the stairs.

Chapter 14

The sun shone brightly through Satin's bed-room window that morning. As the warm rays moved and danced over her sleeping face, she began to stir. Satin loved the sunshine. That was the reason she had a large picture window built into her loft. The owner was a friend of her aunt Selina, so he didn't complain about the remodeling.

Satin sat up in her round, king-sized bed and welcomed the new day. She arched her back to stretch, and exposed erect brown nipples peeking through her sheer nightgown. She slid her long brown legs off the side of the bed and rubbed her manicured feet back and forth over her area rug. There was something about the smooth feel of the smooth Persian material on her bare feet that felt good to her.

When she recalled the details of her date with Lou-Loc, she couldn't help but smile. She had been a little skeptical about the whole affair, with him just popping up and all, but he turned out to be a perfect gentleman. He held all the doors for her, complimented her on her outfit, and never once tried to coax her into intimacy. He got a ten for the evening.

Satin padded across her hardwood floor to her walk-in closet. She didn't have to work today, so jeans and a T-shirt were the order of business. Satin laid her clothes across her bed and headed for the shower. Before she made it to the bathroom, the phone broke her stride.

She answered the phone with a pleasant hello, and was delighted to hear the gentleman's voice on the other end. "St. Louis," she sang, "what the deal, papi? I didn't expect to hear from you so soon."

"I didn't disturb you, did I?" he asked.

"Nah, I was up. Thanks for the good time."

"No, thank *you*. It was different, but I enjoyed it. What you got planned for this morning?"

"Not much. I'm off today, so I'll probably just chill, and catch up on my reading. Why do you ask? You got something planned for me?"

"Can I see you? Maybe take you to breakfast or something?"

Satin wanted to shout, *"Hell yeah, you can see me!"* but she knew she couldn't play herself. Instead she responded, "Nah. But if you wanna come over, I know how to cook a little."

At first Lou-Loc was preparing himself for a rejection, but he was pleased to hear that she was willing to see him. "A'ight," he said coolly, "but since it's ya place, let me cook for you?"

After getting her address, the two hung up. She felt like jumping for joy, but instead she bolted for the shower. Lou-Loc said he'd be there in a half hour, so she didn't have much time. Guess she'd save the jeans for another day. She wanted to look good for Lou-Loc. Martina's time was just about up, she just didn't know it. Hurricane Satin had arrived, and she planned on staying for a while.

Lou-Loc pulled his car over on West Eighth Street and hopped out in front of a pay phone. He dropped a quarter in and punched the number pad. His cell was in working order, but he made it a point never to talk business on it. To do so was just as good as indicting yourself.

After two rings, a female picked up. "Hello?" she barked in a husky voice. "Who the hell is this, and what ya want this damn early?"

"Hey, Kiki," he said pleasantly, "this Lou. Ya brother around?"

"Yeah," she growled. "That no-good nigga in there sleep."

"I need you to wake him up, ma. Tell him it's important.".

"He need to have his ass up anyhow. Muthafucka should be out job-hunting instead of laying up on me and shit."

"You know how it is in the hood, Kiki."

"I got ya hood, nigga. So what's up, Lou, When you gonna come knock the bottom out this here?"

Lou-Loc shook his head. Every time he saw or spoke to Kiki, she was trying to hit on him. At the blue and gray barbecue they had last summer, she even went as far as to grab his crotch when Martina wasn't looking.

"Now, Kiki, you know I can't handle that good loving of yours. You're too much woman for me, ma," he half joked. Kiki was almost six feet tall, and built like a linebacker. She had knocked out quite a few females, as well as a few men. Lou-Loc had never just come out and told her he wasn't trying to fuck wit her because the girl didn't take rejection well. There was no doubt that he could whip her in a fistfight, but her skills with a razor almost surpassed his own. Plus, she was a down-ass chick, and he didn't want to hurt her feelings.

"Yeah, a'ight," she said slyly. "One day I'm just gonna have to get you loaded and take what I want, wit yo' pretty ass." There was no doubt in either of their minds that she meant what she said. Kiki put the phone down, and screamed for her no-good, lazy, dope-selling, fake-ass gangbanging brother to come to the phone. Kiki was a female, but her four-letter vocabulary was more vulgar than most of the homeboys.

After a brief exchange of words, her brother finally came to the phone. "*What!*" he snarled.

"Hold that down, nigga. It's me, fool," Lou-Loc said in a stern voice.

"Oh, my bad, cuz," Pop Top said, realizing who he was talking to. "I thought you was that faggot-ass nigga Breeze calling me 'bout his paper. You know I don't get up till after one, what's the deal?"

"We got a game tonight," Lou-Loc said, speaking in code. "I need the whole team there; the homie Gutter got hurt and can't play."

"What?" Top asked in disbelief. "Is it bad?"

"Yeah, cuz. He might be out for the season, so you know we gotta play hard. I'm talking free-for-all." At the mention of violence, Lou-Loc could almost hear Top grinning through the phone. That boy loved to put in work and Lou-Loc was well aware of it. That's why he called him first.

"I'm on it, cuz. Time and place?" Top asked.

"Home court, baby." By this Lou-Loc meant St. Nicholas Park, which was a popular meeting spot for the Harlem Crips. "I want everyone there at midnight, and I don't mean twelve-oh-one. You and Snake Eyes will be my cocaptains. You'll be in the field and he'll be in the front office."

"Fo sho," Top said, trying to keep his anger in check, "it's on, baby."

"Get them niggaz there, cuz."

"You know I will. Let me get up off this jack so I can make it happen." Without waiting for a response, Top hung up. Lou-Loc knew that if anyone could rally the troops, Pop Top could.

Lou-Loc dropped a quarter into the phone, and moved on to the next order of business. He didn't have Anwar's direct number, so he called the contact who had supplied him with the information. He informed him that the funeral arrangement, which was code for *hit*, would be handled within the next twenty-four hours. The contact thanked him, and said that he could pick up the payment, for the floral arrangement the next evening. With that taken care of, he was ready to go see his sweetheart before he took it to the streets.

Snake Eyes hadn't slept a wink in almost twenty-four hours, and only God knew when he would finally be able to with everything that had transpired since he touched down in New York. His intentions were to surprise his homies with his visit and do some partying, but as it turned out the only party he would be attending was a war party.

After dropping Sharell off, he hopped on the northbound freeway and headed for the Bronx. He really and truly was in a down mood. Not only because his homie was laid up in the hospital, but because of the ripple effect it was having on everyone else. Snake had met Sharell twice before, and spoken to her on the phone dozens of times over the years. He knew she was a good girl and that she loved his friend dearly. He respected her for that. She was in such bad shape that he had to score her some Valium so she could calm down. It was fucked-up when the ones you cared about were really hurting, and there was nothing you could do to ease their pain.

Then there was Lou-Loc. After talking to Lou-Loc, there was no doubt in his mind as to what he had planned. To a lot of people it wouldn't be a big deal; he'd be just one more nigga with a chip on his shoulder, but that's because they didn't know Lou-Loc like he did. Lou-Loc was like a faucet of blood that once turned on there was no way to turn it off. Lou-Loc was one of the kindest dudes he knew, but when he was in kill mode he could be unpredictable and even frightening. Lou-Loc was a master schemer and cold-blooded killer, which is why he made O.G. status so quickly. If you asked for it, you got it and that's just how it was with him. It was strange how someone so intellectual and compassionate about life could take it away so effortlessly. He was like two sides to a coin. Maybe it was the brutal murder of his father that made him like that, or watching his saint of a mother wither away and die. No one really knew what made him tick. Lou-Loc was a good dude; there was no mistaking that, but in his heart lived a killer.

Snake Eyes felt bad for his friend. For as long as he'd known him, Lou-Loc had always been a fair man. It just seemed like life didn't want to be fair to him. The G's in the hood expected so much from Lou-Loc, and no one ever stopped to consider how he felt. To them, he was just a killing machine, but Snake Eyes knew different. Lou-Loc was a tortured soul who— because of his fanatical loyalty to the set—would probably never know peace until he was dead and gone.

Snake Eyes reached the run-down auto shop Lou-Loc had directed him to in the Hunts Point area of the Bronx, and parked his hog around back. The front of the place was littered with beat-up cars and trucks. Some were in need of repair, others hooked up and ready to go.

Snake Eyes entered the auto-body shop and was overwhelmed by the smell of gas fumes mixed in with sweat and urine. Before he got all the way inside, he was cut off by a hulking Mexican wearing a tattered blue overall. From the look in the behemoth's eyes, he didn't want to make nice.

"Fuck you want, homes?" the Mexican asked.

"Name's Snake Eyes," he said matching, his opponent's tone. "I'm looking for Wiz. You him?"

"What you want with Wiz?"

"If you ain't him, don't worry about it."

"I think you better watch your mouth, ma' fucka." said a voice from behind him. Snake Eyes turned to find himself staring at a gorgeous Mexican women. She wore a tight-fitting leather jumpsuit, and her silky black ponytail was held in place by a single blue ribbon. Her brown eyes looked Snake Eyes up and down like a hungry lioness eyeing a gazelle. This woman was the baddest thing he'd seen since his arrival in the Big Apple, but the AK-47 she had aimed at his dick kept him from admiring her for too long.

"Maybe you didn't understand my brother's question, so let me give it a shot. You've got five seconds to tell us what the fuck you want with Wiz or I'm gonna change your gender," she told him.

Snake Eyes had no choice but to spill the beans, but he told himself that the chick would answer for pointing a gun at him. "Listen, honey, my name is Snake Eyes. Lou-Loc sent me up here to pick something up from Wiz."

The girl narrowed her eyes at him and began nodding. For the first time, he noticed a small device sticking out from her ear. After a few moments of debating and mumbling in Spanish, she lowered her gun. "Sorry about that," she said, brushing her hair from her forehead. "You can never be too careful. Our shop is smack-dab in the middle of enemy territory."

"Ain't nothing," he said, relaxing. "I know how it is to live the life. So where is this Wiz?"

"Go on in the back and get yourself a soda from the vending machine. I recommend the orange," she said.

"I don't want a soda. I just wanna get what I came for and bounce," Snake Eyes told her. He was tired and frustrated, so he wanted to get what he had to from Wiz and bounce.

"Just go to the vending machine and get your soda," she said, sounding irritated.

Snake Eyes walked to where the old vending machine sat and eyeballed it suspiciously. The button for the orange soda had a sticker on it that said *out of order*. He looked back at the brother-and-sister team, and they were covering their mouths, trying to keep from laughing. Seeing that he was getting frustrated, they both motioned for him to push the button. With a shrug of his shoulders, he did. That's when the floor fell from under him.

Snake Eyes's heart plummeted as he fell through the floor and down a circular tube. The only thought flashing through his mind was that he was taking his last breaths. To his surprise, he slid out of the tube and landed hard on his ass. As quickly as his good leg would allow him, he sprang to his feet and clutched his cane like a club. He quickly scanned the room and noticed he was in some kind of workshop. The floor was littered with old papers and scraps of metal. There were charts and diagrams covering the walls with a large file cabinet of sorts near the hole he exited. In a far corner of the room was a table with all kinds of equipment on it. They were the kind of things one might see in a chemist's lab. Sitting behind the table was the man Snake Eyes was seeking.

Wiz wasn't at all what Snake was expecting. When he stood up and came around to greet him, he couldn't have been any taller than five feet three or so. He was a short Mexican with slick black hair, wearing a pair of grease-covered khakis with a pearl-white T-shirt. On his face, he wore thick-rimmed glasses that resembled Coke bottles. He looked more like a mad scientist than a gangster, but word around town was that Wiz was a reputable member of the Crips.

"So, you're the lawyer?" Wiz asked, extending his hand.

"Yeah, the name's Snake Eyes," he responded, shaking Wiz's hand. "Lou-Loc sent me for the package."

"Right, right. Hold up a sec." Wiz walked over to a small freezer unit and removed a box. After checking its contents, Wiz placed the first box inside of a slightly larger one. The larger box had what looked like a battery attached to the back of it. "A'ight," Wiz said, handing Snake Eyes the box, "tell Lou-Loc to follow the instructions to the letter. Once he takes these out of the case, he'll only have a little while before they become unstable. One of those bust in his hand and he's gonna have a serious problem."

Snake Eyes looked at the black box suspiciously. He wanted to ask what was in it, but he figured it wasn't his business. If Lou-Loc wanted him to know, he'd tell him on his own. Besides, from the way Wiz was talking, he wasn't sure if he wanted to know.

"Well, then, our business is concluded. That"—Wiz pointed to the file cabinet—"is the elevator. You can take it back to the main floor. Tell Lou-Loc that I said good luck."

As Wiz turned to go back to whatever he was doing, Snake Eyes stopped him. "Say, homie, what's wit that vending-machine shit?"

"Sorry about that." Wiz smiled, revealing a mouthful of braces. "I'm afraid my siblings have a weird sense of humor. That's an emergency entrance to my lab. I guess it was their idea of a joke."

"Very fucking funny," Snake Eyes mumbled as he climbed into the tiny elevator.

Chapter 15

Satin just finished putting the finishing touches on her hair, when her buzzer rang. She saw Lou-Loc when he pulled up in front of her building, so she didn't need to ask who it was. She buzzed him in, and then went about making sure all the scented candles were in place and lit. When she opened the door, Lou-Loc greeted her with a smile and a hug. As he stepped in she sized him up. Even though he was conservatively dressed in a gray sweat suit, he still looked as good as ever.

Lou-Loc openly admired the decor of her small loft. Her walls were lined with pictures of her friends and family. In addition to the pictures, there were artifacts and pieces from various Latino cultures. In the one corner, there was a bookshelf that took up almost an entire section of the wall. In the bookshelf she had everything from Tolstoy to the popular urban author K'wan. Lou-Loc was quite impressed.

When he went into the kitchen, it was Satin's turn to be impressed. He began to empty onto the counter the contents of the shopping bag he was carrying. Inside the bag, there were all kinds of foods. There were fresh fruits, vegetables, pastries, thin steaks, eggs, fresh cheese, and an exotic wine that Satin knew ran him quite a few dollars. She had never had a man cook for her before, and here he was not only cooking, but going all out. This was going to be interesting.

Lou-Loc noticed Satin staring at the bottle, and felt a little ashamed. The morning had given way to the afternoon, but it was still a bit early to be drinking. The last thing he wanted to do was give Satin the impression that he was an alcoholic. "I hope you don't mind. I thought you might like a glass of wine with your meal. I can run out and get some juice if you like."

"No, wine will be fine," she told him.

After washing his hands, Lou-Loc began preparing the meal. By the time he was done in the kitchen, he had prepared quite the little feast. The steak was lightly breaded and sent waves of pleasure through Satin's taste buds every time she took a bite. The cheese eggs were light and fluffy. They almost seemed to melt in her mouth. In addition to the steak and eggs, he had chopped up the assorted fruits and arranged them in the shapes of beautiful flowers. If Satin had any doubts before, she was sure now. She was falling in love with this man.

As they ate, they talked about everything from books to movies to politics. She knew Lou-Loc was intelligent, but she was actually quite surprised at how informed he was. He kept abreast of everything that was going on in the hood as well as in government. After the meal, they moved in to the living room, where they sipped hazelnut coffee and ate marble cake. As the smooth sounds of Billie Holiday seeped from the CD player, Satin couldn't help but to smile at how together Lou-Loc was. He even turned off his beeper and cell phone. He didn't think she was paying attention when he did it, but she was. That was very gentlemanly of him, and he scored big points with her for the act. The morning turned to afternoon, and afternoon started giving way to evening. Satin was having a wonderful time with Lou-Loc. As wonderful a time as she was having, the thought of his girl was nagging at her. It was then that she decided to lay her cards on the table.

"Lou-Loc," she said, touching his hand, "I wanna thank you for such a beautiful day."

"It's cool. I really enjoy your company, Satin. It wasn't nothing for me to come throw a meal together for you. In fact, we need to do this more often," he suggested, sliding a little closer to her.

"I'd like that, but for as much as I wanna fall for you, I have to stop myself. I keep thinking about your girl," she said honestly.

Lou-Loc stood up and pulled her to her feet. He took her in a gentle embrace. "Satin, it's like I told you; I fucks wit her but it ain't like that."

"So why don't you tell me what it's like, St. Louis," she said with attitude.

Lou-Loc took a deep breath and began speaking. "The only thing I've ever been a fool for is love, which is what has me in this twisted situation. To be perfectly honest, I love Martina but I'm not in love with her; haven't been for a while."

"Then why are you still with her?" Satin snapped.

Lou-Loc shrugged. "Just stupid, I guess. I kept trying to tell myself that she would change, but what I'm beginning to understand is that people are going to be who they are and it's wrong to expect them to change, even if it is for the better."

"And you expect me to believe that?"

"Satin, don't take this the wrong way, but I don't too much care what you believe as long as I know my words are genuine. I should hope that you believe me, but if you don't I can't stop living because of it. Things between me and Martina are gonna play out how they play out whether you're there to see it or not, but I would like for you to be there when it's all said and done."

Satin turned her face away so he couldn't see the tears welling up in her eyes. "I don't know, Lou-Loc," she sobbed, "I can't play second fiddle to nobody, no matter how I may feel about you."

Lou-Loc wiped the tears from her cheeks. "Listen, baby," he said softly, "I'm gonna run something down to you, and I hope you don't think I'm a sucker for it. I've only known you for a few days but I feel like I've been searching for you my entire life. I'm falling for you, baby, falling hard and helpless to stop it."

"Stop it, Lou-Loc, just stop it. Don't say things you don't mean."

"Don't mean?" he asked, shocked. "I don't bullshit with my emotions, girl. Soon as my man float me the info I need on this phony-ass broad, I'm in the wind. She can keep the crib and the rest of that funky-ass shit. I'm getting out of this game, and that's real. I got some bread put up, and I plan on doing something with my life. If you were to ask me to pick up and leave all this shit behind just to be with you, I would do it in a heartbeat."

"Just like that?" she asked, suspiciously.

"Just like that," he assured her. "Don't get it fucked up, though, Satin. I ain't no trick-ass nigga, not by a long shot. The only reason I'm laying it all on the table this way is because I believe you're the real deal and not just a passing thing. Now if I'm wrong about you, speak on it. Let me know that I'm full of shit, and I'll be on my way." Satin was silent. "I see," Lou-Loc said, lowering his head. "Thank you for the wonderful day, Satin. I'll always cherish the memories of the brief time we shared together." He broke the embrace and headed for the door.

Satin just stood there for a while, weighing her options. She knew guys were notorious for running game, but something in Lou-Loc's eyes made her want to believe him. Without giving it a second thought she rushed to the door and stopped him. When she spun him to face her she was shocked to see tears in his eyes. "I believe you, Lou-Loc. I may be a fool for it, but I believe you." She wrapped her arms around him. "It may sound silly, but my heart tells me you're being real. Just don't hurt me like the rest."

"I would never," he said sincerely. He was a little embarrassed about Satin catching him in a weak moment, but what mattered was that his words rang true. "Satin," he said, playing with her hair, "I'd rather go blind and broke before I caused you to ever shed one more tear over a nigga like me."

"Stay with me?" she pleaded. "I hope you don't think poorly of me, but I want you to make love to me. Seal the deal and become my man."

Lou-Loc reluctantly broke the grip she had on his neck. "I wish I could," he said, stroking her cheek, "but I got some things I need to handle tonight. But I'll be through to see you tomorrow."

"You promise?"

"Satin, you are my shining diamond amid a field of coal. Light the way for me so I can always find you." Lou-Loc kissed her softly on her forehead, and made his way down the stairs.

Satin felt as if she was floating. In her heart she knew she had made the right choice. Lou-Loc was the kind of man she dreamt about as a little girl, and now she had him live and in the flesh. The fact that he was a gang member didn't even bother her anymore.

She went into her bedroom, removed her rosary from the vanity mirror, and knelt beside her bed and started to pray. "God," she whispered, "I know we haven't spoken much lately, but I need your help on this one. This man that you've sent me is all that I've ever needed or wanted. I might be foolish for falling for him so quick, but if loving this man is wrong, I'll be damned if I'll be right. So if you can find it in your heart to make everything okay, let ya girl come out on top."

Lou-Loc stepped from Satin's building and took a deep breath. He knew it was some bird shit letting Satin see him cry, but fuck it. She had assumed his emotional display was over the conversation they had, but that wasn't the case. When he went into the hallway, he cut his cell back on and found that he had thirteen voice mails waiting. Eleven of them were from Martina, one from Snake Eyes, and one from Cross. He listened to them all and it was the last one that caused him to break down. "The dog was rabid and had to be put down," was all Cross said but Lou-Loc knew what he meant. Lost in his thoughts, he made his way back to where he had parked the car. Just as he reached it, a young kid wearing a red hoodie pulled up on a bike.

"You got a light, blood?" the kid asked him.

Lou-Loc fished his lighter from his pocket with his left hand, and fingered his Glock with the right. "Here you go, cuz," he said sarcastically when he handed the kid his lighter. He knew from the way the kid was dressed which side he represented, but after the positive meeting he'd had with Satin, color didn't seem so important to him anymore.

"Thanks, big homie." the kid said, exhaling the smoke from his cigarette. "You better be careful out here with them colors on, dog. This is LC Blood hood."

Lou-Loc sized the kid up and noticed that he bore a striking resemblance to Satin, but paid it no mind. "Look here, li'l homie, I'm from the old school. I wear what I want and go where I please. Niggaz don't fuck wit me, and they live to see they next birthday, ya heard?"

The kid smirked at Lou-Loc and asked, "You must be a bad man, huh?"

Lou-Loc rolled up his shirt sleeve, exposing his tattoo of a six-pointed star. "Harlem gangsta, anybody killer coming straight out the jungle, so miss me with that East Coast shit. Y'all niggaz in New York better get a clue because y'all set riding and ain't even putting it down right."

The kid puffed up. "What? This is LC, homie." He threw up his hood in an awkward hand gesture.

Lou-Loc gave the boy a comical look and shook his head. "That's just the kinda bullshit I'm talking about, shorty. You rob a few ma' fuckas, or slash some ol' winehead, and you think that's gangsta? Where I'm from to be down with a set means more than busting ya gun or just being a hard ass. We took care of each other and our neighborhoods. Y'all niggaz see an old woman struggling, and instead of helping her, y'all wanna get ya jack on. Y'all dead-rag niggaz got the game fucked up. Take my advice, homie, leave this shit to us grown folks."

During the whole conversation all the kid could think of was how much hood fame he could gain by killing this O.G. Lou-Loc turned to walk away and the kid made his move. From under his hoodie, he pulled a .25 and pointed it at Lou-Loc's back. "Crab ma' fucka," he spat. "I should twist yo' shit for coming through here sideways."

Lou-Loc turned slowly and looked the kid dead in the eye. The kid expected him to be afraid, staring down the barrel of the gun, but in Lou-Loc's eyes he saw emptiness. The cold look in Lou-Loc's eyes made the kid hesitate, and that mistake cost him. With speed born of a lifetime in the streets, Lou-Loc snatched the handgun and knocked the kid off his bike and onto the pavement.

Lou-Loc leaned over and grabbed a handful of the kid's shirt, slapping him viciously across the face. "You think I'm some buster-ass nigga who's scared of this li'l pop shooter? Muthafucka, I am death on two legs," he snarled. Lou-Loc gave a cautious look around to make sure nobody was watching before he finished the kid, but when he looked up and saw Satin's bedroom light come on, he thought better of it. "You gotta be the luckiest nigga in the world, shorty, so make sure you count your blessings before your head touches the pillow tonight." Lou-Loc stuffed the gun in his pocket and released the kid. He was going to let it be, but as an afterthought he kicked him in the side of the head. "If I ever see your mark ass again, it'll be a bullet hole in your head instead of a sneaker mark, bitch!"

When Lou-Loc's car pulled off, the kid sat on the curb and cursed himself for being so weak. He could've made the big time by capping Lou-Loc, but instead he almost got himself killed. He hated Lou-Loc and vowed that he would see him again. And the next time, only one of them would walk away.

Chapter 16

Lou-Loc parked two blocks from the meeting area. His watch read 11:30, so he still had some time before the meeting. Top had rounded up all the troops and Snake Eyes had picked up his package from Wiz. His lieutenants were on point and that's why he chose them. Pop Top was a savage when it came to combat, and Snake Eyes was the voice of reason.

All that was left for Lou-Loc to do was meet Cross to get the details of his stakeout and make good on his payment, which was the location of the two virgin girls in the pictures he'd given him at the bar. Lou-Loc still wasn't comfortable with dealing with his friend's eccentric taste, but Cross's kind didn't deal in money—they dealt in blood. The price for doing business with the Gehenna was a blemish on your soul, if you were lucky, but for as much dirt as Lou-Loc had done over the years one more stain on his soul wouldn't too much matter. Two tears in a bucket. If it got the desired results, it was worth it.

Standing in the shadows of the park, Lou-Loc felt Cross's presence, but didn't see him, which was a side effect of their strange relationship. It was kind of feeling that someone was watching you but you were the only one on the block. Giving substance to his suspicions, Cross came slithering out of the shadows.

"You need to stop sneaking up on people like that, before I shoot you by accident one day," Lou-Loc joked with his friend.

Cross smiled. "If I had a quarter for every time some asshole has shot me, I'd be a rich man."

"So, what do you have for me?" Lou-Loc asked.

For an answer, Cross tossed Lou-Loc a paper shopping bag. Lou-Loc peeked into the bag and almost vomited when he saw the contents. It was a human hand, with a ruby ring on one of the pinky fingers.

"That's what's left of the gentleman Martina was creeping with. I'm sorry, old friend," Cross said sincerely.

Tears welled in Lou-Loc's eyes, but he refused to let them escape. His worst fears were confirmed. "A fool for love," Lou-Loc mumbled.

Cross felt terrible, seeing the hurt in Lou-Loc's face. Even though they came from two different worlds, Lou-Loc was the closest thing Cross had to a friend. The path of darkness was a lonely one, where friends were hard to come by and even harder to hold on to, but for as long as Cross had known Lou-Loc the young gangster had always been true to him, even after discovering the truth about him. Though they were born to different parents during different times, the same blood ran through their veins, which only strengthened their bond.

Cross touched Lou-Loc's shoulder affectionately. "If it makes you feel any better, I took his hand while he was still alive. He suffered a great deal before I released him to death."

This brought a slight smile to Lou-Loc's face, but the pain remained. "Thank you, my friend. Cross, I need two favors from you."

"Just tell me who and they're dead," Cross assured him.

"Not that kinda favor. I have a lot of things I need to do tonight, a lot of bad things. I can get them done on my own but I need that killer edge that only you can help me with. Do you understand?"

Sadness came over Cross's face. "Lou-Loc, don't do this to me. The more of that shit I give you, the more dependant on it you'll become. Eventually you'll be hooked and won't be able to function without it. I've seen what becomes of people addicted to it and it's not pretty."

"I understand and I appreciate your concern. Hopefully, this will be the last time I have to ask you. The second favor runs a little deeper than that."

"Well, don't keep an asshole in suspense, what is it?"

"My nigga Gutter is in Harlem Hospital laid up and sprayed up. He's in bad shape and probably won't make it unless I do something."

"Lou-Loc, giving it to someone as healthy as yourself is one thing, but giving it to someone who is already on death's doorstep could have unforeseen consequences. If it goes wrong it could mean the death of all three of us," Cross said honestly.

"Cross, after all you've done for me I would never put you in a jam, but that's my heart in there. If Gutter was to die and I didn't at least try to do something to help, I couldn't live with myself. That's my heart lying in that hospital," Lou-Loc said emotionally. "Don't make me beg, Cross. I need you to do this for me. Will you?"

"Lou-Loc," Cross said softly, "I hope you realize what kind of position you're putting me in."

"Thank you so much, Cross."

"Don't thank me;" Cross cut him off. "I never said I'd do it. Just know that I might never see another night after this one if I do this thing for you. Lou-Loc, you saved my life when my own comrades wouldn't help me and for this, I owe you a great debt, but let me make something clear to you and never forget it, my friend. Nothing is without its price, especially the gift you are asking for your friend. Always remember what I've said to you this night." Cross closed his eyes and let his thoughts roam. "Damn you, Lou-Loc, for putting this load on my shoulder," he whispered, "and damn me twice, for being your friend."

South of where Lou-Loc and Cross were making their exchange, Cisco sat listening to a young man recounting the events of his run-in with the notorious Lou-Loc of Harlem Crip.

"Are you sure?" Cisco asked the kid while taking a puff of his cigar.

"Yeah, I'm sure," the kid went on, "it was Lou-Loc. When he showed me his crab-ass tattoo, I saw his name under the six-point star. You shoulda heard how that faggot was talking. He was act'n like LC don't hold no weight down here. I was gonna clip his ass, but he snuffed me before I had a chance to pull out on him," he lied.

Cisco absently rubbed the scar on his cheek, and winced from the still lingering pain. "Tell

me this, Jesus; if that was Lou-Loc you bumped
into, what was he doing nosing around Satin's
building? You think Harlem knows we're behind
the hit on Gutter?"

"Nah, I seen them together before. I think he's
trying to fuck, bro."

Cisco's eyes flashed anger. Could Lou-Loc
be fucking Satin? Just the thought of it sent
sharp anger pains through Cisco's temple. He
figured if he couldn't have her, no punk-ass crab
would. Then another thought flashed through
his twisted mind: What would the rest of the
crew think if they found out that their leader's
sister was involved with one of their rivals?

"Jesus, I have a job for you," Cisco said, smiling devilishly. "I want you to keep an eye on your
sister, and find out what the deal is with her and
this crab. Don't let her know you're following
her, and do not alert El Diablo to the problem
just yet. This may work to our advantage. You
do this without fucking up, Jesus, and there's a
promotion in it for you." Cisco saw the greed well
up in Jesus's eyes. He had no idea that Cisco was
using him as a pawn.

"Don't worry, Cisco," Jesus said, heading for
the door, "I won't fuck up."

Cisco sat back in his leather recliner and
clasped his hands together. This was a situation

that would definitely require some watching. Cisco giggled like a schoolgirl as he thought of the look El Diablo would have on his face when he broke the news to him.

Lou-Loc stood atop the jungle gym and looked down at the sea of blue-clad soldiers. Even though it was dark, he could see each and every member in attendance. He made a mental note of those who didn't bother to show, and decided they would be dealt with accordingly. At the last minute, they had decided that having all of the homeboys in the park at one time might draw too much attention. They thought it'd be best just to have all of the captains and their lieutenants present, each with a soldier of their choice. Even with this precaution, there were still a good twenty-five of the homeboys present. When Lou-Loc's voice finally boomed out, all became silent.

"I wanna thank all y'all niggaz for coming," he said, addressing the crowd. "We got pressing business to attend to, so I ain't gonna keep you long. I'm pretty sure all y'all niggaz done heard about what happened to our folk Gutter, so ain't no need for me to go into detail about the shit. When them faggot-ass Brims tried to slab Gutter they played themselves. By them even thinking that they could touch an O.G., they disrespected us. They basically said, Fuck Harlem and fuck the whole C-nation. I know muthafucking well we ain't going for that shit."

Lou-Loc had the crowd in an uproar. There were chants of *fuck Bloods* and threats ridding the world of Bloods. There was a wicked gleam in Lou-Loc's eyes. It had been so long since he had held the reigns of power that he almost forgotten what they felt like. The beast was in control and it howled for blood. The man speaking to the homeboys wasn't St. Louis Alexander the writer: It was O.G. Lou-Loc, head buster and stone murderer.

Lou-Loc waited until the crowd died down before he began speaking again. "Now," he said waving them silent, "we know it was some Brims that did the shooting, but we don't know which set exactly or who gave the order, so I say we ride on 'em all. I want at least one Blood on every set dropped every fucking night from now until they give up the shooters and the muthafucka who gave the order. If they don't do it in a timely fashion then blast their whole muthafucking gang off the map!"

The gathering of young men soon turned into a violent mob and Lou-Loc smiled like a proud father, as he knew his words had hit home. These were his children, and if he asked, they would follow him to the ends of the earth.

After the crowd had died down, Lou-Loc motioned for Pop Top and Snake Eyes to join him. "These are the men you will answer to during these troubled times. All you cats already know Top, he'll be over seeing the troops out in the field, but I want to introduce you to my main man, Snake Eyes."

An unsure mummer went through the crowd as the gangsters took stock of the well-dressed man with his walking stick and glasses.

"I know you see him standing there in his shoes and specs, but make no mistake that he's one of the most cold-blooded studs you'll ever meet. He done saved my ass on many occasions back home in L.A., and done dropped quite a few people, so don't let his appearance fool you. He'll also be providing legal services for those of you who'll need it. He's our minister of defense," Lou-Loc explained. "These are two of my most trusted partners. You show them the same respect that you would show me. Now, y'all niggaz go lay it down. Show these fuckas that the name Crip still mean something in these streets." Lou-Loc threw up his C's and all the homeboys responded in kind. The crowd filed out with murder on their mind. The park had emptied out, leaving only the three leaders.

"That was one hell of a speech," Top said, patting Lou-Loc on his back. "Shit, I'm ready to go bust on something."

"It's gonna be a lot of heat on us, cuz," Snake commented. "A whole lot of muthafuckas is gonna end up on the slab."

Lou-Loc looked at his homie and smiled. "I guess the stock in funeral homes is gonna go up, huh? Remind me to call my broker in the morning."

Top thought that the comment was funny, but Snake Eyes didn't see it that way. Unlike everyone else, the murderous gleam in Lou-Loc's eyes didn't go unnoticed by him. It was a look that he hadn't seen since the night Lou-Loc murdered Stan and it frightened him. "You a'ight, Lou?" Snake asked.

"Never better," Lou-Loc said, entirely too calm. "You got my package from Wiz?" Snake Eyes handed him a duffel bag and stepped back.

"Yeah, I got it," he said. "Man, those are some strange-ass Chicanos you fuck wit, cuz."

"Nah, the twins is cool and Wiz is just a li'l different. Y'all niggaz go home and get some rest. I'll call you sometime tomorrow afternoon." Before waiting for a response, Lou-Loc strolled off into the darkness.

As Snake Eyes watched his friend stroll off, he shook his head. After what happened to Gutter, Lou-Loc's mood seemed to change. He wasn't the ambitious young man that the East Coast was molding him into. He was the Cali killer that he used to be. One thing was for sure, there would be a lot of black-dress buying in Harlem.

After Lou-Loc left the park, he headed downtown and rented a room at the Quarters Hotel. When he signed in, he used his real name. The reason for this was so he'd have an alibi as to his whereabouts. After checking in, he slipped out the back and headed home. When he got there, he had to pause before going inside the house to gain his composure. The voice in his head was screaming for him to kill Martina and be done with it, but he still had feelings for the girl. That and the fact that he didn't wanna make her kids orphans. As soon as he walked in, Martina started up.

"Fuck you been?" she snapped. "I been paging you and trying to call you all damn day. Was you laid up wit a bitch or something?"

"I was busy," he said coldly. Martina wanted to continue the argument, but something in his eyes told her to leave it alone.

Lou-Loc got a can of paint from under the kitchen sink and walked into the bedroom, where he proceeded to collect all the jewelry he had brought Martina over the years and stuffed it into his pockets. He paused when he got to the five-and-a-half karat diamond ring that he intended to surprise her with and shook his head because he had paid a grip for it and she'd never get to see it. Next, he went into their closet and removed all of her furs and leathers. After laying Martina's goods on the bed, he removed his razor blade and proceeded to slash all of her dresses. DK, Versace, Prada,—all turned to confetti. He took all of the clothes he could carry from his side of the closet and placed them in a duffel bag with his jewelry and guns. All of his papers were in a briefcase, so he had all bases covered. Strolling like he didn't have a care in the world, he went into the living room and placed his bags by the door.

"Damn, you just got here and your ass is about to go back into the streets?" Martina rolled her neck. "And what's all them bags for?"

"Don't worry, baby," he said, kissing her forehead, "I gotta drop some shit off to Gutter, and make a run. I'll be back tomorrow, though. But come here for a sec. I got a surprise for you," he sang.

At the mention of a surprise, her whole attitude changed and her anger was replaced by greed. On the walk to the bedroom, the only thing that was on her mind was if it was money or jewelry. He didn't come in carrying any bags, so it had to be either-or. Martina's eyes bulged in disbelief at the sight of her shredded clothes and her minks scattered on the bed. "What the fu—" was as far as she got.

Out of nowhere, Lou-Loc splashed lavender paint all over Martina's belongings. She stood in the center of all the carnage, slack-jawed. Lou-Loc had laid waste to at least 150,000 dollars' worth of goods. Before she even realized what was going on, he had grabbed her by her jaws and lifted her off her feet.

He looked into her tear-filled eyes and spoke in a voice that didn't sound like his own. "Bitch, I go all out for you and your crumb crushers, and you try to put shit on me?"

"What are you talking about, baby?" she stuttered.

With his free hand he removed a ruby ring from his pocket and held it up for her to see. "Does this look familiar?"

"Where did you get that?"

"From the hand of a dead man," he said with a twisted grin. "All this time, and you been creeping with a Brim? I should twist yo' ma' fucking brain." He tossed her onto the bed and put his gun to her heart. "All I wanna know is why?"

"Wait, Lou-Loc, let me explain. He didn't mean anything to me. You were always gone and I needed someone," she pleaded.

"Gone? Bitch, I'm out there on the grind every day throwing stones at the penitentiary so you can live good and that's the excuse you give me?" Lou-Loc drew his gun and pressed it to her chest. "Whore, I should bust your heart wide open the same way you did mine!"

"Lou-Loc, please don't kill me," Martina begged.

"Nah, I ain't gonna kill you." He tucked his gun. "For as much as I wanna pop your stupid ass, you ain't even worth the bullet. Just answer me one question: Is that baby you're carrying mine?"

Martina was silent.

"That's just what I thought," he said in a defeated tone. "I'm gone, Martina. Make due with ya bills the best way you can." He started for the door.

"Baby, wait," she said, running behind him and grabbing his arm. "I know I fucked up, and I'm sorry, but don't leave me. Let's try again, I know we can make it work. I couldn't live without you. I love you, daddy!"

"Un-ass me, bitch." Lou-Loc swatted her hand away. "You can't even spell *love*, let alone know what it feels like."

"I'm sorry, Lou-Loc." She broke down in tears.

"Yeah, the sorriest bitch I ever had the pleasure of meeting," he said coldly. "My advice to you is to steer clear of me, because if I ever see you again I can't be held responsible for my actions." He stormed out of the apartment and Martina's life.

Lou-Loc made hurried steps down the building stairs and to the car. He wanted to get as far away from Martina as he could before he either went back on his word or killed her. Either way, it wouldn't have been good. As he was throwing his stuff in the trunk of his car he heard her screaming at him out the window.

"You ain't shit, Lou-Loc. You just gonna leave me and ya baby? You fucked up my furs and my clothes, but that ain't enough? Youze a crab-ass nigga, but that's a'ight. You gonna regret this shit. Believe me, you gonna regret this," she threatened.

A warning bell rang off in Lou-Loc's head, but he shrugged it off. He figured she was just hurt talking out of her ass. He left her broke and bummy. What the fuck could she do to him? Lou-Loc hopped in his car and hit the highway to Brooklyn.

***

Upstairs, Martina's wheels were already turning. She cursed herself for letting Lou-Loc get away. She had already dismissed the idea of calling Mac because nine times out of ten he was already dead if Lou-Loc knew about him. Her meal ticket had run out on her and she was hotter than fish grease. She needed a way to fix Lou-Loc's ass and it would only be a matter of time before she figured out how. Then it hit her. She dug through the pile of clothes and paint until she found the phone. Within seconds, she had reached the party she was seeking. "Let me speak to Cisco."

Chapter 17

Lou-Loc parked a few blocks from a bar where his victim was said to be a regular. From the backseat, he retrieved his duffel bag and checked the contents. Inside the bag were an old Colt revolver and a small metal box. He opened the box and was greeted by cold air from the cooling system. Inside the box were six bullets that Wiz had made especially for him. The tips were made of a special plastic to contain the corrosive acid that filled the bullets. They were designed to burst on impact and eat away at flesh from the inside out. This had been Lou-Loc's idea to make it harder for forensic teams to trace them back to the assassin.

Lou-Loc placed the gun under his seat and got out of his ride. He walked the few blocks to the bar and stepped inside. There were wall-to-wall people in the place, so Lou-Loc had to look around for a while before he spotted him. He sat at the bar hunched over a drink, surrounded by a few of his peoples. Even in the dim light his bald head shined like a beacon. His white tank top stood out against his dark skin like two ends of the color spectrum. To Lou-Loc, the man they called Born didn't look like he was worth the overpriced fee he had agreed on with the Al Mukalla prince, but if Anwar was willing to pay, he would gladly take the money.

When he turned at an angle, Lou-Loc could see his iced-out medallion swinging from his platinum chain. Lou-Loc figured he might as well take that too. After all, Born wouldn't need it where he was going. But then again, wouldn't he need all the ice he could carry in hell? Lou-Loc chuckled to himself at the little joke and walked happily out of the bar.

After retrieving his Glock as well as the supped-up Colt, Lou-Loc stood in a darkened doorway of a closed auto-body shop and waited. It would probably be quite a while before his mark came out of the bar, but patience had always been one of his strong points. If need be, he would've waited until daybreak for the perfect opportunity to move on his kill, which is what made him such an efficient killer.

Mean while, on 114th Street a group of young men were sitting on a stoop drinking and passing blunts. All of the young were dressed in predominantly red, letting everyone know they were members of the Blood gang. They went about their business as that was their turf and they had nothing to fear, but if any of them had been able to see into the future they might've stayed home that night.

The most animated of the group was a tall, light-skinned cat named Scooby. Scooby considered himself a hard ass who had a sharp tongue and an even sharper blade. He wasn't the nicest with his hands, but in battle had been known to carve his opponents up like Christmas turkeys. Scooby ran his crew with an iron fist, and when he spoke, they listened.

"Fuck them crabs," Scooby said, taking a long swig of his 40-ounce. "Let one of them muthafuckas come through here and it's a wrap. I don't play that shit, dog. I'm the hardest muthafucking damu out here."

"What about them folks uptown, Gutter and them niggaz?" a dark-skinned youth asked.

"Fuck them niggaz," Scooby spat. "You see, I know how Gutter gets down. He's crazy, and that's just that. I know what to expect from him, so I ain't worried. It's his partner that gives me the creeps."

"You mean that nigga, Lou-Loc?" another youth named Bear added. "Fuck that nigga, he pussy. I seen him on a-hundred-and-twenty-fifth one day while I was wit my bitch. I threw my set up, and he ain't even do shit. Lou-Loc is soft."

"That's ya problem, you take everything for face value," Scooby scolded him. "My cousin that lives out in Torrance, he gave me the four-one-one on that nut. That kid is the real fucking deal."

"Yeah," a young boy named B.G. added. "I heard he killed like a hundred niggaz on the West Coast. Shit, they say he went at it with a SWAT team and won!"

"Those are just stories." Scooby said. "Besides, LC hit Gutter the other day. The way it's looking his ass is worm food. As it stands, Lou-Loc is the only thing between me and control of Harlem. The nigga might be 'bout it, but he ain't superman. He bleeds like us."

"You better be careful," Tick said. "You plan on going at Lou-Loc, you better be ready to get down for real."

"Whatever," Scooby said, handing Tick his beer. "Hold my shit, nigga, while I go take a leak." Scooby stumbled around the corner to try and find a dark spot to pee. Little did he know, the shadow of death was right on his heels.

Scooby whipped out his joint and began to relieve his bladder. He thought about the line of bullshit he had fed his peoples. He wished he really was as confident as he had sounded. In all reality, he knew what time it was with Lou-Loc. Scooby wasn't a coward, but Lou-Loc was somebody who he really didn't want a problem with. Scooby's mind was so jacked up off beer and weed that he didn't even see the figure slithering from under a car behind him.

It crept up on Scooby, holding a cord that was as thin as dental floss but made of steel. Before Scooby even noticed that he wasn't alone, the figure looped the cord around his neck. Scooby grabbed for it. As he did so, fire shot through his hand as his middle and index fingertips were severed. The shards of diamond dust woven into the cord severed both flesh and tendon.

The more Scooby struggled, the more excited the figure became. The more excited it became, the tighter the noose got. Scooby tried to scream for help, but all that came out were muffled groans as his life's blood spilled out onto the Harlem street. The cord bit deeper into Scooby's neck until it met bone. Even then, the figure applied more pressure, but the bone wouldn't give. In a matter of seconds, Scooby's head was almost severed, and he was dead on his feet.

After being gone for a while, the others began to worry about Scooby and decided to check on him. All their combined years of street education couldn't prepare them for what they saw when they rounded the corner. Lying on the pavement in a pool of blood was their leader, Scooby. His head hung at a funny angle, and his face still held the mold of a man attempting to scream. The worst part was that Scooby's dick was still hanging out of his pants.

Lou-Loc sat across from the bar, smoking cigarette after cigarette. The sun would soon be forcing its way up, bumping away the darkness, and exposing him. He considered just making the hit inside, but then pushed the thought from his mind. He didn't know the layout of the bar well enough to try that. The last thing he wanted was to trap himself.

Lou-Loc stepped from the doorway to stretch his legs and spotted his mark staggering out of the bar. He was flanked by two rugged-looking characters on either side. Lou-Loc had counted on them being unarmed because they were coming out of a bar, but all hopes of that quickly vanished when one of the bodyguards produced a pistol from out of a nearby Dumpster.

Lou-Loc stuck to the shadows and crept to the trio's left. Keeping his eyes locked on his victim, he removed the bullets from their special case and loaded them into the Colt. With the Colt at the ready he moved toward his victim. It was still dark and they were dead drunk, so they still hadn't noticed him. He was close enough to hit his mark, but he only had six bullets in the Colt, and he only had his Glock for backup, so he needed to get up close and personal to make sure that every bullet hit home, but the open space would expose him and potentially ruin the element of surprise.

As luck would have it, a group of white kids came stumbling out of the bar a few seconds after his mark and provided him with the perfect cover. Lou-Loc blended in with the crowd, faking drunk and moving ever closer to his mark. Just as Lou-Loc got close enough to spit on the mark, he turned around and stared him dead in the eye. This was usually the part where the killer said something slick or boasted to the mark about how he was going to die, but Lou-Loc wasn't much for theatrics. He raised the Colt and squeezed off two shots. The first shot hit Born in the forehead and the second embedded itself in his eye. The bodyguards stood there in shock as the acid did its work. Born lay on the ground with blood coming out of his eyes and ears, twitching and convulsing while his blood-soaked companions looked on in horror. Lou-Loc used their hesitation to his advantage.

Firing the Glock through his jacket pocket, he took down the bodyguard closest to him. The second bodyguard tried to react but Lou-Loc was already spinning on him with the Colt drawn. The bodyguard opened his mouth to shout a threat but Lou-Loc never heard it over the roar of the Colt. The custom bullet hit him in the back of the throat and exploded, melting through his tongue and burning, destroying his vocal cords as the liquid trickled down.

After dispatching the bodyguards, he moved to Born, who was convulsing violently. The acid bullets were making mincemeat of his face but he was still alive. Lou-Loc tucked the Colt and hit him twice in the heart with the Glock. Though he had been sent to kill Born, he had never done anything to him so it seemed wrong to make him suffer. It was only business.

The drunken kids had sobered up when they heard the gunshots and the females began to scream. Lou-Loc turned his Glock on them and purposely fired two shots over their heads. Some scattered, some hit the floor. Didn't really matter to Lou-Loc; he just needed them distracted long enough for him to make his getaway. As he hauled ass down the block, he fired four more rounds over his shoulder so any would-be witnesses would keep their noses to the ground and out of his business.

***

Lou-Loc took his time driving back to Manhattan, making sure to stay under the speed limit. There was no sense in escaping the murder scene only to get pulled over for speeding and blow everything. Before returning to the hotel he'd checked into earlier that night, he pulled over to the side of the FDR and tossed the pistols he'd used into the river. He didn't care about the Colt because it was only to be used once anyway, but it hurt him to part with the Glock. It had been one of his favorite guns and he'd had it since he came to New York from L.A., but no matter how attached he was to the weapon it wasn't worth going to prison for.

When he reached his hotel room, he slipped back in the way he left. The hotel only had cameras in the lobby, so he didn't have to worry about his comings and goings being recorded. Once inside his room, he stripped naked and stuffed his clothes into a duffel bag, which he would get rid of later. Next, he got in the shower to wash off the blood and whatever powder residue that might've been clinging to him. He knew enough about forensic science to leave no stone unturned. After drying himself he lay naked across the bed and reflected on the turn his life had taken.

The contract for the Al Mukalla had been handled, which only left whoever had tried to kill Gutter to be dealt with. Pushing thoughts of murder and revenge, he thought of Satin. Now that he was officially done with Martina he could move forward with Satin and couldn't wait to call and tell her the good news, but it would keep until the morning. At that moment all he wanted to do was get a good night's sleep. Lou-Loc stretched out and fingered the small pistol under his pillow. Knowing that he was safe for the moment, he let sleep claim him.

Chapter 18

In the weeks that followed Lou-Loc's proclamation in the park, the streets were thrown into chaos. There had been sixteen reported shootings and murders and those were only the ones the police knew about. The homies were putting in overtime, dropping bodies left and right. The Bloods fought back, and for a while held their own until they found themselves fighting not only New York City Crips but Crips from the surrounding areas as well. When the war kicked off Lou-Loc starting calling in favors and there were more than a few people who owed the Crip general. Everything was working out just how Lou-Loc had planned it.

During the war he had even filled six more contracts for the Al Mukalla and some of their associates. He hadn't planned on coming out of retirement, but the overpriced hits Anwar and his people were paying for would help him stack the chips he needed to get out once and for all

when it was all said and done—at least this was
what he kept telling himself. The truth of the
matter was that Lou-Loc missed the thrill of the
hunt. For him, committing murder was sweeter
than any drug he'd ever taken and he was on
course to overdose.

On a different note, Satin and Lou-Loc were
getting closer. When he wasn't out killing he was
spending time with her. They went on regular
dates, like to the movies and bowling, but Satin
also exposed Lou-Loc to things he had only
heard about or seen on television like fancy
restaurants, where the menus were all printed in
foreign languages and the theater. The first time
she took him to the opera he was reluctant but
actually found himself enjoying it. Going to these
places was different for him, but it was nice.

Lou-Loc and Satin were like kids falling in
love for the first time. In truth, they were. Neither had ever had someone they could totally
give themselves to until they met each other. To
fall in love was a beautiful thing, and they were
diving in headfirst.

Lou-Loc and Satin strolled down the board-
walk at Coney Island and let the sun beam down
on their faces. He pulled Satin to him and lovingly kissed her eyelids. They had been seeing

each other for over a month now, and it was the happiest six weeks of both their lives. He stared down at her smiling face, and wondered why God hadn't put them together sooner.

"Satin," he said softly, "can I say something and you won't think I'm being corny?"

"Yeah," she said, wrapping her arm around his, "what's that?"

"Until I met you, I thought love at first sight was just a phrase. It might sound crazy, but I think I loved you from the first time I saw you."

"Don't say things like that."

"Nah, I'm serious. I been hurting inside for a long time, maybe ever since I lost my dad. When I met you, it's like the pain just faded. You feel me?"

Satin nodded and walked up a little. Lou-Loc caught up with her and turned her around to face him. The tears on her cheeks sparkled like diamonds in the afternoon sun. Even crying, she was still beautiful to him.

"It's okay," he whispered as he kissed the tears away. "We got each other now."

"You make me feel so special," she said in between sobs. "I don't want this feeling to ever end. Promise me?"

"Baby, you know I'm here for you. How long depends on you, but I ain't got no plans to go nowhere."

Their little moment of tenderness was interrupted by a loud clapping. Lou-Loc spun around
and was surprised to see the same young kid he'd
almost killed in front of Satin's building. He was
dressed in all red, and so were the two boys with
him.

"Bravo," Jesus said, stepping forward. "Man,
that shit was so touching I thought I was gonna
cry."

"Li'l nigga, I gave you a pass once, but now
you're pushing your luck," Lou-Loc snapped,
moving between Satin and the kid.

"A lot of good soldiers are dead because of you,
crab. You got a lot to answer for," Jesus spat.

"Fuck you in yo' bitch ass, sissy. I could give
less than a fuck if all you dead rag niggaz curl the
fuck up and die. When y'all give up who gave the
order on my boy, it all stops. Other than that you
can suck my dick." Lou-Loc grabbed a handful of
his crotch for emphasis.

Jesus went for his gun, but Lou-Loc was quicker.
With a flick of his wrist, a P-89 appeared in his
hand. As he began to apply pressure on the trigger, the unexpected happened. Satin jumped in
between them.

"Satin, what the fuck are you doing?" Lou-Loc
asked in disbelief.

"Oh, you mean Satin hasn't told you?" Jesus
taunted him.

"Told me what?" Lou-Loc asked, turning his cold glare on Satin. "You know this chump?"

"She should, since we dropped out of the same womb," Jesus said, laughing. "Man, this just keeps getting better. If she didn't tell you about me I'm sure she didn't tell you about our older brother Michael. You might know him as El Diablo, king of LC Blood. I can see it now: Me, you, and El Diablo sitting around the table like one happy family!"

When Satin looked at Lou-Loc, she saw the hurt in his eyes. She intended to tell him, but just never got around to it. The last thing she wanted was for him to find out like this. "Lou-Loc, let me explain."

"You ain't got to explain nothing to me because I see just what it is. You popped all that shit about me being honest and not hurting you, but it looks like you're the one doing the hurting."

"Lou-Loc, it's not like that. Just let me talk to you for a minute?" She reached for his arm but he jerked away.

"Baby girl, we ain't got shit to talk about. I'm in the wind," Lou-Loc snapped and turned to walk away. He intended to just leave but Jesus couldn't help stoking the fire.

"Hey Lou-Loc," Jesus called after him, "if it'll make you feel any better, those were my homies who put those holes in your boy Gutter!"

Lou-Loc's temperature shot up 300 degrees. When he turned around his eyes had gone so cold that even Satin took a cautionary step back. The three Bloods stared him down confidently, daring him to make a move. He was outnumbered and he already knew that at least one of them was strapped, but Lou-Loc had slipped beyond the point of logic and the spirit within him called for blood. There were too many people on the beach for him to start a shoot-out, but the led pipe he spotted sticking out of the trash can to his right would do just fine. He moved so quick that the three Bloods never even saw it coming. Wielding the pipe like a sword, Lou-Loc tore into his enemies.

The pipe came down across the face of the closest Blood to him, breaking his cheekbone and jaw. The second Blood reached for the gun under his shirt but he was too slow. Lou-Loc brought the pipe down across his wrist, fracturing it and causing the gun to go off accidentally. The bullet tore through the boy's thigh and sent him spilling to the ground, wallowing in his own blood. Lou-Loc bashed him in the head twice for good measure, knocking him unconscious. With his hands and clothes covered with blood, he turned his attention to Jesus.

Seeing what Lou-Loc had done to his friends, Jesus wanted no parts of it, so he bolted. He had made it several yards before Lou-Loc hurled the pipe after him like a boomerang, connecting with the back of his head. Jesus hit the floor, dazed and in a world of pain, but Lou-Loc was hardly done with him. He picked Jesus up by the back of his hoodie and held him suspended in midair. Jesus tried to offer an apology, but Lou-Loc was too far gone to hear it. Swinging with all his might, he punched Jesus in the face, breaking his nose. Infusing his hands with the hate he carried in his heart, Lou-Loc wrapped his hands around Jesus's throat and began squeezing.

"I'm gonna kill you real slow," Lou-Loc whispered to Jesus, who was gasping for air.

"Lou-Loc, please—don't kill my brother," Satin pleaded.

"Bitch, you ain't really in the position to make no requests, so I advise you to shut the fuck up!" Lou-Loc snapped. Satin grabbed his arm and tried to pull him off Jesus, but his grip was like steel. With a swipe of his hand he sent Satin crashing to the ground. Seeing her sitting on her ass in the sand, holding her cheek, jogged Lou-Loc out of his rage and he dropped Jesus to the ground. Even though she had crossed him, he still loved her. He knelt down beside Jesus and said, "This is the second time your sister has stopped me from killing you and no matter how much I love her I doubt there'll be a third. It's a wrap for all you LC niggaz, you hear me?" Lou-Loc slapped Jesus to make sure he was paying attention. "Tell your brother that when I catch him, it's lights-out." Lou-Loc punched Jesus in the face and knocked him out.

He dusted himself off and walked over to help Satin to her feet. "Listen, I'm sorry for hurting you, but I'm not sorry for what I done to them niggaz here today. By right I should be pissed at you too for lying to me, but I can't find it in my heart to be mad at you, Satin."

"Lou-Loc, you've got to believe that I was going to tell you. I was just trying to wait for the right time. I know how you feel about the Bloods and I was afraid that when I told you who my brother was that you wouldn't want anything to do with me," she explained.

"Satin, let me tell you something and I don't want you to ever forget it. It doesn't matter to me who your family is because I'm not in love with them, I'm in love with *you*. If we're going to be together then we have to be honest with each other, good or bad. Do you think you can do that?"

"Yes, I swear I will."

"Good, now let's get outta here before the police come." Lou-Loc grabbed her by the arm and led her away, leaving the three unconscious men in their wake.

In a different borough several people, dressed in various red garments, sat huddled around a table sipping Rémy and conspiring. These people represented several Blood sets throughout the five boroughs. Each of them were powerful and each of them extremely dangerous.

The man who sat at the head of the table was known on the streets as Hawk, because of his striking resemblance to the winged predator. Hawk wasn't a large man, but he was very well built. This came from years spent on the yard lifting weights in various New York State prisons. He was a brown-skinned dude who stood around five feet nine on a good day, with cunning eyes and wavy hair that he wore cut low with a half-moon part on the right side. He was what you would call a throwback, who survived prison and the crack era while still managing to hold on to his little piece of the rock, but like everyone else sitting at the table, what he built was now in jeopardy because of Lou-Loc.

"I would like to thank you all for coming," Hawk addressed the people at the table. "Before we conduct our business here, I would like to welcome home one of our most outspoken brothers. El Diablo." He nodded respectfully to the man sitting to his right.

"Thank you," El Diablo said, receiving applause from the crowd. El Diablo was draped in a black suit with a blood-red tie and black shirt. "It's good to be home."

"Yeah, what the fuck ever," Ruby cut him off. She was the only woman at the table and one of the most dangerous of the captains. Her skin was the color of autumn leaves with eyes to match. She sported her hair in fishbone braids that were dyed crimson red. "Hawk, you wanna tell us why we're here?"

Hawk gave her an irritated look. "Always the outspoken one, aren't you, Ruby? "Well, being that you asked so nicely, let's get to it. I'm sure no one here has missed out on the latest turn of events concerning the Harlem Crips?"

"Missed out? Shit, they dropped five of my boys, and that was just last week." Bullet spoke up. He was the wiry leader of a small pack of Bloods that operated out of Hell's Kitchen. Bullet was quick to shoot off his mouth as well as his gun, hence the name.

"You're not the only one who has been losing soldiers behind all this," Hawk assured him. "Until now they've been little more than a nuisance to us, but over the last few months or so they've turned the city into a slaughterhouse. Something or someone seems to have agitated them," he said, cutingt his eyes at El Diablo.

"Fuck them and they mamas. I say we roll on them bitches and put them in the dirt once and for all," Ruby snapped.

"We've tried that approach, but it seems like for every one of their troops we kill they drop two of ours. There are people uptown who I've been doing business with for years that can't open up shop anymore without somebody in blue shooting it up," Hawk confessed. "Now the feds and the police are all over the place, shutting shit down because of all of the killing and it's just a fucking mess. I, as well as our friends out west, would like to put an end to this as quickly as possible. Now, we'd like to have a sit-down with their leader Gutter, but due to unforeseen circumstances he's unavailable." He cut his eyes at El Diablo again. "Would someone like to fill in the blanks as to what the hell is going on so we can get this shit resolved?"

"Oh, I'll fill in the blanks," Bullet said sarcastically. "It's that fucking nut job, Lou-Loc, that's who's running the show now and he ain't big on talking," he told them.

There was a twitch in Hawk's eye when he heard the name of Harlem's new general. He knew of Lou-Loc's reputation and was not pleased to hear that he was now calling the shots. "This is bad business." Hawk began pacing. "With Gutter we could've at least negotiated a cease-fire because of all the money getting fucked up by this way, but money don't mean shit to Lou-Loc. To him this is a blood debt and can only be settled in blood."

Ruby shrugged. "Then let's make the nigga bleed and be done with it."

"Apparently you've never dealt with Lou-Loc," a young, dark-skinned brother named Cano spoke up. He was originally from San Diego but had recently relocated to New York City. "Over the years there's been exaggerated stories about some bad-ass Crips, but Lou-Loc is the real deal. Plenty of squads have been sent to hit him but it seems like he just refuses to die. Some of the older heads from our hoods in SD used to joke that he made a pact with the devil and can't be killed."

"Fuck Lou-Loc!" Cisco spoke up for the first time. "This crab is a man just like all of us here, but you're speaking about him like he's some kind of God. He can die; you fuckers just haven't tried hard enough."

"Big talk from the Latin Infection," Ruby sneered at Cisco. "Gutter and Lou-Loc have been a pain in LC's ass since they came here from Cali and y'all ain't did shit about them yet, but talk about what you're gonna do. You talk real big, Cisco, but your follow-through is way suspect."

"Who the fuck do you think ordered the hit on Gutter?" Cisco said with a smile.

"And you fucked that up," Ruby shot back.

"I met Lou-Loc back when they signed the treaty in '92," Hawk cut in. "He's an efficient killer, true, but he's not a violent man. Even though we were both two little bad-asses from opposite sides of the track, he still treated me with courtesy. He was provoked, and that's what opened this faucet of blood. Now the question is, How do we shut it off?"

"Fuck it," El Diablo started. "I say we pool our resources and put him down."

"You crazier than a shit-house rat," Bullet said. "That boy is protected from on high. He gets his props from both sides of the coin."

"Bullet's got a point," Hawk added. "I made a few long-distance phone calls to get the four-one-one on our friend Lou-Loc. The word is, he and Gutter are operating independently. The thugs he called in are putting in work out of love for him and Gutter, not their gang. This shit LC done started is personal."

"What the fuck—he's ordered the assassinations of more than two dozen of our number, and we're supposed to not do anything? I say, Fuck that nigger!" El Diablo snapped.

"Watch your mouth, spic," Bullet shot back.

"Gentlemen," Hawk interrupted, "slinging racial insults among each other isn't going to solve our problem. This mass killing is going to fuck us. We need to come up with a reasonable solution before the law shuts us all down."

"I say we toss him Cisco or somebody from LC to put an end to this shit. They started this petty-ass war so I say let them roast for it so we can get back to this money," Ruby suggested.

"Fuck you," Cisco hissed.

"The both of you need to shut the fuck up," El Diablo said, looking at Cisco and Ruby. "Listen, if we stand our ground maybe we can wait them out and end this without taking any more losses. I have no love for the Crips uptown, but I am with Hawk in the thinking that continuing this feud is only going to hurt our pockets."

Cisco looked at El Diablo in disbelief as he knew it was because of him that the war was started in the first place. He decided to take a dig at El Diablo. "I would expect you to be slightly more sensitive over this than the rest of us considering your little sister and Lou-Loc are involved."

El Diablo's eyes widened in shock, as did the rest of the eyes of the council. "What did you say?" El Diablo snarled.

"Please forgive me for bringing it up at such a venue," Cisco said sarcastically. "I wanted to wait until I was sure before I brought it up. Lou-Loc has taken quite an interest in little Satin."

"Why do you mock me at a time like this, Cisco? This is not the time or the place for rumors."

"I assure you, Michael, it's all true. If you don't believe me ask Jesus."

El Diablo collapsed in his chair as if all the strength was drained from his body. Never in his life would he have even considered his sister to go over to the other side. She wasn't gang-affiliated, but she knew who her peoples were and she was loyal to her family.

"Hey Mikey, does that mean you've got a little blue in your blood now?" Ruby mocked him.

"Now, now," Cisco said, standing. "it isn't his fault. El Diablo had no idea that his sister was seeing Lou-Loc. This however, has brought me to our solution. A friend of a friend has provided me with the means to get at Mr. Untouchable. Lou-Loc is a dead man."

"Cisco, even though Lou-Loc is out there raising all types of hell, he's still an O.G., which means he's a made man. If he happens to end up dead, and anyone can trace it back to you, there's going to be some really unhappy campers out west."

"I'm not worried. All I need is the support of my brothers on the matter."

"I ain't touching that one," Ruby said flat-out. "That kid is connected to some heavyweights. I heard a rumor that the big boys were talking about putting the hurt on whoever hit Gutter. The worst part about that is our superiors don't have a problem letting it happen. They too feel like someone should've been consulted before an attempt was made on Gutter's life. To make a long story short, the shit LC pulled was fucking dumb. We've kept the peace with them boys for a while, and you fuck it up cause LC wanna be greedy."

"Whatever. LC will handle it."

"You're right," Hawk said, standing. "LC started this shit, so it's up to LC to finish it. No disrespect to you, El Diablo, but I feel that if we went with you on this, we would be dragging the Bloods as a whole into this feud. It ain't worth the headaches or the casualties. I'm sure my fellow council members will agree with me on this one." Everyone nodded in agreement. "Now that that's settled, I have a message from our friends in the UBN. I was told to deliver it to whoever was responsible for causing all this. The gist of it is: This thing will be settled quickly and quietly. If we can't settle it, then they will send someone who can. In short, gentlemen and lady, when this is all said and done, some of us will find ourselves out of a job and on a slab."

Chapter 19

Lou-Loc sat on the passenger side of Satin's jeep, fuming. In his rage he'd almost forgotten that they'd rode her whip to Brooklyn. If he had actually stormed off during their fallout instead of listening, he'd probably had to hop in a taxi, if he was lucky enough to stop one.

Satin clutched the steering wheel with both hands as she switched lanes without signaling. She kept one eye on the road and one eye on the bulge under Lou-Loc's shirt. She wasn't scared, but she was still shaken a bit by the little encounter between Lou-Loc and Jesus. Never before had she seen a man go off like that. He was like a wild animal, tearing into the trio. She wondered if she hadn't been there, would Lou-Loc have spared Jesus?

"So," Lou-Loc said, breaking her train of thought, "you said you wanted to explain. I'm still waiting."

Satin shifted in her seat and tried to find the
right words, a way to explain the madness that
was her life. If only he could look into her heart,
all would be clear. She loved this man, but didn't
know how to express it. "Lou-Loc," she said
softly, "I really don't know what to say, so I'll just
be honest with you."

"That would be cool as hell, considering you
been lying so far," he said sarcastically.

"Lou-Loc, please? This is hard enough for me
without you making smart-ass comments. Now
I wanna tell you the real-to-real, but I ain't gotta
kiss yo' ass while I'm at it. Michael and Jesus
are both my brothers, but it's not like we're the
Partridge Family. None of us are that close.
Until a few weeks ago, I hadn't seen Michael
in years, then he just pops up, and all this shit
starts happening. Jesus, he's a good kid, but the
streets have poisoned his mind. I'm afraid my
baby brother has been lost to me for some time.
Can't save everyone, huh? The only person I
had in this world was my aunt Selina, God bless
her. Then you came along. Lou-Loc, the reason I
didn't tell you is because I didn't want to run you
off. I was feeling you, and I know you wouldn't
have fucked with me if you knew who my peoples
were."

Lou-Loc spared a sideways glance in Satin's direction, and saw the tears stream down her face. "Satin," he sighed, "try to understand where I'm coming from. We're at war with these muthafuckas and I find out that they yo' peoples. How am I supposed to feel? I told you what I just went through wit this bitch Martina, and yet you still holding back secrets? At this point in my life, I can't afford to have people keeping shit from me, especially the ones I love."

"Lou-Loc," she sobbed, "I know you love me— at least I hope you do, because I damn sure got it bad for you. If you love me the way you say you do, then leave this war and get out of the life."

Lou-Loc pulled at his hair in frustration. "Satin, you know I can't just up and bounce, the set needs me right now."

"I need you too."

"I know, Satin, and I need you, but you gotta understand."

"Lou-Loc, the only thing that I understand is that you're the best thing that's happened to me in a long time. I know all about your unfinished business, Lou-Loc. I just don't want the business to finish you. The night we were at my house you said that if I asked you to we could pick up and go, Well, I'm asking you now. I've got some money saved that I could put with whatever you have, and I could sell my jeep. We could just go away from here and never come back, okay?"

"Satin," he said, touching her cheek. "if only it were that simple. If I were to leave here now, there would be nobody to lead the set. With the way things have heated up over the last few weeks that would be like leaving a pack of rabid dogs loose on Times Square. They'd run wild, and things would only get worse."

Satin parked in front of her building behind Lou-Loc's car. When Lou-Loc reached for the door to get out, she grabbed his arm. "Lou-Loc," she said, wiping her eyes on her sleeve, "where is this relationship going? I mean, I've laid all my cards on the table, I've come clean with you about how I feel, but what have you given back? Where are we going with this, Lou-Loc? If I'm setting myself up for a letdown, tell me now, and we can go our separate ways."

"Satin, why are you putting me through all this drama?" he asked in a frustrated tone.

"Because I want to know where I stand, where *we* stand. In my heart, I know you're the person I want to spend the rest of my life with, but how do you feel? You say you love me, but do you love me enough to get out of the life?"

Lou-Loc looked into her eyes to see if she was putting game on him, but she was dead serious.

From the moment Lou-Loc first laid eyes on this Latina beauty, he knew she was special. He knew that Satin was someone he wanted to know more intimately, but he hadn't considered a lifelong commitment. He had only begun to think that far ahead with Martina, and that was after two years. Now here was this amazing woman, whom he had only known a little over a month, asking him to walk the path of eternity. At that moment, everything in Lou-Loc's life became crystal-clear to him. He knew what he had to do.

"Listen, Satin," he began, "right now I can't promise you anything, but it'll all be sorted out in a minute. Once I know Gutter's okay, we can go wherever you want. I'm getting tired of New York anyway. I hear Florida's nice, so maybe we can set up shop down there."

"You mean it?" she asked, smiling.

"Satin, it took a while for me to recognize love when I saw it, but you taught me what to look for. I can bend on this one, boo. Just give me a few days to tie up some loose ends and we'll give some serious thought to our future. Now that we've applied for your subscription to *Modern Bride*, I gotta move to make."

"Lou-Loc," she said, stopping him short, "before you leave, there's something I have to give you."

"Okay," he said, shrugging his shoulders, "give it here."

"I can't, it's upstairs."

"Okay, but I gotta dip, so let's hurry."

Lou-Loc followed Satin into her loft apartment, not suspecting a thing. Satin continued to play it off like nothing was up, but there was something definitely up. When they got inside she instructed Lou-Loc to have a seat while she went and got his surprise from the bedroom. Lou-Loc sat on the couch and thought about what his plans were for the future. He had been so caught up in all of the madness over the last few weeks that he'd forgotten that he was the one who was supposed to be trying to get out of the life. It took a woman like Satin to remind him of where his priorities lay.

That Satin is one hell of a catch, he thought to himself. Sure, he was a little salty for her not being up-front with him, but he wasn't actually as mad as he'd acted. He was more hurt than anything, so he had to give her a hard time about it. Even though he had told Satin he would give it some thought, there was no doubt in his mind about leaving New York. He reflected on his life and how it would change now that he had her in it. One thing was for sure: He had to go legit. Satin wasn't trying to fuck with him if he was still banging, and he respected her for it. At this point in his life he was just hustling for kicks anyway; it wasn't like he was hard up for money.

Lou-Loc had always been wiser than his comrades when it came to managing his money. While they were buying cars and clothes he was making investments. He owned a barbecue joint in Carson that his aunt and uncle ran and used the money made from that to take care of his sister. Even though they never asked him for anything, Lou-Loc made sure to send them a few dollars every month just to let them know that he appreciated them.

Unbeknown to most people—with the exception of Snake Eyes and his father—Lou-Loc had quite a bit of money tied up in legal businesses. In addition to his barbecue spot, Lou-Loc was one of the financial backers in a hip-hop clothing line. That alone would've put his sister through college and still kept them well-to-do. Overall, his more modest source of legal income was probably security. Lou-Loc was the silent partner in a small security company on the West Coast called Blue Light Protective Services. The company not only provided security for the well-off and wealthy, but they also provided services to the dealers who solicited them.

Lou-Loc was also one of the few brothers who gave back to the hood. He would donate large sums of money to different charities and community organizations under assumed names. He felt what he was doing was his responsibility, considering he was one of the people helping pump drugs into the hood and putting bodies on the slab. With all that Lou-Loc had on the ball, he could've walked away from the game and never looked back. If most people knew the kind of bread he was handling, they'd have called him a fool. He wasn't Bill Gates or even close, but he had more money than a lot of white folks in the game. With all that, Lou-Loc still chose to live among the dealers and other parasites. After all, they were his people.

After a few moments had gone by, Lou-Loc began to get impatient. Satin had been gone about fifteen minutes and he was beginning to worry. Just as he got up from the couch to go check on her, she came out of the bedroom and Lou-Loc thought his heart would burst. He was prepared for anything except what he saw.

Satin stepped into the living room wearing a sheer bathrobe that stopped above the knee. Beneath that, she was wearing a transparent gold teddy with the matching garter belt and stockings. When she moved toward him, her dark nipples seemed to be staring him down through the fabric. Lou-Loc stood there, slack-jawed and speechless, staring at the heart-shaped muff of hair that became slightly visible as Satin placed one of her toned legs on the arm of the sofa.

"Well," she said in a seductive tone. "You just gonna stare at me all day or what?"

Lou-Loc was too dumbfounded to say a word, so she took the initiative. Slow and gracefully, Satin moved toward Lou-Loc and pushed him back on the couch. She placed one leg on either side of him and slid down onto his lap, where she proceeded to grind back and forth.

"St. Louis," she whispered while nibbling his ear, "I want you to know how special you are to me. Am I special to you?" she asked while massaging his penis. All Lou-Loc could do was nod his head in agreement. "Tell me!" she demanded.

"Ooh, yeah," he moaned. "You special, baby."

"How special?"

"Very."

"Oh yeah?" she teased while grinding harder. Lou-Loc tried to be cool about it, but looking at her perfect body made him want to bust all in his boxers. Even though they had been seeing each other for a while, they hadn't had sex yet. That was the way she wanted it and he really didn't mind. He could get sex from any bitch in the hood he chose, but with Satin, it wasn't about the sex. He loved who she was and what she was about.

"Lou-Loc, baby," she said while licking his neck and lips, "I love you so much. I want to ask you something, baby, and please don't tell me no. You know how I hate rejection."

"Anything," he panted.

It was then that Satin did the unexpected. She reached behind her neck and let her hair down, but to Lou-Loc's surprise it wasn't a hair clip that was holding it up. Satin held in her hand a platinum men's wedding band. Crisscrossing all around the outside of the band were the prettiest blue diamonds. "Marry me?" she whispered.

Lou-Loc's eyes got as big as saucers and as damp as a London street. He was so shocked, he wanted to break down and cry. But him being gangsta, he didn't. Satin asking Lou-Loc to marry her caught him off guard. A woman asking a man to jump the broom wasn't the traditional way it went, but it was a new millennium and women were bolder about the way they did things. Truth be told, Lou-Loc had toyed with asking Satin what she thought about the idea, but he didn't want to sound like a cornball or anything. It was just a strange twist of fate that she sprung it on him first.

"This what you want, baby?" he asked in his Billy Dee voice.

"More than anything," she replied.

"Then you got that," he said, kissing her nose.

Satin put Lou-Loc in a bear hug that would rival even Big Kiki's. When she had first purchased the ring a few days prior, she felt like she was playing herself. She had only known Lou-Loc for a short time, but he felt right to her. Before dropping it on him, she feared that it would scare him off. She had wanted to sleep with him, but she didn't want to be just another piece of ass. She wanted to take what they had to another level. The marriage proposal to him was the final test, and he passed with flying colors. If he had said no, she probably would've fucked him anyway, but after that, she would have kicked him to the curb. *Fuck it. Life goes on.*

A week ago, when the idea of proposing to Lou-Loc first popped into her mind, she immediately asked her aunt Selina what she thought about the idea. Selina raised her frail frame in the cast-iron hospital bed and looked at her favorite niece through her cloudy gray eyes. Even as an old woman, there was still something regal about her.

Selina was once the object of many a man's affections. Old age had stolen her beauty and much of her health, but it couldn't rob her of her wisdom.

"Marriage," she asked in a heavy Spanish accent, "how long ju know dees man?"

"For a short time, tía, but I know he's the one."

"And how ju know dees, mees smarty pants?"

"Because my heart tells me so."

"Good answer," Selina said, patting Satin's hand. "Does dees man love ju as well?"

"He says he does."

"A man can tell ju any ting he wan, Satin. What he do to proof his words?"

"Many things, tía. He's rearranging his whole lifestyle to be with me, because it's what I want."

"Mmm hmm," she said suspiciously. "More talk. What he do that mean something?"

"He spared one of Jesus's stupid little friends, even after the boy try to kill him."

"Satin, ju would be with a man who bring death into the world?"

"No, no, it's not like that. You see, Michael, and Jesus's people tried to kill his brother because they are from rival gangs, and—"

"He es a gang meember?" She cut her off. "Ay, Satin, I did no raise ju to be stupid. Ju see what these gangs have done to your brothers, why you geet involved with these people?"

"Tía, you don't understand. He is a gang member, that much is true, but he's not like the rest. He cares about life and about people. He's getting out of the life, so he and I can be together. He loves me, and I love him."

For a long while Selina didn't say a word. She just sat there studying Satin. In her niece's eyes, she saw true love. "Satin," she finally said, "I know jour heart because I've helped you put it back together many a time, after it broken. I see ju really love dis man."

"Oh, I do," Satin said excitedly. "I love him enough to marry him."

"Now hold on," Selina said sternly, "ju moving kinda fast, no?"

"No, tía. I love this man and want to spend my life with him. He says he loves me also. Me asking him to marry me will be the final test of his loyalty. If he says yes, then even you can't deny that we were meant to be."

"So ju say," Selina responded. "But what about him? Let heem tell me to my face that he love my niece as much as she love heem. When he come tell me, I know if es true."

Satin's lips parted into a wide grin, exposing two rows of perfect white teeth. "I thought you might feel that way. Wait here for a second." Satin jumped up from the bed. After a few minutes, she came back into the room leading Lou-Loc by the hand. "Tía, this is my friend, St. Louis."

"Como está usted, senora?" he said in perfect Spanish.

"Buena," she responded. "I see ju speak Spanish?" she asked, impressed.

"Yes, ma'am. In California it's a mandatory second language."

"My niece tells me many things about you."

"I hope they're good things?"

"Some good, others not so good."

"Well, Miss Selina, I won't lie to you. I've made some poor choices in life, but your niece is trying to help me correct them."

"Good answer. So, Meester St. Louis, what are your plans for my baby?"

"To make her as happy as possible."

"Another good answer. She coach you on what to say to me?"

"No, ma'am. I'm just speaking from the heart. I would never attempt to deceive someone as lovely and as wise as you. Even if I could, I wouldn't."

"So far, so good," she said, looking at Satin. "I'm just going to come right out and ask you, Meester St. Louis: How do you feel about my niece?"

The question caught Lou-Loc off guard, but he didn't fluster or hesitate. "I love her, ma'am. I only want to do right by her, for as long as she allows me to."

Selina studied Lou-Loc for a long moment. She looked him dead in the eyes to see if there was any hint of a lie in what she was seeing. But in Lou-Loc's eyes. all she saw was sincerity.

"Meester St. Louis," she said, holding his hand in hers, "for a long tine I've looked after this girl. I've watched her come from a tree-climbing little girl, to a beautiful young lady. I am an old woman now, and I fear that my time is short in this world, but I no sad. I know that when I leave here, I will be with my lord and savior. I need you to promise do something for me."

"Sure, if I can," he said, sounding a little dumbfounded.

"Take care of her," she said, teary-eyed. "Allow me to pass on to the kingdom of heaven knowing that my niece is in good hands. Promise me that you will try to do right, and treat her like the queen that she is?"

"I promise," Lou-Loc said, sounding a little emotional himself. "You have my word." The three of them shared a warm hug and exchanged a few tears. Selina knew that Lou-Loc would stay true to his word.

As Satin and Lou-Loc made to leave, Selina called her back. She pulled Satin to her and whispered into her ear, "You've made a fine choice, little one. The heart never lies. God bless you both."

Satin left the hospital feeling pleased with herself and her man. To her, a blessing from her aunt was as good as a blessing from God. She was pleased that Selina hadn't mentioned Michael during their visit. She hadn't yet gotten around to telling Lou-Loc about her affiliation with the rival gang. That was a week ago.

Lou-Loc and Satin spent a long time exploring each other in the shadows of scented candlelight. It was as if it were the first time for both of them. Not just their first time with each other, but their first time with anyone. Lou-Loc was very gentle with her. Each time his tongue stroked her skin, she felt her nerves come alive. He kissed and sucked his way from her eyelids down to her belly. When he got to her vagina, she felt like sparks were going to pop out of her scalp.

At first, he did it slow and sensual. He licked around it and grazed her clit with his tongue. When she tried to push his head down, he just pulled away and continued to tease her. When he finally did start handling his business, she was in another world. The way his tongue worked his way in and out of her spot, she thought she was going to pass out. She began to see spots and blurs with every stroke. It was the first time a man had ever made her orgasm, let alone with his tongue. She was into it and didn't have any shame in her game about showing it. "Oh, that's it baby!" she shouted. "That's that shit! Oh, you nasty nigga you!"

After about twenty minutes and a few orgasms, it was time to return the favor. Satin wasn't as experienced as Lou-Loc in oral pleasure, but she wasn't no slouch. The warmth from her mouth felt so good to Lou-Loc that he wanted to cum prematurely, but being the type of nigga that he was, he wasn't going to let that happen. Her teeth scraped him a few times, causing him to flinch, but she still satisfied him. He actually respected her more for not knowing how to give head. That showed that she had either never done it before or didn't have much practice, unlike Martina, who was a pro.

After a few moments of oral, Lou-Loc decided that it was time for him to bust her out. He carried Satin to the bedroom and laid her gently on the bed. Lou-Loc slipped on a rubber and tried to penetrate her. Even with the lubrication from

the condom, she was still too tight. He dropped
down to his knees and began to lick her spot in
an attempt to add more moisture to the mix.
Once she was thoroughly lubricated, he eased his
way inside of her.

He had only gotten it about halfway in when
she began to whimper and cry. "You want me to
stop?" he asked, concerned.

"You better not," she said seriously. "You
don't know how long I've been waiting on this.
Just keep going; I'll be all right."

So keep going he did. It felt like it had been
quite some time since anyone had been inside
Satin, and Lou-Loc loved her tightness. He
stroked her slowly and with care at first, but once
they had gotten into a rhythm she begged him to
give it to her harder. Lou-Loc was only too happy
to accommodate her.

They went at it for a good forty minutes before Lou-Loc reached his climax. After a brief
intermission they were at it again. This time,
they both went at it like wild animals, each one
trying to out-savage the other. Satin tore chunks
of flesh from his back and arms while he plowed
into her like a man possessed. Six position
changes and an hour later, they lay in each
other's arms and reflected on the lovemaking
they had just shared.

It was strange for Lou-Loc. For the first time in his life, he felt content. The burdens of the set weren't hounding him, he wasn't looking over his shoulder, and nobody was dying. Even if only for the few moments in the arms of this beautiful woman, he was free.

"What ya thinking about?" Satin asked, looking up at him.

"Life," he said, smiling. The way Satin made him feel was something he'd been searching for most of his life. It was like this brown goddess was the piece he was missing. It felt so good that he wished it could go on forever. But why couldn't it?

Since he'd been old enough to bang, Lou-Loc had been putting in work for the set. He avenged his father's death a dozen times over and amassed a fair amount of paper. With the money he had put up and his investments, he was good. Why not lay up with this bad-ass bitch and live?

Lou-Loc had a good run in the game, but time was getting short. All his niggaz was getting killed or getting football numbers in prison and Gutter getting shot hit too close to home. It pained Lou-Loc to think of his ace all tore up and shit, but he had to face the reality of the life he was living. He and Gutter had come up under the same codes, doing the same shit. Lou-Loc might have killed a few more people, but Gutter wasn't no saint. He had much blood on his hands. The situation could've been reversed, and that could've been Lou-Loc with all those tubes running in and out of him. Satin coming to him was like God had taken a chance, and given his fallen angel a second shot at life. Hell, if that was the case, Lou-Loc had no intention on wasting it. He was going to take it and run with it.

"Satin," he said, stroking her forehead, "I been . . . you know, thinking about what you said."

"And?"

"Well, I ain't gonna lie, you asking me to marry you was some weird shit, ya know? I don't mean *weird* in a bad way. I mean, it caught me off guard."

"Yeah," she said, getting up, "I played myself, right?"

"Nah," he protested, pulling her back down, "it ain't like that. But are you sure that this is what you want?"

"Listen boo," she said in a serious tone. "Life is too short to be pondering over things your heart is already telling you is right. You the one, baby. I don't mean to sound thirsty or like I'm desperate, but that's just how it is. I got a jones for you, St. Louis Alexander, and I know you got one for me, so why fight it?"

"Damn," he said, nodding, "that was straight-forward and confident. You deep, girl."

"Lou-Loc, you know how I'm living, ain't no shame in my game. You're somebody I can build something with. You ain't some simple-ass corner nigga still trying to hustle up that Benz. You got yo' shit together just like me. You and I could be serious together, as lovers and as partners. But you gotta understand, I can't get wit no street nigga. I know you gonna be you, but let's do it the right way. Ya feel me?"

Lou-Loc just sat back and smirked. This was a side of Satin that he hadn't had the pleasure of meeting yet. She was a bull when it came to something she wanted. It was an asset to her numerous other qualities. This was definitely someone he could be with.

"Ma, you make a lot of sense. These streets put age on you quick. I ain't even twenty-four yet, and I done been through enough shit to last me two lifetimes. Maybe it is time to give the streets a rest," he said.

"That's what I'm trying to tell you, Lou-Loc. This shit is for the birds. Baby, write ya books and be the star you supposed to be. I've read your work, and I know you can do it."

Satin's words of encouragement gave a boost to his ego. Not only had she taken the time to read the work he'd given her, but she liked it. Martina had never had time to read his work, let alone critique it. There was something special about her. Even though her peoples were from the other side of the color line, he decided to get over it and accept her.

"Satin, I want to give you something," he said, reaching into his knapsack. He handed her a purple velvet box. When she opened the box, she was enthralled with the crater-sized diamond.

"Lou-Loc," she squealed, "this is so beautiful. When did you—hold up? I know you ain't trying to pass nothing off to me that you bought for that other bitch you was with?"

"Nah," he lied, "that's just something I bought a while back. I always said I was going to save it for the day I met someone special enough to have it. Lo and behold, here you go." It was a little white lie that he told her, but technically it wasn't that far from the truth. He had bought the stone for Martina, but she had never actually owned it or even seen it, for that matter.

"That was sweet of you," she said, hugging him. "I'll cherish it."

"Just think of it like this," he said while putting their two rings side by side, "we gonna jump the broom, but not no time soon, we gotta get it together first. In the meantime, these rings will be a symbol of our devotion to each other. When I get my affairs in order I'm gonna cop you a rock so big, that you'll need a wheelbarrow to carry it around."

"You're silly," she said, kissing him on the cheek.

"Now, I got some moves to make, Satin. I'll come by to check on you tomorrow."

"Lou-Loc, don't go?" she pleaded.

"Baby, you know I gotta handle business. I gotta get my affairs in order so we can do us. Within the next few days, we gonna put some distance between us and this shit hole."

"You serious, Lou-Loc?"

"Am I serious? Baby, let me tell you how serious I am. When you wake up tomorrow, you go on down and tell your landlord that you'll be moving out soon. I'm gonna float you the bread to pay off your last months of rent, so you shouldn't have no static wit the old bird."

"Baby, if you ready to pull up, we can leave tonight," she said eagerly.

"Nah, honey." He waved her off. "We gonna do it right. Take care of your crib and your gig. Within a week we outta here, straight gangsta."

As Lou-Loc headed for the door, Satin stopped him short. "Lou-Loc," she called out. "I want you to promise me something."

"Anything, boo. What is it?"

"Promise me that we'll always be together? Baby, if I put my feelings into this like I want to, I wanna know that it's something solid, and not just a fling?"

"Baby," he said, pulling her close, "you're the rainbow at the end of a storm. I wanna wake up and see your baby-doll face next to me in the morning for a lot of years to come. You will forever be my heart, mama. In this life or the next, you'll be the only girl for me."

"Then promise me, Lou-Loc. Tell me that you'll never leave me, and I'm not a fool for loving you?"

"Satin, honey, that's a guarantee. Now, I gots to raise up and get right.'

She didn't want him to go, but she knew a man had to be a man, so she kissed him good night and let him go. She loved the shit out of Lou-Loc. Her biggest fear was that the streets would take him away from her before they really had a chance to appreciate each other. She had always been psychic about things like that.

Chapter 20

The penthouse of the Golden Arms apartment building off of Central Park West was about as plush as they came. The decorator, who was imported from France, laid it out to look like a Chinese palace. The walls were decorated with various artworks from around the world. They were only prints, but it still gave the apartment an eccentric feel. As opposed to curtains, the windows were all fitted with bamboo shutters. Expensive furniture filled every room of the apartment. Even the toilet was handcrafted to certain specifications. A red carpet ran from the front door to the living room, giving those who entered the feeling of being a celebrity. The owner liked to stroke his ego that way. This was the domain of El Diablo.

El Diablo paced back and forth over his plush living-room carpet, while Cisco looked on and smiled.

"Michael," Cisco crooned, "you're going to upset your ulcer if you don't calm down."

"Calm down?" Diablo snapped. "You announce in front of those fucking apes on the council that my sister is seeing one of the men I'm trying to have assassinated, and make me look like a complete fool and I'm supposed to calm down?"

Cisco leaned back in the recliner and lit a cigarette. He knew he couldn't overplay his hand for fear of ruining everything. He had to nudge El Diablo. LC Blood would be his, but he had to be patient. "Michael," he said, exhaling a cloud of smoke. "I did things the way I did for your benefit. For one, if I told you in private, would you have taken me seriously? I told you at the council because I knew that would help you to realize the seriousness of the situation. For two, I wanted all of those fucking eggplants to respect our gangsta. The streets are watching. Not only are they watching, but they're talking. Some of our comrades feel that since you haven't been on the scene for a while, that you might've gone soft."

"Soft?" El Diablo asked in disbelief. "I have spilled more blood on these streets than any ten of your best soldiers, Cisco. I have paid my dues."

"Oh, it's not to me that you have anything to prove. It's these fucking street rabbles that are trying to tarnish your good name. Then you got this meatball-ass nigga from the other side sporting your sister on his arm, which is only making things look more suspect. If you let this slide, then it's only a matter of time before you have these fucking tar babies lining up to challenge your authority." Cisco sat back and watched El Diablo pace the room as his words sank in.

"You're right, Cisco. This will not go unpunished. When El Diablo allows his own family to become Judas, he is no longer fit to lead."

"Just what I was thinking," Cisco mumbled under his breath. "This is what I suggest, Michael: Give me a day or two to get with my contacts and I'll have this Lou-Loc situation taken care of, but in the meantime you need to talk to Satin. We definitely have to resolve this situation, but we have to do it right."

"Yes, I agree. I'll talk to Satin and if she doesn't go along with what I say, then I'll blow her boyfriend's fucking brains out and put my foot knee-deep in her ass!"

"Now that's the El Diablo I know," Cisco continued to put the battery in him. He stood up and prepared to leave. "We'll get this worked out, Michael, I promise you this." As Cisco made his way to the elevator he had to fight back the smile that was forming on his lips. Things were working out better than he had originally planned. Soon

Lou-Loc would be dead and El Diablo would either be dead or in prison. Either way, LC would be his again.

Lou-Loc dipped his car in and out of traffic like it was legal, feeling himself. He was on top of the world. He had some paper, a bad bitch, and a plan. In his mind he was good and no one could bring him down—or so he thought.

The first call was to his crooked-ass financial planner. He informed her that New York was no longer going to be his residence, and that he would need some cash to travel with. She assured him that he would be receiving the cash within twenty-four hours, and the necessary paperwork would be taken care of. The next call was to Pop Top, telling him that there would be an emergency meeting of the set leaders taking place that night. Top kept asking him what the deal was, but Lou-Loc wouldn't give. He knew a lot of the homeboys wouldn't be too happy about him getting out, but fuck it. If niggaz really felt that strongly about it, they could see him in the streets. It's not like he was abandoning them, he was just retiring while retirement was still an option.

The hardest part would be saying good-bye to Gutter and Sharell. They were the only family he had on the East Coast, so the bond between the three was strong. Sharell had always tried to tell Lou-Loc about Martina, but he wouldn't listen. The first thing he would do when he met with her at the hospital was tell her that she was right about the broad, before he made his peace with Gutter and went on with his life.

By the time Lou-Loc made it to the hospital, the sun had set. Looking at the new evening made Lou-Loc think about Cross. He wondered if he should track his friend down and tell him that he would be leaving soon, but decided against it. He had put Cross through enough as it was and it was probably best if he let him be, at least for a time. When he finally did decide to stab out he would tell his friend, but that night he needed to see Gutter and lay it all on the table. There was still no telling which way the wind would blow with his condition, so he wanted to lay it all out for him while he still could.

As Lou-Loc made his way through the hospital lobby, he tried to find the right words, but he couldn't. How do you tell your best friend, who happens to be in a coma, that you're leaving and you'll probably never see him again? There was no easy way to say it. Lou-Loc promised himself that no matter where he was, if Gutter came out of his coma, he'd be on the first thing smoking back to his friend's side. When he got off on Gutter's floor, Sharell greeted him with open arms.

"Where you been, boy?" she asked, giving him her Sunday-service smile. "I ain't seen you in so long, I almost forgot what you looked like."

"Ain't nothing, sis. I just been out trying to get my life together."

"Oh yeah? I hear that. So you and that fast-ass Spanish chick finally parted company?"

"Yeah, how you know?"

"Boy, you know Harlem ain't but so big. She was all out on the block crying and shit. She was talking 'bout how you left her for some square-ass young girl."

"Yeah, that's my boo."

"Mmm-hmm."

"What you mean by that?"

"St. Louis Alexander, you in love?"

"Girl, you know me better than that."

"Yeah, I know you and that's why I said it. I knew from the first time you told me about her that she was something special. You know, I prayed on it for you, Lou-Loc. I asked the lord to send you someone to set yo' ass straight, and in comes Miss Satin."

"Yeah, Sharell. Satin is all that. She opened my eyes to a lot of shit. I'm trying to find a way out of this hell without doing it the way I've been doing it. We've even talked about getting married."

"Not you, mister player! Marriage so soon— she must've put that thang on you?"

"Nah, it ain't even like that with us. I mean we did the do, but that was after I'd been with her for a while. She's a good girl, Sharell."

"Praise the lord. I'm so happy for you, Lou-Loc. You need a good woman in your life. But how do you plan on truly making this girl happy if you're still caught up in this madness?"

"That's kinda what I came to talk to y'all about," he said timidly. "Sharell, I'm getting out of the game and leaving New York. I'm done. I'm just hoping you don't think I'm being a coward for leaving before my man wakes up."

Sharell's eyes welled up with tears. She rushed to Lou-Loc and embraced him. "Lou-Loc, I would never think you a coward for trying to survive. This is what you've always wanted and Kenyatta knew it. There ain't no shame in being tired. We all get that way if we go through enough. The important thing is you're getting out by choice instead of by bullets or bars."

Hearing Sharell's approval of his decision made Lou-Loc feel a little better. He had always had a lot of respect for her. She wasn't no hood bitch, yet she wasn't some stuck-up chick either. She was just a young lady who had her shit together.

"How's my boy?" Lou-Loc asked.

"Well, it's hard to really say. Some days he's good, others not so good. The doctors say his condition is stabilizing, but he's still unconscious. I'm scared, Lou-Loc. What if he doesn't wake up?"

"Don't fret that," he said, patting her hand, "that boy tough as they come. I've seen Ken pull himself out of more shit than this. It's a small thing to a giant, ma. Bank on that one."

"I hope so, Lou-Loc."

"So, how y'all doing as far as bread, honey?"

"We straight, baby, thanks for asking. You know I work everyday and Ken has got bread in the stash, so we're okay," she told him.

"Okay, but what about the medical bills? I know Ken ain't got no insurance and the hospital is gonna charge a grip for all this."

"Some bigwig friend of Gutter's is taking care of that. I told him that he didn't have to, but he insisted. He said he owed Gutter's family a favor," Sharell said, shrugging.

Lou-Loc was surprised to hear this. The last few times Gutter had met with Anwar he had never mentioned it to him, but the little prince seemed to be full of surprises. Lou-Loc would thank him later, but he wanted to stop in and see Gutter first. "Sharell, I'm gonna spend a few with the kid and get some things off my chest."

"Okay, Lou-Loc. Take your time, I'm gonna run downstairs and grab something to eat. You want me to bring you anything?"

"Nah, I'm straight."

"Okay, I'll be back in a bit." Sharell grabbed her purse and headed toward the elevator.

Lou-Loc made his way down the corridor, trying to figure out what to say to his brother. It was best to just open his mouth and let the words flow freely. When he entered the room, he almost broke down. Gutter was laid out in that iron bed looking like death warmed over. There were tubes running in and out of damn near every hole in his body and a machine helping him breathe. His beautiful dark skin was ashy and drawn in. His hair needed to be braided over and he had lost quite a few pounds. This was not the man he knew.

At first, he was mad at Cross. The man had the means to save Gutter and did nothing. But once reason took over, Lou-Loc realized there was no reason to be mad at his friend. It was not meant for man to interfere with what God had planned.

Cross was just playing his part in the natural
scheme of things and to be upset with him was
selfish.

Lou-Loc pulled up a chair beside his bed and
took his friend's hand. "What up, cuz? This ya ace
boon, Lou-Loc. Man, so much shit been going on
since you took ya little vacation. The homies been
putting in work like a ma' fucka. We done rode on
damn near every Blood set in New York. I found
out them little marks that put the paper on you
was from LC. I put the hurt in their leader's little
brother, and two of his peoples. I took care of
that nigga Born too, cuz. In return, Anwar made
good on his end and knocked Scooby out the box.
We set up the new spots out in Brooklyn, and
baby boy, the money is coming in. I got li'l boo
and his peoples looking over shit out there cause
that's where they peoples is from. Peep the fly shit
though, cuz; remember that chick, Satin? That's
El Diablo li'l sister. Wait a second before you start
preaching, she ain't on it like that. She don't fuck
wit them niggaz. She ain't got nothing to do wit
the life, she a good girl. That's my boo now, cuz.
It's like you always said, that bitch Martina was
dirty. Come to find out she was fucking wit that li'l
slob Mac. He ain't putting his li'l dick in nothing
no more, though, cuz. Guess I should get to the
point though, huh?" Lou-Loc hesitated, as if his

friend would answer him. "Me and Satin, we in love, cuz, and it's the real thing and I wanna see where it goes. Them niggaz that tried to one you is dead and buried and Harlem Crip has established itself as an official powerhouse, so for the most part my work is done. I'm gonna hang up these pistols and live me a nice, square life."

Lou-Loc sat for a minute, just listening to the sounds of the machines in the room and Gutter's labored breathing. The longer he sat there it seemed like the more depressed he got. Seeing his friend like that was hard on him and he wasn't sure how much longer he'd be able to take it. "Cuz, I'm sorry for what happened to you, Lord knows I am. If we could've traded places, it'd be me in this fucking meat factory instead of you, but it didn't play out like that." He composed himself. "G, I know you're probably salty with me for getting out, but we both know I didn't intend to play this game forever. I'm tired and I need some peace in my life." Lou-Loc took Gutter's hand in his. "Cuz, before I make this move, I need to know that we're square." He felt Gutter's hand twitch slightly, and then tighten around his. Gutter was letting him know that he was free. Tears began to well in Lou-Loc's eyes and this time he let them flow.

Lou-Loc cried like a baby as he held the hand of his dearest friend. He cried for his father, who was gunned down in a mall parking lot. He cried for Gutter's father and grandfather, who died for what they believed in. He cried tears for every man he had ever murdered and the mothers who had to bury their children. He cried for the youth of black America.

As Lou-Loc was hunched over his friend, crying, he didn't notice someone watching the exchange and shedding their own tears. These were not tears of sorrow, but tears of vengeance. Cross now knew what he had to do. When he wiped the tears away with the back of his hand it came away smeared with blood.

Chapter 21

Satin was on top of the world. The evening breeze was warm on her face as she carried her small bag of groceries back to her loft. Hell, it could've been pouring rain and she wouldn't have cared. Her life was finally beginning to get better. She had been skeptical about coming at Lou-Loc the way she did, but her forwardness had paid off.

It was like her aunt used to always say: "Love is an unpredictable thing. When in doubt, follow your heart." Those words rang true in her situation. She followed her heart and hit a home run. She knew she loved Lou-Loc from the first time she laid eyes on him. Their hearts called to each other and now they would become soul mates.

Satin's thoughts were interrupted when she saw Michael's car parked in front of her building. This drama she didn't need. She was a grown-ass woman, and Michael could go fuck himself if he had a problem with her being with Lou-Loc.

Before she could get to the car, he hopped out and started toward her.

"Satin, what the fuck is up with you?" El Diablo snapped.

"Nice to see you too, Michael," she said sarcastically.

"Don't play with me, Satin. What's this I hear about you fucking this nigger from the other side?"

"First of all," she said, pointing her finger, "his name is Lou-Loc. Second, he's not a nigger, he's a writer, and third, we're not just fucking—that's my man."

"Your man? He's a killer! Lou-Loc personally executed two of my peoples. Satin, how you gonna fuck with somebody that broke our little brother's nose?"

"Michael, please. Jesus brought that shit on himself. He started fucking with Lou-Loc and got his little ass kicked. The only reason he didn't get himself buried was because of me. Lou-Loc loves me, so he let Jesus live."

"Loves you?" Michael said, rolling his eyes. "You poor misguided child, he's just fucking you to get at me. This shit is like a fucking slap in the face. You know how stupid this has me looking among the other Blood generals?"

"Michael, you're making yourself look stupid pressing this shit. If you recall, Lou-Loc and his peoples didn't start this shit? Y'all cast the first stone."

"Satin, you don't know shit about shit as far as this goes."

"Michael, don't play me, okay. You don't think I know it was LC who shot Gutter? Jesus already let the cat out of the bag. Shit, why you think he got his nose broken?"

"Damn, Satin. If I didn't know any better, I'd think you were siding with them black bastards."

"Oh, please. You know I don't get down with that gang shit in no kinda way. All this sides shit don't mean nothing to me, so miss me with it. I could care less if the police killed or locked up every one of them dumb-ass so-called gangsters. For your information, he's getting out of the gang so we can be together. Lou-Loc is my man, and that's just the way it is."

"Ya man? Satin, that black son of a bitch don't love you. To him, you another notch on his belt, a fine-ass piece of Spanish pussy!" Michael didn't mean it like he said it, but it was too late to take it back.

That last comment hurt Satin deeply. She and Michael had their differences, but he was still her brother. If anything, she wanted him to be happy. She didn't expect him to accept Lou-Loc, but she wanted him to at least understand how she felt.

"Fuck you, El Diablo." she said coldly. "I could give a fuck what you think."

"Now, you listen," he said, grabbing her by the arm, "I'm your big brother and I know what's best for you. I forbid you to see this spook anymore. I forbid it."

Satin threw her head back and burst out laughing. "You can't be serious. I'm not the little girl you remember asking for dollars. I'm grown, Michael. *G-r-o-w-n*, so you can bump your head with the dumb shit."

Satin turned to walk away but El Diablo wasn't done yet. He spun her around and slapped her across the face. Satin dropped her groceries and stood there in shock. Michael had never put his hands on her before, but there was a first time for everything. "Satin," he said, reaching for her, but froze when she drew her gun and aimed it at him.

"You dirty motherfucker," she hissed. "Ain't no man ever laid hands on me, not even our father. Let me tell you something, you dope-peddling snake. I don't give a fuck what you say— this is my life. Me and Lou-Loc are going to be together, and that's a fact. Now if your small, racist brain can't accept that, too fucking bad! That's the way it is. And if you ever raise your fucking hand to me again, I'll empty this clip in your worthless ass. Now, can you dig that?" Before he could answer, Satin was strutting toward her building. Before she went through the lobby door, she took another jab at her brother. "The next time I have to pull a gun on you, it'll be to take your life." She disappeared into her building.

Michael stood there, at a loss for words. What the fuck was his family coming to? The same little girl he raised had just threatened to kill him. All he wanted to do was look out for his sister's feelings. There was no doubt in his mind as to whether or not his sister loved his rival. But did Lou-Loc feel the same? El Diablo knew he had to bring some clarity to the situation, and quickly. This shit was getting out of hand.

Cisco stood on the corner of 125th and Park under the Metro-North station waiting for Tito to show up. The excitement had him so worked up that he wanted to jump up and down. El Diablo had called and told him about the altercation with Satin and asked his opinion. Cisco played the role of the concerned counsel, but inwardly he jumped for joy. The mighty El Diablo was playing right into his hands. Within the next day or so, he would be the sole controller of LC Blood. Before Cisco could fantasize further, his cell phone vibrated.

"Hello?" he sang.

"Cisco," purred the seductive voice on the other end.

"Martina, what a pleasant surprise," he said, lying. In all actuality, Cisco had no love for her. She was loose and had no loyalty. She would sell her mother out to the highest bidder. As foul as she might've been, he still needed her. She would be a key player in his scheme.

"So, what the deal, mami?"

"You know the deal. You got my paper?"

"Listen, sweetheart, don't put the cart before the horse. You'll get ya bread when the job is done."

"I know you got me, Cisco. I just got shit I need to do, that's all."

"Yeah, me too."

"Cisco, why don't you swing by my crib before you turn in for the night?"

"Oh yeah, for what?"

"Just to chill, you know? Gosh, a bitch can't just wanna hang for old time's sake?"

"Yeah, right. Martina, I know you too well. You always got something up your sleeve."

"Nah, it ain't even like that. But if one thing leads to another, you know?"

Cisco couldn't help but to laugh. Here this bitch was pregnant as all hell, and still scheming on cock. Cisco and Martina had hooked up on occasion, but the way things stood, he wanted no part of her. The bitch was a stone snake that didn't have a preference about who she bit. If she was willing to cross a nigga she was supposed to love, imagine what the fuck kinda shit she would get him into? Cisco was arrogant but he wasn't stupid.

Martina was going on and on about the good times they used to have, but Cisco wasn't really listening. He was too preoccupied with looking for Tito. Just as Cisco was about to bark Martina's head off, he spotted Tito coming down the steps from the Metro-North. "Martina, baby—I gotta go handle something and make sure everything is set for tomorrow. Make sure you handle your end. When you make all the arrangements, call me." He ended the call without waiting for a response.

"Damn," Tito said as he walked up, "these fucking people out here wanna overcharge you for everything."

"Don't sweat it, my man. It ain't your bread anyhow. So we clear on what's up?"

"Yeah." Tito lit a cigarette.

"Good, good. Make sure they make the train when it's done. Now for our other problem: Sometime tonight our friend the giant is going to meet with an accident. Nothing serious, just enough to sideline him. I'm gonna volunteer you to stand in as El Diablo's bodyguard. When he gets my call, you'll know what to do from there."

"Damn, Cisco, you one cold motherfucker. I'm glad we on the same side."

"Tito, you've kept it more than real with me from day one. Didn't I always tell you that I was gonna take care of you? Once I'm running the show, you'll be my number one."

"What about El Diablo? He sure as hell ain't gonna like this."

"Fuck Diablo. As long as you do what I say, he ain't gonna be in no position to do shit. The N.Y.P.D already got a hard-on for that nigga. They're gonna jump for joy when this shit pops off. Hell, they're gonna put him under the jail. Just make sure you put them things where they need to be when you go to pick him up."

"I got you, Cisco. Everything gonna be gravy."

When Lou-Loc arrived at the park, the rest of his lieutenants were already there. There were six of them in all. There was Li'l Boo, who ran the shop in Brooklyn; B.T. Gangsta, from 145th; Moe, from Wagner, and High Side from St. Nicholas Projects. With Pop Top and Snake Eyes overseeing everything, the gang was all there, so it was time.

"What it is, fellas?" Lou-Loc greeted everyone.

"Life is good, homie, and you the reason for it." Li'l Boo replied.

"Hell yeah," Moe chimed in. "Shit, these ol' slob-ass niggaz is on the ropes, cuz. You Cali ma' fuckas lay it down for real. Them niggaz that you had out here tore shit the fuck up. That shit had me hyped."

"Right, right," High Side cosigned.

"So what's up, Lou-Loc?" Pop Top asked. "I know you ain't called a nigga way down here for nothing?"

"Fo sho, my man. I got something to say to y'all niggaz. Some of y'all might not like it, but it's just the way shit is," Lou-Loc said.

"Well spill, nigga," Top said.

"Well, it's like this," Lou-Loc started, "I been banging for the hood for the last twelve years. I done put in work and earned my stripes. As all of you can agree, I'm one of the realist cats in the whole Crip gang, on the east or west. I'm the last of a dying breed, which is what makes this so hard for me to say." Lou-Loc sighed. "I'm out the game."

The park went so silent you could've heard an ant fart. There was a look of utter shock on all of the homies' faces, all except Snake Eyes. The thought of Lou-Loc leaving the gang was inconceivable. He was one of— if not the— baddest niggaz on any set. Pop Top was the first one to break the silence. "What you mean, cuz?" he asked sorrowfully.

"I mean what I said," Lou-Loc responded. "This shit here is wearing on my nerves, cousins. All this killing, it can drive a motherfucker batty. It just ain't for me, cuz."

"How you gonna bail on us like that?" High Side asked. "I know how you feel about all this, but you and Gutter started this shit. Y'all showed us how to bang accordingly. That man done did a lot for us, but you the real power behind Harlem Crip, Lou-Loc. In this little bit of time, you've established us as the strongest set in the five boroughs. You that nigga right now and you just wanna give it all up?"

"Easy, homie," Snake Eyes butted in. "This nigga here is a ghetto superstar. He got more stripes than most niggaz in the game, and he still here to talk about it. That shit in itself is a blessing. There comes a time in a man's life where he just gets tired, and I guess the homie Loc has reached that point."

Some of the homies thought it odd that Snake Eyes was speaking up for Lou-Loc. They figured that it was because of their long-standing friendship and them both being from killer Cali, but it was much deeper than that. Lou-Loc had wanted to get out of the game for a long time and Snake Eyes was well aware of that. They had many discussions on the topic, and he felt his friend's pain. This was one of the main reasons that Snake's father had helped Lou-Loc wash some of his money.

"Listen," Lou-Loc started. "it's like this. I'm always gonna be a Crip, that's just a given. But as far as being active in the field, that shit is over. I've killed many a man and caused many a man to get killed. I've put in enough work to earn my freedom. Straight like that."

"Straight like nothing," B.T. said harshly. "We all know when you get in a gang it's for life. This ain't no fucking job where you can put in your two weeks' notice."

"Ay, watch ya mouth, nigga," Top checked him.

"Nah," Lou-Loc said, waving Top off, "let the homie speak."

"Look," B.T. continued, "all I'm saying is this shit ain't kosher. You come all this way to build up your street credibility, and now you just wanna walk away? This shit don't sit right wit me, cuz. Maybe the things niggaz is saying is true."

"Like what?" Lou-Loc asked defensively.

"Well," B.T. sighed, "word is that you done hooked up wit Diablo's li'l sister. Niggaz is saying that this slob-ass bitch got ya nose open. What up wit that shit?"

The tension in the air had suddenly become very thick. The knowledge of Lou-Loc and Satin's relationship was limited to a select few. Sure, some of the homies had seen them together, but no one had ever questioned it. That was Lou-Loc's business. By trying to put Lou-Loc on blast, B.T. was asking for trouble. There had always been bad blood between the two, but it was always kept to ranking on each other. B.T. was testing him, and it didn't go unnoticed.

"Why don't y'all niggaz just chill?" Snake Eyes said, placing his hand on B.T.'s shoulder.

"Man, fuck that," B.T. said, jerking away from Snake Eyes. "Nigga, I don't even know you like that for you to be making suggestions. Only reason ma' fuckas in the hood even gave you a little respect is because Lou-Loc said you was cool. Shit, the way this nigga acting, I'm starting to question his judgment."

Lou-Loc's eyes became dark and glassy. Pop Top and Snake Eyes had seen this look in his eyes before, so they stepped back. It was a look that only came over him when he felt a nigga needed to be taught a lesson.

"Listen, B.T.," Lou-Loc said through clenched teeth, "I don't think you really know what's up, so I'm gonna clarify it for you. Satin is my shorty, period. Yeah, I know her brother is a mark-ass nigga and always gonna be one, but that ain't on her. She a square and ain't got nothing to do with this war or me wanting to get outta the game. If you was down from the gate like Snake and Gutter instead of a li'l know-nothing-ass nigga, you'd know this. As far as who I'm wit, and why I'm wit 'em, that ain't none of your never mind. Let this be the first and last time I gotta remind you of that, cuz."

B.T. matched Lou-Loc's stare without blinking. He was a bad-ass nigga in his own right. If Lou-Loc wanted to get stupid, he'd have got down with him. As tough as he was, he didn't want no drama with Lou-Loc if he could avoid it. But B.T., being the type of nigga he was, couldn't allow Lou-Loc to play him in front of the crew. "Let me tell you something," he said, putting his finger in Lou-Loc's face, "I ain't scared of you, nigga. I know who you are and how you do, so the respect is there, but don't you think for a fucking moment that I wouldn't hesitate to put something in yo' ass. This is New York, and we don't play that ol'—"

That was as far as he got. Once again, the beast had reared its head and Lou-Loc was in battle mode. He grabbed B.T.'s finger and snapped it like a twig. High Side moved to break it up, but Lou-Loc moved with near-inhuman speed. With his free hand he pushed High Side, sending him skidding a good five feet. All of the homies looked on in shock. High Side outweighed Lou-Loc by at least twenty pounds, but Lou-Loc tossed him like a small child. B.T. opened his mouth to scream, but Lou-Loc silenced him with a straight jab to the lip, busting it wide open.

"Now you get this straight," Lou-Loc snarled at his bleeding opponent, "I'm through wit this shit. It's little fuck-ass niggaz like you that's fucking the game up now. I'm done, you fucking hear me? I want my life back and ain't nobody gonna stop me from being happy!"

All B.T. could do was cough blood and shake his head. He wanted to put on a show for the homies, but he had no intentions on setting Lou-Loc off. He knew the man's reputation for killing and wondered if he would be the latest addition to his list of kills. Luckily for him, Snake Eyes took Lou-Loc's arm and pulled him away.

"That's enough, old friend," Snake Eyes whispered. "He ain't worth it. You free, my nigga, and I'll back you on that. Let it go and live your life."

The sound of Snake Eyes's voice seemed to bring Lou-Loc back from wherever he had been. The madness had receded and he was himself again, at least for the moment. Lou-Loc looked around at the sea of frightened faces and felt ashamed of what he had done. These were supposed to be his peoples, yet instead of understanding, he saw only fear. He knew it was time for him to get out.

"I'm sorry," he said, addressing his peoples. "We're supposed to be down for each other, and look what the fuck I do. I'm an O.G., and I ain't supposed to conduct myself in this manner. I'm supposed to be showing y'all younger G's a better way, but instead I personify the old ways, the violent ways. This ain't how it's supposed to be." Lou-Loc sounded defeated. "After tonight, it's a wrap for me, cousins. I'll always be a Crip, and I'll always love y'all niggaz, but I'm done with this shit. Pop Top will be the acting leader of Harlem Crip until Gutter recovers. I'm trusting you with this shit because I know you can handle it. Do the right thing, cuz."

"Hey, you know I will," Top said, grinning. He had finally got his chance to hold the reins of power, and he intended to run with it.

"One last thing," Lou-Loc said, raising his hand. "This muthafucka—" he pointed at B.T., who was still rolling around on the ground— "he ain't fit to run shit. He still Crip cause that's his right, but he will no longer be a set leader. From here on, let it be known that B.T. has been stripped of his rank and title. Top, I don't give a fuck who you get to replace him, but he's a fuck-ing nobody on set, ya dig?" Pop Top nodded. "I wish you niggaz all the best that life has to offer after I retire. Call on me for guidance whenever you feel necessary. The homie Snake can tell you how to reach me. Now let it be done."

All of the lieutenants who were still able to stand gathered around Lou-Loc and embraced him. They were sorry to see their homie step down, but they knew that's what he wanted and they respected his wishes. Lou-Loc had nothing left to prove. In the years during his run, he had held the set down and put in much work. In all their eyes, Lou-Loc was a stand-up nigga. If he wanted his freedom, he was more than welcomed to it. He'd earned it.

In another part of town, everything was all good. The Giant staggered out of the East Village pub with two young girls on his arm. He had spent a good part of the night, as well as his bankroll, on the girls, getting toasted in the bar. He had big plans for the two.

Whether they wanted to or not, he planned on fucking.

Being that he was too drunk to perform the task, he decided to let the older of the two girls drive while he freaked off in the backseat with the other. He handed the first girl the keys and watched her shapely little ass as she climbed behind the wheel of the hog. Next, he let the other girl into the backseat and started around the other side to get in. In his mind, he went over the various demeaning tasks he would have them perform.

As a young man, the Giant never had much luck with women. He was an oversized teenager who wore hand-me-down clothes. His shoes would always be busted at the seams because of his oversized feet and his clothes were always too small. The kids had called him all kinds of cruel names, from *tree trunk* to *mighty-tighty*—and these were some of the nicer names. When El Diablo found him, he was a poor brawler who fought for money in backroom bars and underworld basements. El Diablo took pity on the young man and gave him a job. No longer would the Giant have to wear hand-me-downs or fight in back rooms just to eat. El Diablo had made him somebody, a man of power and standing. For that, he would be forever grateful.

As the Giant made his way around the car, he didn't notice the vehicle speeding toward him from the opposite direction. As soon as he stepped into the street, the car clipped his leg, sending his large body flying over the trunk. The Giant landed hard on the curb with a sickening *thud*. The two women jumped from the car, wailing like banshees. All traces of the liquor they had consumed were gone as they looked upon the twisted hulk lying on the sidewalk. He lay sprawled on the ground with his leg twisted at an odd angle. He didn't scream, nor did he cry. The pain was too intense for him to utter a sound. As consciousness fled him, his last thoughts were, How would he serve his boss as a cripple?

Chapter 22

B.T. sat in the emergency room looking at his twisted finger, waiting to be seen. Lou-Loc had done him dirty and it was his fault. If he'd just kept his mouth shut none of this would've happened. Whether he was right or wrong, Lou-Loc was going to get his.

With his good hand, he pulled out his cell phone and dialed a number. "Yo, what up?" he said into the receiver. "This B.T., kid. Peep game; remember that thing we talked about? Well, the nigga done finally played himself. It's time for our boy Lou-Loc to take a nap, permanently." The caller said something on the other end, to which B.T. nodded in approval and ended the call. He felt a little better about every thing now. He had probably lost the use of his finger, but it was okay. Before the night was over, Lou-Loc would lose his life.

Lou-Loc sat in the passenger seat, puffing a blunt, while Snake Eyes drove. He felt a little fucked-up by what happened, but B.T. asked for it. If he hadn't tried to be a big shot. . . . Fuck it, it wasn't his problem anymore.

"What's on ya mind, player?" Snake Eyes asked as they pulled up in front of White Castle.

"Ain't nothing, just thinking," Lou-Loc said, exhaling the smoke. "Man, I can't believe I'm finally getting out. This shit don't even feel real to me, cuz!"

"It's about fucking time, nigga. You can't run the streets forever. Eventually, the shit catches up with you. Just be glad you're getting out on two feet instead of on ya back."

"I know that's right." Lou-Loc gave Snake Eyes dap.

"So what you gonna do, cuz?"

Lou-Loc shrugged. "I can't say for sure what the future holds, but for right now me and Satin are gonna get outta the city. I figure me and Satin can get a li'l place somewhere and trying to focus on living the right way."

"Well, I'll be headed down to Miami soon to start work at my dad's firm. Maybe you could come down and work part-time for him until you finish school," Snake Eyes suggested.

Lou-Loc chuckled. "Cuz, you know damn well I ain't about to get no job, but Miami move don't sound like a bad idea. The weather is always nice and the property ain't too expensive. I'm sure Satin would love it."

Snake Eyes was silent for a few moments. "Can I ask you something, cuz?"

"Go ahead, man. You know you my nigga."

"You and this girl serious?"

"As a heart attack, cuz. I don't know why everybody is tripping off me and Satin hooking up, like I'm some kinda fool," Lou-Loc said defensively.

"Lou-Loc, calm down. I know you ain't nobody dummy, but you've only known this girl a li'l while. All I'm saying is that maybe you're rushing it a bit, like with Martina."

Lou-Loc looked at his friend seriously. "Snake, these are two totally different situations. Let me tell you something about love, homie: There ain't no instructions or early-warning signs to this shit. When you find somebody and it happens, you just know."

"Yeah, Lou. I can dig it. As long as you happy, I'm happy for you."

"And that's why you'll always be my nigga."

The two friends shared a manly hug right there in front of White Castle. They didn't care who was looking or what they thought. To them, it was the end of an old life and the beginning of a new one. But their precious moment was short-lived as a car screeched to a halt behind where they had parked their car.

"Ay, which one of y'all niggaz is Lou-Loc?" someone shouted from inside the car.

Without even thinking, Lou-Loc stepped forward. "You know me, cuz?" For an answer, the back windows of the car slid down, and all that could be seen were the flashes from gun muzzles.

Snake Eyes was the first to react. He dove and knocked Lou-Loc to the ground. Before Lou-Loc could clear his gun from his belt, Snake Eyes was already on one knee, firing his .380. His bum leg didn't hinder his aim at all as his bullets slammed into the car, shattering its windows and striking one of the gunmen.

The driver tried to peel off, but Lou-Loc stepped out into the middle of the street. Seeing his target, the driver stepped on the gas in an attempt to mow him down. Snake Eyes shouted a warning but if Lou-Loc had heard him, he gave no indication. He stood there smirking as the car sped toward him for the kill. At the last possible second Lou-Loc leapt into the air, smashing into the windshield and rolling over the hood. The driver thought he had surely finished Lou-Loc, but found out differently when the rear windshield shattered. He looked over his shoulder and saw Lou-Loc clinging to the back of the car, laughing insanely, trying to get a bead on him with his gun.

The terrified driver swerved from side to side, trying to dislodge him from the vehicle, but he held tight. Lou-Loc dumped shot after shot into the car, shattering the windshield and sending shards of glass flying into the driver's face, temporarily blinding him. His vision cleared just as the car was jumping the curb on course to slam into a streetlight. The impact slammed the driver's head into the steering wheel, dazing him, totaling the car and sending Lou-Loc flying over the car. The driver drifted in and out of consciousness, trying to ignore the pain of the dashboard that had been forced into his chest on impact. He could hear people screaming and the faint sounds of sirens in the distance coming ever closer. He was in bad shape from the crash, but at least he had succeeded in killing Lou-Loc.

Through the smoke billowing up through the busted radiator, the driver could see movement and he thanked God that help had arrived. Any hope that he'd had in his heart abruptly died when his vision cleared and he saw that the figure moving toward him wasn't a paramedic, but Lou-Loc. His mind told him that it was impossible for Lou-Loc to have survived the crash, but there he was, limping in his direction and slipping another clip into the pistol. The driver had heard the stories about the legendary resilience of the man who refused to die, but dismissed them as exaggerated. Seeing it firsthand, he wondered if there was some truth to Lou-Loc's pact with the devil.

The driver tried to scream for help, but because of his broken ribs couldn't find the breath to do so. He lay there helpless, watching his intended target yank the door from the hinges. Pain shot through the driver's chest as Lou-Loc snatched him from the vehicle and threw him roughly to the concrete. He opened his mouth to try and barter for his life, but when Lou-Loc shoved his gun down his throat he knew it was pointless. The driver had rolled the dice and lost.

Lou-Loc leaned in close enough for the driver to see the unnatural glint in his eyes. "When will you amateurs learn?" Lou-Loc asked before pulling the trigger and putting the driver's brains on the curb. After the adrenaline had worn off and the tainted blood was no longer flowing through his veins, the severity of his injuries kicked in. He dropped to one knee clutching his ribs, which felt like they were busted. He would be in a world of pain for the next few days, but he would live, which was more than he could say for his would-be killers.

Snake Eyes came hobbling across the street, gun drawn, and ready to finish the men who had killed his friend. He couldn't hide the shock on his face, seeing that Lou-Loc had not only survived, but killed the assassin. "Damn, cuz, I thought they finished you."

"These novice muthafuckas can't do nothing with me, Snake." Lou-Loc tried to stand but it felt like his legs wouldn't support his weight.

"We gotta get you to a hospital," Snake Eyes said urgently, helping Lou-Loc to his feet.

"Fuck a hospital, man. Just get me outta here before the police come." Lou-Loc leaned on his friend for support and they made tracks for the car. When they were safely away from the scene of the crime, Lou-Loc turned to his comrade. "Cuz, I done had enough of this shit. How soon do you think we could make moves for Miami?"

Satin paced around her loft, fuming. Her earlier encounter with her brother had her shaken. She didn't know whether to be angry or afraid. El Diablo had always been stubborn, but never unreasonable. "Who the fuck does he think he is?" she asked no one in particular. Michael must've been out of his mind to get up in her mix like that. Satin reasoned that she was a grown woman and could fuck whomever she chose, be it Lou-Loc or the man on the moon. It was her pussy and her heart.

She touched the sore spot on her cheek where her brother had slapped her, and it only fueled her anger. She wasn't hurt by the slap itself, but it was the fact that he had even been bold enough to raise his hand to her at all. In all her years, neither Michael nor any other man had laid hands on her. One guy she had dated a few years back had grabbed her arm, and that alone landed him in the hospital with a broken nose. Satin might have been petite, but she was far from fragile. Michael had enrolled her in martial-arts classes when she was young, so that she would always be able to defend herself.

That fool really had some nerve trying to dictate who she could see. Talking 'bout "He forbid it"—was he out of his mind? But what if he tried to do something to Lou-Loc? As soon as the thought entered her mind, she pushed it out. Lou-Loc had always been a pussycat around her, but she wasn't fooled. She could tell the man was dangerous, even before he kicked Jesus's little ass. He had always let her assume he was a drug dealer, but it didn't take a rocket scientist to know what the deal was. He was a killer. Lou-Loc was the type of man that when he came walking down the street, you got the fuck out of his way. His mere presence exuded menace.

Lou-Loc was by far one of the most intelligent and talented young men she had ever met. The disturbing thing was that he was street poisoned. It was sad when you thought about it. He watched his father get murdered in cold blood, and then the cancer took his mother. All he had left was his sister, and he cherished her. Satin had never met her personally, but they had spoken on the phone on several occasions. Sometimes they would just talk on the phone for hours. Not about anything of any relevance, just girl stuff. Malika was like the little sister she never had.

She wasn't the typical sixteen-year-old little girl, but was very well mannered and polite. She always said *please* and *thank you*. Whenever she called the house, it was never, "My brother there?" It was always, "Hello, Satin, how are you today? Is my brother available?" She thought the world of her brother and the same could be said for him. They were very close, despite their age difference. Satin had promised her that when they got settled, she could come and visit with them.

Satin's thoughts were interrupted by the phone ringing. She wondered who could be calling her at that hour of the night. It wasn't really late, but it wasn't early either. She didn't usually receive calls after ten o'clock. Her heart was suddenly filled with dread. She hoped nothing had happened to her aunt or her man.

"Hello," she answered.

"Hey, boo," Lou-Loc said on the other end. "I didn't wake you, did I?"

"Oh, no," she said, perking up. The sound of his voice on the phone or in person always made her feel good. "I was just thinking about you. Nothing's wrong, is it?"

"Nah," he said, more confident than he was. "I just wanted to touch base with you. Hey, listen. We might be pulling out sooner than we thought."

"Lou-Loc, what's wrong?"

"Nothing for you to worry about. I broke the news to the homeboys about me retiring."

"Oh, how did they take it? They didn't have to jump you out or anything, did they?"

"You silly. Nah, it wasn't nothing like that. The real soldiers took it like G's. I had to whip that lil nigga B.T. out for talking slick, though."

"Lou-Loc, you said no more violence."

"Hey, I didn't start. That ma' fucka had it coming."

"So, Mike Tyson, did you decide where we gonna go?"

"Fo sho, li'l mamma. What you think about Miami?"

"Oh baby," she squealed. "I've always dreamed about living somewhere like that. Are you serious?"

"As a heart attack. Snake Eyes is setting everything up."

"Oh, baby. I can't believe you're taking me to Florida!"

"Yeah, and I was thinking—well, if it's okay with you? Maybe we could fly your aunt and my li'l sister down that way once we're settled."

"Yeah, that's cool with me. It'd be nice to have them visit with us. That way, the people we love can get acquainted."

"Yeah, ma, plus I'd like for my sister to be the maid of honor when we get married next month."

Satin was stunned by the announcement. "What did you say?"

"Satin, honey. I know we said that we'd wait for a while, but maybe we shouldn't. I love you, ma, and I want you to know it."

"Lou-Loc. You don't have to rush and marry me just to prove you love me. Baby, you've given up your whole way of life to be with me. That's proof enough."

"I know, I know, but I want this. I made a promise to myself a long time ago, that if I ever found that special someone, I'd hold on for dear life."

"That is the sweetest thing I've ever heard. If I hadn't already put that thang on you, I'd think you were trying to get into my panties." They both laughed at that. "So, when do you wanna leave?"

"Like tomorrow." he said seriously. "We'll probably catch a flight tomorrow afternoon or in the evening."

"Tomorrow, why so soon? Something's wrong, isn't it?"

"Nah, I just need to get away from this place. Too many memories and too many hostile feelings. I just wanna bail before I end up hurting somebody."

"Damn, I haven't even finished packing my stuff."

"Don't worry about that, ma. Just pack a few things, and whatever's personal to you. Don't worry about the rest of your clothes. We starting off fresh, remember? When we hit Miami, we both are going shopping. Before we leave, I'll give your key to Snake so he can have your furniture put into storage."

"Well, what about our cars?"

"My other car is already sold, and I'm having my lowrider shipped to Florida."

"And my jeep?"

"Fuck it. I'll have Snake sell it and send you the money. I'll buy you another car once we get settled."

"You got it all figured out, huh?"

"You know I do, baby. Look, I'll be by to pick you up in the morning. We gonna swing by the hospital to see ya aunt, then we gone. You okay with that?"

"Well, I guess so. You not coming over tonight?"

"Nah, boo. I got some loose ends to take care of. The dude that's buying my car is also buying my guns. Shit, I'm retired so I don't need them and I couldn't get them on the plane anyhow. Don't worry about anything, just get some rest tonight and be ready to roll out. Tomorrow marks the beginning of a new era for us. Sleep well, boo. I love you, Satin."

"And I love you, Lou-Loc." With that she hung up.

Satin sat on her bed with tears in her eyes. Everything was happening so suddenly. Everything that Lou-Loc said, he did. He left his gang and was moving her to the beautiful shores of Miami. This was too good to be true. Soon she would be married and living in a beautiful city with the man she loved. After all the heartache she had endured, Satin was finally going to have the storybook life she had always dreamed of.

Chapter 23

The loud chirping of his cell phone woke Lou-Loc from his much needed rest. When he looked at the caller ID, he recognized the number. "Hello, Pam," he said sleepily.

"Well, good morning to you too, Mr. Alexander. I hope I didn't wake you and if I did, too bad. Now you know how it feels."

Lou-Loc laughed. "Do you have good news for me, Pam?"

"Don't I always? As per your instructions, I've had most of your accounts transferred to Miami First National. I did some calling around, and arranged for you to meet with a no-questions-asked Realtor next week. He says he has some nice beachfront property that you might be interested in. I still haven't found a buyer for your security company, but I'm working on it. I've sent you a travel package with three dummy credit cards via express mail, so it should reach your p.o. box sometime today. Our friends at the shipping company said you can have your car dropped off tomorrow, and they'll have it in Miami no later than next week. Overall, I'd say we're set. Anything else, Mr. Alexander?"

"Yeah, stop calling me Mr. Alexander. Love you, smart ass."

"Yeah, well, act like it and hit a sister off wit a li'l something, something."

"I got you, Pam."

"Yeah, whatever, nigga. Bye."

Lou-Loc loved Pam like a sister. She was crooked as hell, but also the best at what she did. Pamela Sparks was one of the best money managers on the West Coast. She was a sister from the hood that had finally clawed her way out. She was ghetto as hell, but also very professional. Sure, she skimmed a little and helped drug dealers launder their money, but we all gotta eat. The way Pam was jacking the commission on the brothers in the hood, she was eating like a muthafucka.

Pam had a house in the Hills, two Mercedes, a Navigator, and game. That's what makes the world go round. The nigga wit the most cake is the nigga wit the most game. A lot of people thought it was all about heart or education, but that was all bullshit. It was all about game and who got the most of it. If yo' game was tight, then you were good.

Lou-Loc stretched his aching muscles and strolled over to the window. The weatherman had said it was going to be sunny, yet the sky was cloudy. A bad omen, but Lou-Loc chalked it up to the dumb meteorologist. Last night's meeting had gone well. Big Mike had given Lou-Loc 15,000 dollars for the car and 2,000 dollars for the guns. Considering that it was all cash, he was good. He had agreed to let Lou-Loc use the car for the day, so he was set for transportation. Even though Big Mike wasn't a Crip, he was folks, and that was just as good. Big Mike was good peoples.

Lou-Loc flipped his phone open and dialed Snake Eyes. After about three or four rings, he picked up. "What it is, cuz?" Lou-Loc said happily.

"Ain't nothing," Snake Eyes said, yawning. "Today's the day, huh?"

"Yeah, cuz. I'm putting this life behind me and starting over fresh."

"Cuz, you don't know how proud I am of you."

"I be knowing, pimp."

"It's a whole different ballgame you stepping into, Loc. I'm gonna introduce you to a totally different hustle, cuz. Them crackers got this game sewed, but slowly but surely, we getting in there. I got big plans for you, Lou-Loc. All you gotta do is be willing to put the time in, and we good."

"Hey man, I'm always willing to learn. I'm gonna do the right thing by this girl, Snake. I didn't tell her yet, but I plan on opening up a li'l boutique or something for her in South Beach. It's gonna be a surprise wedding present for her."

"Damn, nigga. You got it bad."

"Fo sho. I'm in love, cuz."

"Well, Mr. Lover-man. You just make sure you have your ass at the airport by twelve o'clock. Your flight leaves at one-fifteen."

"Cuz, I can't tell you how much I appreciate what you've done for me."

"Man, go 'head wit that sucker shit. We kin, it's all good. You just make sure you get yo' ass back in school, and do right by that girl. We gonna get ya money all washed up, and then you gonna ball like you supposed to, ya heard?"

"Loud and clear, big player. So, I'll meet up with you at about eleven. I'll hit ya phone to let you know where."

"A'ight, cuz. I'm taking my ass back to sleep. Be careful out there, Loc."

"I'm out the game, Snake. The rules don't apply to me no more. As of today, I'm a square."

"Yeah, well, you still watch yo' ass, Lou-Loc. You got a strap?"

"Nah, I sold 'em all to Mike."

"Damn, nigga. I'm 'bout to come through there and lay one on you."

"Be cool, Snake. I ain't going anywhere. When I leave this room, I'm going to pick Satin up and then I'm coming to meet you. You gonna take us to the airport so you can drop the car keys on Mike. It's cool, baby."

"I ain't feeling this shit, Lou-Loc, especially after what happened last night. At least let me send somebody over there to hold you down."

"Snake, this is me. If I say I'm cool, then I'm cool. Good looking, though. I'll give you a call later, homie. Out." Before Snake Eyes could protest, he hung up.

All of Lou-Loc's bags were still packed from the breakup with Martina, so he didn't have to worry about that. All of his guns were gone as well as the excess jewelry he wouldn't need. It was time to go pick Satin up and get on the road.

Cisco got up especially early. Normally he didn't stir from his plush water bed until about eleven or twelve, but today was different. Today was the day he would put an end to Lou-Loc and El Diablo. He felt like a kid on Christmas. Late last night, he had gotten the call about the Giant's accident. It was a wasted call, because he already knew. He set it up.

Cisco picked up his antique phone and set the ball in motion. The first person he called was Tito. During the brief phone conversation, Tito had informed him that the goods were in place and he was en route to pick up El Diablo. With that taken care of, he called Martina. He could hardly bear to stay on the phone with the woman but for so long. If he didn't need her, he would've just said *fuck it*, but this wasn't the case. In order for everything to go accordingly, she had to play her part. It was a damn shame what some people would do for money. Martina was going to sell her soul—as well as her ex's—for a funky 10,000 dollars.

The phone had barely rung twice when Martina snatched it up. "Hello?" she said, out of breath.

"What up, Martina? This is Cisco."

"I was wondering when you would call. You got my paper?"

"You don't waste any time, do you?"

"Life is too short to waste time, especially when it comes to money. Now, do you have mine?"

"You'll get your money when the deed is done. We gotta make that happen fast, as in *today*."

"Shit, that ain't a problem, pa. I'm about to make the call in a little while."

"Good girl. I owe you one, ma."

"Don't get it fucked up, you owe me ten—ten thousand! So listen, when this is all done, how about—" She didn't get a chance to finish her sentence as the line went dead in her ear.

Martina sat back on her bed and smiled devilishly as she thought on how she was going to fix Lou-Loc. When Cisco's people caught up with him they were going to give him a good beating—at least that's what Cisco had told her. She should've felt bad, but she didn't. He had hurt her heart and her pockets when he left her and she wasn't going to stand for it. After they beat him up she would be there to nurse him back to health and Lou-Loc would see that Martina was the girl for him and the chick he was seeing would be an afterthought, at least to Lou-Loc. After Martina had her baby she intended to track the girl down and show her what she did to little bitches that got in her mix. She had something for Cisco too. There was no doubt in her mind that once Lou-Loc recovered he was going to kill Cisco, removing the only person who could connect her to the setup. When it was all said and done Martina would be the only winner in the little game.

"You just wait, Lou-Loc," she said, rubbing her belly. "You'll come back to your senses, and I'll be right here waiting on you."

Chapter 24

Lou-Loc sat on the couch puffing on a Newport as Satin put the last of her things into her shoulder bag. He looked her up and down, and couldn't help but think how lucky he was. She looked so good, even dressed down. Satin was sporting a pink Rocawear sweat suit with a pair of pink and white Nike Air Max. Her silky black hair was wrapped around her head and held in place with pink and white hairpins. Satin wasn't as thick as Martina, but what she lacked in thickness, she more than made up for in character. Lou-Loc's girl was the baddest thing on the streets and he was proud to have her.

"Damn, boo, I can't believe we're really leaving," Satin said as she took one last look at her apartment.

"Well, believe it," he said, picking up her suitcase. "I told you I was taking you away, and I always keep my promises. Now let's get this shit down to the car." Before Lou-Loc was completely out the door, his cell went off. When he looked at the caller ID, he knew just who it was.

"What?" he snapped.

"Damn," Martina whined, "good morning to you too. What's up, boo?"

"First of all, I ain't ya fucking boo. Second of all, what you want?"

"You ain't gotta be all stank and shit, Lou-Loc. What's the matter, papi, that bitch you wit ain't treating you right?"

Lou-Loc sucked his teeth. "What goes on with me and mine don't concern you, so don't worry your wicked-ass brain over it. Now what the hell do you want?"

"Damn, what's with the attitude? Are you in a rush or something?"

"Oh, I guess you ain't heard? As of today, I'm out the game. Not only am I out the game, I'm out this city."

"What?" Martina asked in disbelief. "What you mean?"

"Damn, I forgot you kinda slow," he said sarcastically. "It's a wrap, Martina. I'm putting some distance between me and this rotten-ass apple. You smell me?"

"Well, let me and the kids come with you. Maybe we can work it out?"

"Girl, you crazier than a shit-house rat. Me and my boo is gone from here, so you can keep ya drama, ya games, and yo' kids. I hope you have a nice life."

"How you gonna do this to me, Lou-Loc?" she said, breaking down. "What about us? What about the baby?"

"Bitch," he said coldly, "don't even play me. You know damn well that ain't my seed, so miss me wit it. Matter of fact, is there a reason for this fucking call?"

Seeing her man about to lose, it Satin intervened. "Lou-Loc, calm down. The girl is upset, so try to be a little sympathetic to her situation. Be the bigger man that I know you are."

Satin's words calmed him a little, but the anger was still there. "What is it, Martina?" he asked in a slightly softer tone.

"I didn't call to bug you, Lou-Loc," she said, trying to sound sincere. "The reason I called is because I'm having a problem with the lease. The apartment is in your name and the landlord is being an asshole about switching it over unless you sign off on it. He says that if you don't, then once the lease is up he's gonna put us out."

"That ain't my problem. Work that shit out."

"Lou-Loc, I know you're salty about everything that went on with me and you, but the kids ain't got nothing to do with it. Don't make them suffer because you're mad at me. Look, it'll only take you five minutes to sign the papers and then I won't bother you anymore. I promise," she said sincerely.

A warning bell went off in Lou-Loc's head. Something about the way Martina was coming at him didn't seem right. "Look, Martina," he started, "I feel for you and all, but I ain't got time for this bullshit. I'll call you sometime during the week and give you a p.o. box address to mail the papers to. I'll sign them and send them back. Outside of that I ain't got shit for you."

"Oh, word? You hate me that much that you'll let me and my kids get thrown out into the streets?" she shouted into the phone. "You a dirty nigga, Lou-Loc."

"Martina," he said, getting angry again. "I'm trying to be nice about this shit, but you ain't making it easy. You want me to come all the way from where I'm at to sign a lease? Fuck outta here. It ain't my fault y'all asses is getting put out. As a matter of fact, you can go straight to—" Satin pinched his arm, and kept him from finishing his sentence.

"St. Louis Alexander," she said in a stern voice. "I know you ain't gonna do that girl like that? I know she's a bitch, but she got little ones. Don't do it for her, do it for her kids. They're innocent in all this. Don't stoop to her level."

"Satin, come on. We still gotta stop by and see your aunt and some more shit before we dip to the airport and I don't wanna miss this flight."

"We can do that after you sign the lease. It shouldn't take you but a few minutes. We can go to the airport from the hospital."

"Okay, Satin. You lucky I love you," he said playfully. Lou-Loc composed himself and put the phone back to his ear. "Okay, Martina. I'll be there in about a half hour. Have the paperwork ready. I'm signing the lease, then I'm gone."

"Thanks, Lou-Loc. I—" The phone went dead. For the second time that morning, Martina had been hung up on. It was okay, though. Mr. O.G. Lou-Loc was about to learn a very important lesson: Hell hath no fury like a woman scorned.

Lou-Loc dialed Snake Eyes's cell but didn't get any answer. He left a message on his answering machine, informing his friend on where he was going. He had intended on having Snake Eyes meet him there, but he'd just have to try him again later. After Lou-Loc put the last of Satin's bags in the car, they hopped on the highway and headed uptown. He felt uneasy about dipping through the hood without any type of firearm, but there was nothing he could do about it now. He would be in and out, so he didn't really think anything could go wrong. Besides, that was his hood. Niggaz knew better than to fuck with him.

Cisco hung up his phone, and a wide grin formed on his face. Things were going well. Now it was time for him to set phase two of his plan in motion. First he called his hired help and gave them their instructions. The next call he made was to El Diablo's cell phone.

"Diablo," he said in a frantic voice, "I hate to bother you, but we've got a problem I thought you should know about."

"What's wrong?" El Diablo asked, concerned.

"It's your sister, Michael."

"Satin—what about her?"

"One of my ladies just called me. She said that fucking ape, Lou-Loc, is uptown kicking your sister's ass in the street, like some whore."

"That motherfucker," El Diablo snarled. "I'll kill that nigger bastard. Where is he, Cisco?"

"It's going on right uptown in front of his old building. It was Martina who called and told me. She said that Satin found out they were still seeing each other, and wasn't happy about it." Cisco giggled to himself as he heard Diablo relaying the info to Tito.

"I'm on my way," El Diablo said, out of breath.

"I'll meet you there," Cisco lied and hung up the phone. He sat back in his recliner and turned on the twenty-four-hour news channel and waited. There was no doubt in his mind that the plan he had put in motion would make headlines.

Lou-Loc pulled up in front his old building and got out. As soon as he stepped onto the pavement, a cold chill ran down his spine. He shrugged it off as the jitters and continued to stare at the building. He had some good times on that block as well as some bad ones, but it had been home for him. This was going to be his last time seeing this building or Martina's funky ass. Good riddance to them both.

"You okay, boo?" Satin asked from the passenger-side window.

"I'm cool," he assured her. He didn't want to spook Satin, but something didn't feel right. He looked up at the window and saw Martina looking down at him. They were supposed to meet in front of the building, so why the hell was she still upstairs?

"Come on so I can get outta here," Lou-Loc yelled up at her. Martina looked down at him and grinned, but made no move to come down, which only aggravated Lou-Loc. He knew what kind of games Martina liked to play, so if she thought that she was going to dupe him into coming up, then she had another thing coming—and apparently so did Lou-Loc. He spun around just as the Cadillac pulled to a screeching halt at the curb.

Martina watched Lou-Loc get out of the car and stoop down to talk to Satin. *So, that's his new bitch, huh?* she said to herself. As Martina looked at the features of the small woman in the car, she had to admit that the girl was pretty. As Lou-Loc strolled toward the building, she put on her brightest smile. Mr. Lover, lover was about to get his.

Martina saw El Diablo's red hog bend the corner and suddenly felt as if something was very wrong. Cisco never said anything about El Diablo being involved. When she saw the gang leader hop from his car and rush at Lou-Loc, she knew that Cisco had played her.

"You fucking tar baby, what have you done to my sister?" El Diablo fumed as he rushed Lou-Loc.

"Huh?" Lou-Loc asked, dumbfounded by the man in the suit running toward him.

El Diablo swung a wild punch at Lou-Loc, which he easily sidestepped. Without trying to gain his balance, he swung another blow. This time Lou-Loc grabbed his arm and rabbit-punched him in the stomach, folding him. El Diablo had quite a rep with a blade or a gun, but he wasn't a very good fighter. "Y—you, bastard, I'll kill you for what you did to my sister," he wheezed.

"Man, what the hell are you talking about? I don't know you or your sister," Lou-Loc told him.

"Michael!" Satin yelled, getting out of the car.

Suddenly the pieces fell into place for Lou-Loc. "Wait a second, this goofy muthafucka is the notorious El Diablo?" Lou-Loc couldn't help but to laugh. "You can't be serious."

El Diablo sat on the ground, looking from Lou-Loc to Satin in a state of confusion. His sister didn't have a mark on her. Her hair wasn't even out of place. Somebody had looped him and he knew just who it was. El Diablo was about to get up and explain himself when he noticed two young boys running up behind Lou-Loc. Everything that happened next seemed to go in slow motion.

"What's up now, Blood," one of the boys shouted, raising a .45.

Instinctively Lou-Loc reached under his shirt where his gun would normally be, only to find himself clutching air. "Shit," was all he could say.

The first boy cut loose with the hammer, hitting Lou-Loc in the gut and staggering him. Lou-Loc looked down at his bloodied shirt, confused, and then up at the boy who had shot him. His face twisted into a mask of anger and he staggered toward the boy. The boy hit him again, this time in the shoulder, but Lou-Loc kept coming. He could hear Satin screaming but for some reason he couldn't see her anymore. Everything was getting blurry, but anger willed Lou-Loc on and he tried to close the distance between himself and the boy, who looked bewildered at the fact that Lou-Loc was still standing.

A second boy joined the first, this one carrying a machine gun, at the same moment Satin came into view. She was standing between them, shouting something that Lou-Loc couldn't understand. In what felt like slow motion, Lou-Loc saw the boy raise the machine gun and point it at her. He heard the distorted sound of the first of several bullets expel from the machine gun. With the last bit of strength he had, he shoved Satin out of the way and received the bullet that was meant for her.

Time sped up again and the machine gun roared to life. Bullet after bullet slammed into Lou-Loc, lighting him up like the Fourth of July and finally dropping him. Even as his body was ripped to pieces as the boys dumped rounds into him, his killer's instinct continued to will him forward. On hands and knees Lou-Loc crawled toward the boy, determined to keep their attention off Satin. When he reached them he grabbed at one of the boy's pants legs futilely and was rewarded with a kick to the face, putting him on his back. Lou-Loc was trying to say something, but the only thing that came out of his mouth was blood.

The boy carrying the .45 knelt beside Lou-Loc's body and pointed the gun at his face. "This is what you get for fucking with El Diablo," he shouted loud enough for everyone to hear. "You got any last words?"

Lou-Loc fought through the pain and found the words. "Harlem Crip, faggot." He spat blood into the boy's face.

The boy wiped the blood from his face with the back of his shirt. "Fuck you and Harlem Crip," the boy said, pulling the trigger. He dumped shot after shot into Lou-Loc until he finally stopped twitching. For good measure he dumped two slugs into his face. "Long live El Diablo. LC

Blood for life," the boy threw up his set and spat on Lou-Loc's corpse. With that, the two gunmen took off running.

El Diablo, who had been shielding Satin, tried to hold her back but she broke loose and rushed to Lou-Loc's side. "Lou-Loc," she whispered as she watched her man's lifeblood run into the gutter. His handsome face was torn to shreds and his clothes were soaked with blood. "Oh, baby," she sobbed as she knelt beside him. Blood soaked through her sweat pants but she didn't even seem to notice. "Get up, Lou-Loc, we've gotta catch the plane to Miami." She shook him, but Lou-Loc was silent. "Look what they did to my St. Louis. They even messed up your braids," she said as she stroked his bloody skull. "It's okay; I'll just do them over when you wake up. Oh, Lou-Loc, why you leave me, papi? You said we were getting married— what happened? You said you always kept your promises."

Snake Eyes pulled up just in time to see his friend stretched out on the ground. When he got Lou-Loc's message about going to Martina's, he knew something was fishy. He had renewed the lease a few months ago so there was no way it could've presented a problem just yet. Tears welled up in Snake Eyes's eyes as he watched Satin kneel over Lou-Loc with a vacant look in her eyes. Of all the times he had pulled Lou-Loc's ass out of the fire, this was one time he couldn't.

El Diablo walked up timidly and reached out to his sister. "Satin, I'm sorry for your loss," he said sincerely. El Diablo extended his hand to try and help his sister up.

Satin looked up at her brother as if she was seeing him for the first time in her life. The words of the shooters that had connected El Diablo to the assassination played over and over in her head. Suddenly the look of sorrow on her face was replaced by rage. "This is your doing," she hissed.

"Satin, I swear on everything I love that I had nothing to do with this," El Diablo tried to tell her but it was as if she couldn't hear him.

"All he wanted to do was walk away from this color war, but you couldn't see it. You just couldn't see me happy, so you took the only man I've ever loved," she snapped. "We were going to get married on the beach, did you know that?" she asked, holding up her now bloody ring. "We were to be married in Miami, Michael. We were going to buy a house and fly Aunt Selina down to take care of her, did you know that? You took him from me, you bastard," she snarled, eyes suddenly glazed over with madness.

The look in Satin's eyes frightened El Diablo and he began to back up. This was not the little girl he knew, but a woman who had just lost her lover and blamed him for it. He looked to the car to motion for Tito, but he was long gone. It was just brother and sister.

From the car, Snake Eyes watched the whole thing unfolding. When he realized what was about to happen, he moved to stop it, but with his bum leg, he was too slow. Satin's hand dipped into her purse, and she came out with her pistol. Without so much as blinking, she squeezed the trigger. She was so distraught that she didn't release the trigger until the clip was empty. Snake Eyes made his way to Satin and took the gun from her, but it was too late for El Diablo as he lay on the ground with six holes in his 3,000-dollar suit. His little sister, whom he had raised and nurtured as a child, had sent him home. For him, the game was over.

The police arrived on the scene too little, too late as usual. Snake Eyes wasn't there from the beginning, so he couldn't really say what happened, but you know how people in the hood are. They love an opportunity to get a story ass-backwards on the news. Snake Eyes was so distraught by the loss of his friend; he didn't much care what they said. He had one brother in a coma and one in heaven. He had seen it so many times that he was numb to it. Another young brother claimed by the streets.

Snake Eyes walked over and looked down at his mutilated friend. Tears flowed freely down his cheeks and he didn't care who saw. "You're free now," he whispered. "Go on home, cuz. The pain is gone and you're free. I love you, my nigga, and I'm glad you ain't gotta suffer no more. Go on and rest."

Satin walked in a daze as two female officers escorted her to a blue-and-white, reading her rights. If she understood what they were saying, she made no indication of it. All Satin did was sob and repeat Lou-Loc's name over and over. Snake Eyes knew that no matter what she told them that she was going to jail. Regardless of how it went down, she was a young Latina with a gun and that was all they needed to build a case. He would provide her with whatever legal assistance he could, but it didn't look good for Satin. If they were lucky she would spend the next few years of her life in a mental institution instead of prison.

Chapter 25

Lou-Loc's funeral was held at midnight at a large funeral home on the west side of Harlem. Normally they would've never agreed to the late-night service, but Snake Eyes had called in quite a few favors to make it happen. No one understood why Snake Eyes had scheduled it for such an odd hour and when he was asked, all he would say was, "So that those closest to him can say their good-byes. This is how he would have wanted it." What he meant only Snake Eyes and Lou-Loc knew and neither of them would tell.

It was supposed to be an intimate gathering for friends and family to send off their loved one, but it turned into a huge event as ballers and other criminal elements from every coast came to pay their respects to one of God's most thorough soldiers. They laid Lou-Loc out in a solid gold casket, with a six-pointed star carved into it. Because of what happened, they had to make it a closed-casket funeral, but there were pictures of him all over. Snake Eyes took the picture of Lou-Loc and Satin at Six Flags, and put it in the casket. He would've wanted her close to him.

Martina, of course, showed her ass at the funeral. She was crying and falling out in the lap of any nigga that was willing to keep her ass from hitting the floor. On two separate occasions, Snake Eyes and Pop Top had to keep Sharell from swinging on her.

Snake Eyes and Pam took Lou-Loc's money and did the right thing with it. With part of the money, they started the St. Louis Alexander Scholarship Fund for underprivileged children who couldn't afford to go to college. With the rest of the money, they set up a trust fund for Malika, so she would have all the advantages life had to offer.

As expected, the police gave Satin a hard time about the murder of El Diablo. Snake Eye was prepared to go as hard as he could to defend Satin on his own, but as luck would have it he didn't have to. When his father had gotten wind of all that had gone down he came out of retirement to take the case and brought his old legal team with him. They couldn't get the charges dismissed completely, but they were able to get them significantly reduced. The girl was a shell of her former self and most days all she did was stare out the window or weep until the point that she had to be sedated. After several interviews with Satin the state's psychiatrist deemed her unfit to stand trial. After some bartering they agreed to place her in a mental institution, where she could be cared for properly. They all prayed that one day Satin would snap out of it and return to her former self, but it didn't seem likely.

Snake Eyes's last order of business was Lou-Loc's work. All his thoughts, memoirs, and everything he put to paper were typed up and put on files, which were submitted to different publishers. At the time there wasn't really a market for the street stories Lou-Loc wrote, so the publishers thumbed their noses at them, but this didn't stop Snake Eyes. He and Pam put some money together and started Harlem Publications, which specialized in stories about urban communities and the people who came from them. Within a few years everyone was trying to get on the bandwagon that would go on to be called urban lit, but it was Harlem Publications that was the blueprint for the fledgling genre.

Pop Top came out of the restroom and spotted Snake Eyes in the doorway of the funeral home, speaking with a man he had never seen before.

From the way he was dressed in a black-leather duster and motorcycle boots, Pop Top knew he wasn't a part of the set. As he approached, Snake Eyes and the man hurriedly finished their conversation and the man walked out.

"Who was that?" Pop Top asked.

"Nobody for you to stress over, cuz," Snake Eyes told him and walked back inside.

Pop Top's curiosity got the best of him and he stepped out into the cool night air to see if he could get a better look at the man, but there wasn't a living soul on the streets. It was as if the man had vanished, and with him, whatever secret he and Snake Eyes shared.

A little further north in the intensive-care unit of Harlem Hospital, Gutter was still laid up. To the doctors and everyone else who came to visit him, he seemed to still be in a catatonic state, but what they couldn't see was that his brain was working overtime.

In his mind's eye, he replayed his attempted assassination over and over. He could see himself walking down the street, focused on his scratch-off and the shadows began to close around him. He knew what would come next, but was powerless to stop the slug that tore into his side. Glass rained on him as he collapsed on the floor, clutching his side and praying for it to be done with. For as much as he wanted to just lie on the ground and die, this wasn't how the story was to play out.

As his body relived his attempted execution, his teeth clamped down so hard that he almost punctured the breathing tube. Small fires exploded all over his body as the wounds flared in accordance to how they'd been received. It seemed like it had gone on forever, but slowly the cool darkness was starting to return and take the pain with it. His mind drifted like a blade of grass on a soft spring breeze, as the mental reel in his head reset itself and prepared to play the movie again, but this time it wouldn't play until the end.

Gutter's eyes snapped open so fast that he lost several lashes to the crust that had been building in the corners of his eyes. His whole body felt like it had been set on fire, but he was too weak to do anything but flap around like a wounded fish. He would have rather suffered a dozen of his violent dreams than deal with the pain of being awake. He tried to raise his head, but a powerful hand covered his mouth and nose, cutting off his air.

"If you scream, you die, those are the rules," a distorted voice warned. Gutter's vision was still blurry, but he could make out the shape of the speaker's face and a set of menacing green eyes—not the money-green of his own, but more like raw jade. "Do you understand?" the speaker pressed, applying more pressure to Gutter's face. Gutter was finally able to manage a weak nod. "Good," the speaker said, removing his hand from Gutter's mouth. "We haven't much time, so be still while I work." He removed Gutter's breathing tube.

"Who?" Gutter croaked, just below a whisper. His tongue felt like sandpaper and each breath he took threatened to collapse his dry throat.

"When the medication works its way out of your system it'll come to you, but right now we've got business between us. Raising you from this bed settles a debt between an old friend and myself, as well as ensuring that the enemies of my brother will die. Lou-Loc is dead and so is Diablo and I think we both know who orchestrated it."

"Cisco." Gutter was becoming more alert.

A half smile spread across the speaker's face. "He didn't have the nuts to handle his own dirt, so he got other people to do it for him, but I trust Cisco's time is about up." It was more of a statement than a question.

"I'm gonna kill that muthafucka," Gutter wheezed, trying to get up. He had made it into a sitting position before he collapsed back on the bed. Fire shot up through his spine and smoldered at the base of his neck.

"You won't be doing much of anything in the condition you're in, which is where I come in. Before it's all said and done, you're gonna do more killing than you'll be able to handle, but not before you're healed. Our enemies will still be there waiting for Crip justice, I'll see to that. All we have to do is come to an understanding."

"What's your deal, man, what you want from me?" Gutter asked, his voice getting some of its bass back.

"Blood," the speaker said simply. "I want you to rally your army, gang lord. Gather up your minions and wash the streets of Harlem in the blood of your enemies. That is the price for your life. Do you think you can handle that?"

"To settle the score for my homeboy I'd gladly march into hell," Gutter said seriously.

"Good, because that's what you're about to do." The speaker laughed, injecting red fluid into Gutter's IV. As soon as the liquid hit Gutter's bloodstream it felt like his veins caught fire.

"Nigga, did you poison me?" Gutter grasped at the IV, but the speaker held him still.

"Nah, but you'll wish I had when you realize what you just signed up for." The speaker shook his head and started for the door.

"At least tell me who you are?" Gutter called after him.

He slowed and looked back at Gutter. "I don't recall what my mother named me, but these days I'm called the Cross."

Chapter 26

The seasons changed and made way for the summer; it was back to business as usual. Cisco was especially feeling himself. After the death of El Diablo, he took over as leader of LC Blood. For the most part his plan had gone off without a hitch, but it still didn't play out quite like he'd planned it. Cisco had Tito place two guns in El Diablo's Cadillac that had been used in a series of unsolved murders. The original plan was for the police to find the guns in the vehicle and charge El Diablo with the murders, but Satin snapping and killing the old bastard had changed the outcome. Still, El Diablo was gone and Cisco was now the new king, so it was a victory nonetheless.

With Lou-Loc dead and Gutter being a vegetable, Harlem Crip was coming apart at the seams. Pop Top found that inheriting the mantle of leadership was one thing, but holding onto it was something else altogether. Harlem Crip was now little more than the pack of different sets that it was before the unification, all vying for dominance. It was chaos and Cisco loved it. He figured even if Gutter were to one day wake up from his coma, he would be little more than an invalid, hardly capable of restoring the gang to its former glory. LC Blood was once again at the top of the food chain.

Cisco stood on the sidelines of the West Fourth basketball court, sipping his bottle of water. He liked to come down to West Fourth to watch the different kinds of people come and go. At this particular moment, he had an eye on this fine little black nurse, pushing a man in a wheelchair. The man seemed to be in a nod, with his bathrobe and dark sunglasses. He wore a large-brimmed hat to shade him from the sun. The nurse was a nice little cinnamon thing with an ass that just called his name.

"Hey, mami," he said, trying to sound cool.

"Hey yourself," she responded.

"What's up wit you, ma? It's a beautiful day and you're stuck pushing a wheelchair?"

"Yeah, it's a drag, but I gotta pay my bills."

"Ma, I could pay your bills, plus give you multiple orgasms."

"You must be some kinda big man, huh?" she said seductively.

"I'm the biggest man. The name is Cisco, supreme general of LC Blood."

"Oh, I've heard of you. They say you're that nigga," she said excitedly.

"Nah, I'm that spic, but what's the difference?"

"Oh, you all that?"

"And then some. Why don't you ditch the cripple and come back to my spot?"

"Sure, I'm wit it," the man in the wheelchair said, shocking Cisco. Moving swiftly, the man in the wheelchair pulled a butcher's knife from his robe and plunged it into Cisco's gut. He thrust the knife in and out of Cisco almost a dozen times before finally letting him fall to the ground. Cisco lay on the ground bleeding, looking up at the man in the wheelchair as he stood up. When the man removed his sunglasses, Cisco recognized those green eyes. It was Gutter.

Gutter wiped the tears from his eyes and knelt beside Cisco with the bloody knife. "You took my brother's life, so it is with great pleasure that I snatch yours, you rat fuck." Gutter plunged the knife into Cisco's chest, shattering his breastbone and spearing his heart. He continued to put his weight on the knife until Cisco's life expired.

Gutter left the knife in Cisco's chest and wiped his hand on the robe, which he peeled off and tossed into the wheelchair. With tears in his eyes, he looked to the heavens and spoke to his friend. "All scores are settled, my nigga, and that's on Harlem."

Sharell moved beside him and looped her arm around Gutter's waist. "It's over now, baby."

Gutter looked at his lady lovingly and kissed her softly on the lips. "Nah, this ain't over. I'm just getting started."

Epilogue

It was 9:00 p.m. when Martina walked into her apartment with her newborn son. The kids were with her sister, so it was just her and the baby. She put the baby in the bassinet, and stripped down to her panties and bra. It had been a few months since Lou-Loc was murdered, but she still thought of him. If only she hadn't called him that day, he might still be alive. Though he may have lived, there was no doubt in her mind that he would still be with Satin. Lou-Loc loved her in a way that he would never love Martina and that was obvious to everyone. For as sad as Martina was at how it played out, at least she was ten grand richer for it.

Within minutes the baby was asleep so she decided to take a quick shower. Grabbing a towel, she headed into the bathroom and set the water. The hot water spraying from the custom shower-head felt like heaven compared to the lukewarm drip from the shower in her hospital room. She stepped out of the shower and wiped the mirror with her hand to admire the body she hadn't seen in nine months. After she had given birth, the baby weight seemed to shed instantly and she was ready to get back to the game. She would miss Lou-Loc dearly, but a ghost couldn't pay her bills so she needed to find herself another sponsor.

As she was checking her reflection she saw something move behind her. Martina spun and strained her eyes, trying to peer through the steam. "Who's there?"

"Death has come to pay a call on you," a familiar voice spoke from the steam.

Martina found herself staring into a pair of sinister green eyes through the steam. The eyes moved toward her and a face she thought she would never see again materialized in front of her. "Gutter," she gasped.

"What's the matter, ain't you happy to see me?" Gutter taunted her, stalking forward.

Terrified, Martina stumbled backward and had to brace herself on the sink to keep from falling. "This can't be. They told me you were dead."

"And they told me you loved my brother, but I guess the fact that we're standing here like this proves you can't believe everything you hear, huh?" Gutter raised his pistol.

"Please don't," Martina whimpered.

"Any sympathy I might've had for yo' tramp ass died with my homie, bitch. When you meet up with Cisco in hell tell him he forgot these."

Gutter shot Martina twice in the face. He didn't even wait for the body to hit the floor before he left the bathroom.

In the next room, Cross was standing over the bassinet, tickling Martina's baby and smiling. "Is it done?" he asked Gutter without bothering to look up from the baby.

"Yeah, that bitch is dead as a doornail." Gutter came to stand beside Cross.

"You did what you had to do, gang lord. Her death was a necessary one, just as it will be with the others. Blood is the price for the gift I have given you, always remember that."

"Don't worry, Cross, you're gonna be swimming in more blood than you know what to do with once me and my people touch them streets."

"So what are you gonna do about the kid?" Cross nodded toward the baby.

Gutter stared into the bassinet. Instead of seeing an innocent child all he saw was Martina and the hate he would carry for her for the rest of his days. "Fuck that li'l nigga. I got Brims to murder," Gutter said and left the apartment.

It was three days before Martina's sister found her corpse in the bathroom. The stench of the rotting form was so putrid that the first officer on the scene lost his lunch. The only clues to what had taken place were a bloody cross smeared on the wall and an empty bassinet.

More titles by K'wan available at:

http://kwanfoye.com